IDENTITY

Book 2

An Eomix Galaxy novel

CHRISTA YELICH-KOTH

IDENTITY (An Eomix Galaxy novel)
Second Edition: November 2018

Published by CYK Publishing
Oregon, USA

ISBN: **978-0-9883470-9-0**

Cover art: Creative Alchemy Inc. and CYK Publishing

Reviews for ILLUSION
Book I

"As the pieces of the plot unfold, you are tossed around at guessing who is the true evil."—Twin Cities Geek Magazine

"When I read science fiction, I need to be sucked right in or I grow bored. Illusion hooked my attention right off the bat in the first few pages."—Lorena Angell, international bestselling author of The Unaltered series.

As as sit here writing this, is occurs to me that Illusion is one of the better books I've reviewed. I read until I could no longer stay awake, and finished it as soon as I could. [...]Christa succeeded in creating an interesting story, one that I wholeheartedly encourage everyone to read. It's definitely one of my new favorites!" –Reviewer Joe Hinojosa.

"I love all the conflict and the big reveal. ... Energy fingerprints—this is really interesting. You have such a great imagination!"—Holly Kammier, bestselling author of Kingston Court

THANK YOU

A huge thanks to you, the reader,
for bringing my story into your life and wanting more.

Sandra Yelich: For your constant support, feedback, and editing. You helped make Daith's world a reality.

Tom Koth: For your amazing encouragement and insight.

Conrad Teves: For bringing my original cover idea to life.

Creative Alchemy Inc.: For helping design my new beautiful cover.

Jessica Therrien and **Kat Ross**: For being part of such an incredible editing team!

And special thanks to Stu Tighe: I'm still surprised at how I can be a writer and fail to find words to express your importance to this book's journey

CHAPTER I

DAITH IGNORED THE chimes to her quarters, along with the tendril of fear climbing her spine. She adjusted her posture, feet tucked underneath her butt, back straight.

A darkened datapad lay in her hand—its smooth surface reflected the lights above her, set into her room's ceiling. They shone bright white, illuminating the grey walls, metallic bed, and deep red carpet. Daith's dark hair lay over her pale shoulders, highlighted by the harsh lights. Recirculated air hissed quietly through the vents.

Irritated, Daith pushed her hair behind her, her focus broken for a moment.

She closed her eyes and concentrated, letting her power fill her. Heat throbbed inside her gut, crawling through her insides like a flame climbing a tree. The fire filled her arms and trickled down into her fingers. She directed the energy into the datapad, searching for the pathways that would lead her to the information stored on the device

1

without having to turn it on.

The datapad's surface bubbled and melted, its insides crackling. With a growl, she twisted the device and the plastic piece grew gooey under her fingertips, stretching apart.

A drop of blood slid from her nose, trickling over her lips. It hung for a moment on the edge of her chin before it dripped to the floor.

The chimes rang again. Daith's forehead creased.

"What?" she snapped at the interruption. Eyes now open, she hastily brushed the blood from her face. She moved her knee to cover the spot on the floor as her visitor entered.

"Daith?"

"Yes, Trey?" she asked, looking up at him from the floor.

Trey cleared his throat, his dark blue eyes narrowed, searching. "How are you?" He stood tall and straight, his uniform pressed, his short, brown hair cropped and neat.

Daith tossed the destroyed datapad towards a pile on the floor in front of him before reclosing her eyes. Clattering filled the quiet room as the datapad bounced off of the others, all half-melted in the same fashion. "I'm fine." She heard him shuffle his feet as he moved toward the datapads. She could picture his perfectly polished shoes, a contrast to the worn carpeting.

"This looks promising, but Daith—"

"I know," she interrupted. "We only have two standard weeks left. I'm working on it."

Trey muttered something she couldn't understand before she heard the door slide closed.

Daith expelled a breath in the now empty room.

She knew Trey expected her abilities to have progressed. During several sessions with her previous doctor, Dru, she discovered she had unique mental and emotional powers, but without him to guide her, she didn't know how to learn anything new.

And her attempts to do more came at a price. Her headaches, nose and ear bleeds, and irritability had increased since she started working on her own four standard days ago.

Since Dru's death.

A tickle of sadness touched her throat, but anger swiftly took over. Emotional motivation should enhance her abilities. She learned that anger made her more powerful and fear more precise. But no matter how she pushed herself, she couldn't do any more than what she already learned with Dru—heal herself, destroy inanimate objects, and sense basic emotions and thoughts from others.

If she planned to help Trey stop the Controllers—those who killed her family and murdered Dru—she had to be able to do more. Who knew what they might be up against, what type of fight the Controllers would bring? She needed to be ready for whatever they threw at her.

And the clock seemed to tick faster and faster.

Daith palmed the wet rag next to her and rubbed at the spot on the carpet—the cloth already spotted red from her previous work during the day. She picked up the next datapad.

The tendril of fear crept once more.

* * *

Commander Trey Xiven blew a frustrated breath through his teeth. The air whistled in the vacant corridor outside Daith's quarters. What under the stars was he going to do?

He strode through the familiar hallways of the *Horizon*, toward his office, located two decks below him on the five-level spaceship. He focused on the problem at hand—the hum of the ship's engines background noise to his thoughts.

How could he accomplish anything if his weapon didn't work?

Trey entered his office through the swish of the opening door. He took a seat behind his smooth, metallic desk, polished free of prints and dust, tapping his fingers on the arm of his chair. A blinking light caught his attention, indicating a message on his vidlink.

Trey's stomach unclenched with hope and he let the recording play.

The screen filled with the image of a stunning woman—skin white as stars, hair ebony with subtle rainbow highlights, and eyes black like the emptiness of death.

"Commander Xiven," the woman said, her voice sultry, but forceful. "I have entered the coordinates to meet your courier. The six ships promised to assist you will be there. Once your payment clears, the fleet will escort the courier to the designated time and place for the final demonstration. Exarth out." The vidscreen went blank—the message deleted immediately from the sender's side.

Trey's stomach dropped as Exarth's video ended. He hoped the call had been Kircla, the assassin he hired four days ago to kill a witness from when his crew abducted Daith. Kircla said it wouldn't take long, so why hadn't he heard from her yet? With her background qualifications, he'd invested a lot of money into securing her services.

Not that Trey could give Kircla much of a description of her target except a blond haired, caramel-skinned male who attended the same school as Daith.

Still...he hoped to have heard back by now.

Regardless, Exarth's continuance with the contract bode well. Although Trey wondered what her wrath would be if he couldn't produce on his end of the deal.

How could he push Daith, make her abilities progress, without her losing control? Trey's head pounded at his cluttered thoughts. He hadn't been sleeping well, not since the old recurring nightmare of his mother's death returned. He started taking dream-deflector pills again, but Daith needed them as well.

If only Doctor Ludd was still around.... But it was no use. Doctor Ludd had fled, having a change of heart about the entire operation. Without the good doctor, Trey didn't know where to get a fresh supply of the illegal medicine. Once they ran out, Daith would begin to dream again, and may remember her identity, which would destroy everything he had worked to accomplish. Trey only hoped they could both make it through the next two standard weeks.

After they reached Sintaur, dreams would be the last thing either of them would care about.

CHAPTER 2

SMOKE.

Heat.

Darkness.

He couldn't see. He couldn't move. He couldn't breathe!

Torrak Spirtz gasped as he emerged from unconsciousness. Bright yellow lights and the smell of heavy-duty cleaners overwhelmed his senses.

"What's going on? Where am I?"

A pair of pale green eyes looked at him from underneath a mop of curly red hair. "You're in Fior General Medical Center."

Torrak glanced at his friend. "Kalil? What am I doing in the hospital?"

"A student on campus found you lying in a field. Your burns were so bad, the physicians couldn't identify you. They called Central Authority, who tracked you down through the school, and then they contacted me since we're roommates." Kalil pursed his lips and sat on the edge of the hospital bed. "The doctors tried to make *me* seem like the bad guy, asking why I hadn't filed a report you were missing. I told them you planned to stay at the Academy's Study Quarters until finals were over. Like I knew you were in a hospital for the past three weeks."

Torrak could hear the guilt in his friend's voice. "What did the doctors say after that?"

"Not much. Mostly mumbled under their breath." Kalil paused. "So what happened to you?"

Torrak rubbed his fingers over his caramel-colored arms, a crusted mess from the applied anti-burn medication. "I—I don't know. I don't really remember."

"The field looked like it had caught on fire. But why would you have walked into it?"

"I didn't. I mean, I was there already and then, then I felt heat and dust and, and she screamed!" Torrak jerked into a sitting position. Memories slammed into him, disjointed like jagged chunks of rock.

He'd been walking with someone, her face blurred, and then a silver ship landed in front of them. Two men emerged from the craft in blue jumpsuits—one a huge man, like a solid wall, the other tall and thin. They pushed him aside, and rushed toward his friend, grabbing her. His memory of their faces distorted into wavy lines when she stood nearby. Torrak regained his balance and one of them restrained him—the behemoth. The woman screamed for help, her face a shapeless impression. He remembered trying to get up when a blow from behind forced him back to his knees.

Then she was gone. Torrak recalled the flash of a yellow syringe and a sharp pain in his arm. The huge man grinned—full lips chapped and flaky. He remembered thick, yellow liquid, full of orange blobs, dripping off his elbow.

The memories became erratic after that. Torrak remembered

running into a field of tall grass. Lying down. A skull-shaking hum. A wave of heat. His arms and legs felt limp, unable to hold up his body. They sunk into the dry dirt, kicking up clouds of dust.

And then blackness.

Torrak realized unconsciousness must have engulfed him at that point. He tried to remember the name of the girl he'd been with, but to no avail. The events floated away from him when he tried to grasp them. Except one image of terror etched onto the girl's face.

That he saw with perfect clarity.

Torrak had to find her, to help her, though he had no idea where to start. All he knew was a small ship had taken her.

"That must have been how the fire started—the grass must have lit when the ship took off."

"What under the stars are you talking about?" Kalil asked.

Torrak fought with the covers to get out of the bed. "The ship— it took her—she was kidnapped—and I saw it—"

"Slow down. You're doing that 'speaking too fast' thing again. Help who? Who are you talking about?"

"I need to get out of here first. I'll explain later. Let's go home. I need to use your computer system." Torrak struggled into the clean clothing Kalil had brought. His arms and legs wobbled under his weight, the muscles atrophied from lying in the hospital bed for three weeks.

"You know you'd have better luck if you put the pants on one leg at a time," Kalil joked.

"Will you sign me out of here so we can go?"

Kalil flinched at the harshness of Torrak's words. "What are you yelling at me for? I just want to know what's going on."

"I will tell you when we get home. I just need to think."

"Fine."

Unusually silent for the two talkative friends, the ride home consisted of Kalil fuming on one side of the vehicle and Torrak mentally urging him to go faster on the other. Torrak's head spun, a feeling he wasn't used to. Normally able to figure out complex puzzles and situations, he found it unnerving to have parts within his memories missing.

They finally arrived at the small, white, domed two-bedroom house—standard living quarters for Academy students. The two walked straight past Torrak's room decorated in beiges, tans, and browns, into Kalil's. Clashing bright colors covered each wall.

Torrak walked over to the right wall, trying to ignore the dizzying green and magenta stripes, and initiated a computer program. A large, holographic screen came up.

"Okay I need your help now," Torrak said.

Kalil set his jaw.

"I don't have time for this. Are you going to help me or not?"

Kalil crossed his arms, still silent.

"What is your problem? Why won't you just help me?" Torrak felt furious, but not really at Kalil. He was angry with himself for letting his friend get kidnapped, for almost getting himself killed, for putting Kalil through the worry about what had happened to him, and for not being able to remember almost anything.

"You finished with your temper tantrum?" Kalil asked.

Torrak opened his mouth to yell and then closed it with a click of his teeth. He forced out a long breath. "I'm sorry."

Kalil's tone softened. "What's going on?"

Torrak recounted what he could remember. He tried not to let himself get too frustrated with the fact he couldn't remember everything. "I need to find this friend of mine, a girl, but I can't remember her name. I know you have some kind of locator program that can help me."

"Shouldn't we contact Central Authority to report the kidnapping?"

"I don't want to bother them if she's home safe and sound. Besides, what can I report? Some girl got kidnapped three weeks ago? 'No, officer, I don't know her name or where she lives or how I know her.' Yeah, that won't get an immediate vidlink disconnect. I used to deal with reports like this all the time and more often than not the missing individual was just fine."

"I guess it won't hurt to find out who she is and if she's home first." Kalil activated the search program. "Okay. I need you to describe her with the best detail possible."

"Well she probably attended the Academy since the field they found me in is right off campus."

"And what does she look like?"

"Long, brown hair and green eyes. Pale skin." He looked up at Kalil whose fingers flew over the flashing buttons.

Kalil entered the parameters and waited a few moments. He frowned at the results. "There are seventy-one matches of women with brown hair and green eyes at the Academy. We can either go through them all, or else you have to give me something else."

Torrak stopped to think. "Maybe we had a class together?"

"Hold on. I'll cross reference this with your schedule," said Kalil. Tracing his finger along the holographic screen, he eliminated a couple of the options and highlighted a few others. "Okay. That brings us down to thirteen matches. Let's see if she's here."

"That's her," Torrak said at the ninth picture. "That's the one." He looked up at her name. "Daith Tocc. I can't believe I forgot her name."

"*Daith* was kidnapped? You didn't tell me that!"

"I didn't know it *was* her, remember?" Torrak snapped.

"Sorry...it's just... you talk about her all the time. Well her and her sister. I figured this was some random girl you saw while walking by, not Daith."

Now that he'd seen her face, bits of memories sparked inside Torrak's mind. He remembered dinners at Daith and her sister, Valendra's, house. He remembered laughing in class. He remembered her reluctance at wanting to meet Kalil or any of Torrak's friends, though she never specified why. "What's wrong with me?"

"Well you did almost get burned alive. Maybe you hit your head on a rock or something in the field?"

Torrak thought about it. "Maybe. Something feels wrong though. All the events feel blurred—like a bad vidlink connection. I remember some things and not others. Like I can picture her face from that instant, but right now, I can't seem to remember anything else about her. I can remember the man who tackled me, but whenever Daith is in the scene, he and the other man's faces look hazy and distorted. Everything that happened is perfectly clear, except when she was there." Torrak stared at the picture. "You know, they did inject something into my arm."

"What? The doctor's didn't say you had any drugs in your system."

"Some of the liquid dribbled down my arm. But I've never seen anything like it. A yellow, viscous fluid, with darker orange blobs floating inside. It doesn't even sound like anything I saw from my days working for Central Authority. It could be a new drug, I suppose. Something modified to target memories that deal with a certain trigger, like a name or face."

"A serum that can find all the memories you have about her and erase them, but nothing else? That's beyond any technology I've heard of." Kalil paused. "If that's the case, why do you still remember some things about her, like the way she looks?"

"I don't know. Maybe I didn't get a full dose." Torrak's brow furrowed. He didn't like not knowing exactly what had happened. The more he thought about it, the more he wanted to see Daith.

Perhaps she would have answers, if she was all right. "Could you find out where she lives?"

Kalil brought up the address. Torrak memorized it. How could he have forgotten? He'd been to Daith's house many times, visiting her and her sister, Valendra.

"Thanks, man. You're the best." Torrak started to leave.

"Hold on," Kalil called out. "You're going *now*?"

"Of course I'm going now. Why?"

"Um—maybe because you got out of the hospital a few standard hours ago after being incapacitated for three weeks and now you're happily skipping out the door to find some girl you think might have been kidnapped by thugs who tried to erase any memory you had of her—*and* left you for dead."

Torrak took a step back into the room. "You want me to wait? She still could be missing or hurt or dead. I can't sit—her house is just—if she's home then everything—"

"Slow down."

Torrak inhaled, held it, then released it. His brain analyzed things so quickly that sometimes his mouth couldn't keep up. "Her house is just past campus. I have to see if she's home. If she isn't there, I'm going to file a report right away. But I can't do that until I know if she's all right or not. Okay?"

"Whatever. I hope you know what you're doing."

Torrak waited for a moment in the doorway. "Kalil?"

"What?"

"Thanks for your help."

Kalil rolled his eyes. "If you throw a fit the next time, I'll send you to the hospital myself."

CHAPTER 3

DAITH DREW HER knees into her chest and wrapped her arms around her legs. The floor of the engineering room was ridged and cold, but she barely felt it. Her gaze rested on the unique engine—two massive violet-orange silari trees wrapped up by long, metal tubes. The tubes slurped up the trees' sap, silari gel, from a deep pool at the lowest point of the floor, which fueled the ship. The liquid glowed a rusty orange and rippled in an indiscernible pattern, quivering from the motions of the ship.

Entranced by the trees, her eyes followed the curves of their trunks, the whorls in their bark. Part of her believed that somehow, being the only living things on board besides the crew, they could give her inspiration. Void of family or friends, Daith found it difficult to feel connected to anything. She hoped the beautiful trees might reveal their secret—why they kept living while surrounded by metal hollowness.

But the trees remained silent, their sap milked into the pool below them, glistening in the amber glow of the light's reflection. They offered her nothing.

"Back again?"

Daith turned her head toward the voice. "Am I in the way?"

A short, albino man squatted next to her—his white hair cropped, his grey eyes inquisitive. A black smear marred his cheek, residue from his dirty hands. His blue jumpsuit sported matching dirt and grease marks.

"Of course not," the chief engineer said. "I told you you're always welcome here." He hesitated. "Anything I can do for you?"

Daith shook her head and dug her chin into her knees. The man stood to leave.

"Byot?" she asked.

"Yes?"

"The silari sap fuels the engines, correct?"

"Yup."

"If one of the trees died, would the other supply enough?"

Byot shifted his gaze to the massive silari. "One would have enough, if it survived. Unfortunately, if one died, the other would as well. Their roots are interconnected. We have an extra pair in suspended storage, just in case."

"The other one would die," she stated.

Byot nodded.

Daith thought of Dru. Only four days since he'd been killed and her whole life had changed. She never imagined such a strong connection could happen with someone in such a short period of time. Something powerful and meaningful had been lost and she didn't know how to move forward without him. Just like the silari trees. Bonded to another until one of them was gone, ripped away suddenly by death.

Daith tightened her jaw. "That's not fair, to be connected to something mortal, having your life be dependent on another's."

Byot's raised an eyebrow and he looked back down at Daith. "I suppose. But they don't *know* that."

Anger rumbled in her stomach as she stared at the massive trees, their purple-orange trunks tall and lean, bark carved into intricate swirling patterns. Her chest ached. These trees didn't have a choice. She didn't have a choice. How could she have known how easily it was to talk to him? How safe she would feel? And now nothing remained except a longing for someone that no longer existed.

She stood abruptly, stormed up the black ramp, and out of engineering. "It's not fair," she muttered.

* * *

Torrak slowed to a walk. He approached Daith's house. The cream-colored dome looked similar to Torrak's rented student housing, but the bright green paneled windows and half-worked garden beds gave the place an "owned" feel. He stopped halfway up the path to the door when he saw his reflection in the door's glass.

He looked awful.

And creepy.

They'd washed him at the hospital, but his blistered burns made him look half melted, his normally caramel-colored skin had a yellowish tint, his cheeks gaunt from dehydration. *I should have tried to vidlink her.*

Before he could decide whether he should leave, a woman peeked out from the front door.

"Can I help you?"

Torrak stammered at her beauty. "H-hey, Valendra."

Valendra blinked repeatedly, puzzled at the scarred man in front of her. "Torrak?"

He nodded.

She flipped her long, honey-streaked hair over her shoulder—her pale brown eyes wide with alarm. "You look awful! What happened to you?" She held open the door and motioned for him to come forward.

He walked inside the main room and took a seat on their squashy, smoke-colored couch. Pale blue curtains swayed in the breeze through the windows, casting shadows across the modest furniture. The bare, dark grey walls stirred up a flash of a memory in Torrak, that Daith and Valendra had never really settled in, like they wanted to be sure they could leave in a moment's notice. "I'm here to see Daith. Is she home?"

"Daith?"

"Yeah. Is she around?"

Valendra sank slowly into a puffy, grey armchair across from him, her forehead creased. "Who are you talking about?"

"Uh...your sister?"

Valendra half-smiled. "Very funny."

Torrak frowned. "I'm not trying to be funny. I'm actually worried about her. Have you seen her lately?"

"Torrak, I don't have a sister."

"What are you talking about? Of course you do. Daith. Your younger sister. Brown hair, green eyes."

Valendra shook her head with a giggle. "You know I don't have a sister. I live here by myself. What's this all about?"

Torrak stared, dumbfounded. Bits and pieces of memories flickered in his mind. "That's impossible. She lives here. I've been here when she's been here. There are pictures of her on the..." Torrak trailed off as his gaze turned toward the mantel. He stood abruptly and walked over to it. There were indeed pictures—Valendra and her friends, a younger picture of Valendra and a beautiful woman with intense green eyes, a photo of Valendra with her previous pet—but none of Daith.

"I don't understand," he said, turning to face her. "Your sister, Daith. She attends the Academy with me. We're best friends. She's invited me over to have dinner here countless times."

Valendra blushed. "I know you've been here for dinner, but it's only been the two of us."

Torrak sat back down. "This doesn't make any sense."

Valendra sat next to him on the couch, eyeing his injuries. "Torrak, what happened to you? Did you get into some kind of accident?"

With shaking hands, Torrak ran his fingers through his hair. "Yes...sort of. I came from the hospital."

"Why were you in the hospital?" Her words lilted in soft and soothing tones. She placed her hand on his. Warm and pale, her skin stood out against his darker pigments.

"There was an accident—it involved your sister. This may sound insane, but I think someone kidnapped her."

"But I don't *have* a sister!" She snatched her hand away and stood. Her fingers snapped repeatedly toward the pictures on the mantle, their surfaces reflecting the lights. "See? I'm an only child. Me, my mom, and....and..." She trailed off, her eyes staring past the picture into nothingness.

"Valendra?"

The young woman traced the picture of her younger self with the older, similar-looking woman. The two figures stood to the left of the picture—the right side possessed an empty gap. Big enough for another child.

"Torrak?" she whispered.

He stood and touched her elbow. She jumped at the contact, her eyes cloudy with tears. "Torrak, I don't understand what's going on.

And...I received a vidlink message, about two weeks ago...." She shook her head, her honey-blonde hair dancing. "It was strange. It came from Central Authority."

"What did it say?"

Valendra grasped the picture with her slim fingers as if to gain comfort from its image. "They asked me to call them about a Missing Citizens report I'd filed. I had no idea what they were talking about. When I contacted them the next morning, the officer told me she didn't remember leaving me a message. There wasn't any record of the missing citizens file I'd reported. She assumed someone activated my vidlink connection by mistake. She apologized. I haven't thought about it since."

"So they said you filed a report about someone missing, but you don't remember doing that. Then when you returned the call, they said *they* didn't have anything on file. And now I'm here with fuzzy memories about a sister you can't remember being kidnapped."

Torrak's mind burst into a fury of thoughts. He began with Valendra's first comment, about her receiving a vidlink message. He pictured it in his mind, Valendra opening the file, the look of confusion on her face. His mind added other pictures: the missing report, the yellow liquid dribbling off his arm, the apologetic officer. Torrak held the thoughts in his head like pictures on a flat surface. He connected them to each other and then forced himself to fill in the blanks with other pictures of what happened between those moments.

If his memories had been erased about Daith, and Valendra couldn't remember Daith, perhaps she'd had her memories erased as well. And if Valendra reported Daith missing, they must have erased her memories after the kidnapping. As well as the officer's, since there was a call about a report, but then the next day the file was gone.

Sparks popped inside Torrak's mind as the pieces clicked into place. But a hole remained—something vital he couldn't grasp.

Someone must be orchestrating the use of a memory modification drug *and* be able to infiltrate Central Authority. But who had that sort of power?

"Valendra, is there anyone you know who would want to kidnap your sister?"

Her jaw muscles tightened. "I told you I don't have—"

"Sorry," Torrak said, waving his hands defensively. "How about you then? Or harm you in any way?"

Valendra sunk into the chair, her eyes back on the picture. "Um, no. I don't think so," she replied. "All I can think of is—but there's no way that's possible."

"Please. Anything might help."

Her words came slowly. "I can't believe I'm telling you this, but..." She drew in a shuddering breath. "Tocc is not my real name. My real surname is Jaxx. Jacin Jaxx was my father."

Torrak's breath caught in his throat. He couldn't believe it. Jacin Jaxx? The man who'd helped save dozens of worlds with the telepathic, empathic, and telekinetic abilities seen above and beyond anyone in their known galaxy, whose army had mercilessly killed anyone who opposed him. If he was Valendra's father, Jacin Jaxx must be Daith's father, too.

And Daith had never told him.

"About ten standard years ago, two years before my father's death," Valendra went on, "my mother sent me to live on Debbing. She told me my father had become unstable and I needed to stay away from him for a while. She planned to meet me after she took care of some financial business, but she never showed." Valendra's lower lip quivered.

"I'm sorry, I didn't know."

Valendra continued. "I lived on my own for almost a year with the money my mother left me. But then, someone attacked me. I don't know if they wanted to hold me hostage or take me to my father or what, but I never got a chance to find out." Valendra shook her head again, her eyes blinking furiously.

"It's so hard to picture what really happened," she continued. "They entered the room and shot some sort of gas. I couldn't see anything. I heard their weapons discharge and I dropped to the floor. I remember I bit through my lip when I hit the ground. Someone grabbed me and then..." Valendra closed her eyes.

"Then what happened?" Torrak asked gently.

"I screamed and everything went black and silent. When the lights came back on, three men with weapons lay face up on the floor, their eyes glazed. I could see three more bodies in the hallway, all with the same expressions." She shuddered.

"They were dead?"

"No. They just lay there, staring ahead, not blinking. Completely immobile. But I didn't do it. I didn't do anything." Valendra's words came in between shallow breaths.

"It's okay. Whatever happened, it's over."

She placed the picture back on the mantle, her hands shaking. "Torrak, you don't understand. I remember being really scared *for them*. Like I knew something had happened to them. Something terrible, that needed to be kept secret. But I can't remember what."

CHAPTER 4

COMMANDER XIVEN'S INTERNAL ship's communication monitor pinged. He reached across his immaculate desk to turn on the com.

"Yes, Chief Engineer Byot? What is it?"

"Commander, it's about Daith."

Trey's cheek muscle twitched. "What about her?"

"She came to the engineering section again."

"And?"

"She asked about the trees. Then she got really angry and left. I don't think she noticed, but she melted her handprints into the engineering floor."

"Thank you, Chief. Keep me posted." Trey ended the call. Daith's power existed, so close to the surface, but she couldn't control it. He needed to refocus her somehow—keep her grounded, but still unstable.

Trey laughed at the paradox.

If only his brother hadn't been so foolish, Dru would still be here, guiding Daith, building their connection. His death would have been so much more terrible for her—her revenge on the Controllers that much swifter. But Dru turned against Trey earlier than he'd thought. And Trey had been forced to kill him sooner than expected.

Perhaps someone else on board could help with Daith. Trey had to maintain the image of her leader, guide her with specifically planned information about the Controllers. Byot seemed to have a foothold, but Byot would be too busy dealing with engineering. He couldn't be spared to babysit.

Trey tapped his fingers on his desk. He hated this place, this ship. He'd been stuck on it for years, surrounded by an inept crew, with too many varying possibilities. This vessel had become a part of his existence as he watched the downfall of his idol, saw everything he'd worked for vanish at the hands of jealous, ignorant fools.

He couldn't wait to be free, to live his life in the shadows—finally in control. Everyone believed having and using power meant standing in the spotlight, but Trey knew better. He'd seen what happened to those who led the charge. Either their egos got them killed or they became targets to be hunted. However, the general commanding the troops from off the field controlled the situation and the soldiers.

For Trey to do that he needed to get off this ship and onto the sidelines. But keeping Daith on the edge of rage and insanity, without her falling into the abyss, was proving harder than he thought.

And then it came to him. The perfect individual to help Daith become more stable, all the while fueling her anger toward the Controllers.

* * *

"Creepy. You had a bunch of unconscious men lying all around you, but you don't know how they got that way?" Torrak contemplated the facts. If Daith had been wiped from Valendra's memory, perhaps she'd been there during the attack. "What happened then?"

Valendra rubbed her forehead. "I moved to another city and was hunted down again, but this time a second group came to fight the first one. While they were occupied with each other, I escaped. After that happened, I got a job on a vacation vessel under a fake name and made my way here to Fior. I've been here ever since with my new last name, Tocc. But that's the only trouble I've ever had with the Aleet Army. Besides, they disbanded eight years ago after my father's death. There's no one left."

Valendra's words whirled inside his head, building ideas, possibilities. He jumped around through the thoughts, forcing them to connect. The army had tracked her and Daith down a second time. But why? To use as bargaining chips against Jacin? Or were they after something else? Something Valendra wasn't supposed to remember.

Something about Daith.

"Valendra, I don't want to alarm you, but what if the Aleet Army hadn't disappeared completely after Jacin's death, but instead went into hiding?"

"For what reason? Only my father had special abilities. There would be no point in keeping the army together without someone like him running it."

Lightning thoughts flashed through Torrak's mind. He closed his eyes, steadying himself from the dizziness. They would need someone like Jacin. Someone with his abilities.

What if those abilities had been passed down to Daith?

Torrak stood. "I know you want—but the Aleet Army might—not unthinkable—check on activity..." Torrak stopped at the look of confusion on Valendra's face. He forced himself to slow and started again. "I know you want to deny it, but maybe involvement of the Aleet Army isn't that farfetched. It may not seem plausible, but I think this is worth looking into."

"I don't see why," Valendra said.

"I know this is difficult, but you *do* have a sister. You just can't remember her. I think she's been a part of your life the whole time you were on the run from the Aleet Army. I think they've been trying to find her again. And I think they took her three standard weeks ago."

Valendra's lip quivered. "Torrak, what are you saying? I have a sister I don't know about? How is that even possible?"

"I think someone erased your memories of her."

Valendra sunk back into her chair and drew her knees into her chest. She closed her eyes, breathing shallow breaths.

Torrak crouched in front of her, wishing he could make her feel better.

The breaths slowed and Valendra opened her eyes. She smiled. "I'm sorry, I must have dozed off for a moment. What were you saying?"

Torrak frowned. "I was saying how I think someone erased your memories of Daith."

"Daith?" Valendra blinked. "Who's Daith?"

* * *

Lieutenant Commander Cenjo left the simulation room with a grunt. He'd just finished a training session with his most seasoned trainees, but they were mediocre at best. Half didn't seem to have an interest, only there because Commander Xiven required it, and the other half simply didn't have time to practice. Cenjo knew they had hectic schedules since they ran the ship with a skeleton crew, but they couldn't expect to keep their bodies in prime condition if they didn't practice on their own time.

Cenjo's fingers combed through his slicked, black hair—the fingertips digging in to relieve some of his headache. It wasn't fair to the trainees. They couldn't help their schedules. Xiven simply refused to hire anyone else and with his lack of forgiveness and easy dismissal of crew members, their numbers had diminished significantly in the past few weeks.

Now the commander wanted him to get Daith involved in training sessions. The crew barely wanted to associate with her already. She represented a ticking bomb.

But orders were orders. At least for now.

The door to his office swished open and Cenjo entered, leaving the lights off. He made his way to his desk under the dimness of a three-dimensional holographic picture that hung from the center of the ceiling. The piece rotated slowly, showing each side of a red and orange sphere, splashed with currents of gold that wound their way like rivers through the solid borders. The lights reflected off his shiny metallic desk and darkened vidlink station. Datapads, stacked on one edge, mirrored the light in warped waves.

Staring for a moment at the piece, Cenjo admired the artistic take on his homeworld, Katala. His younger sister, Brial, had designed and created the art. It had hung in her bedroom in secret for weeks before she'd revealed it as a gift on his birthday. She'd blushed at his genuine admiration of her work.

He blinked, hard. His chest tightened at the thought of her.

Cenjo sat at his desk below the swirling globe, his thoughts returning to the day's work, away from the painful memories of his sister, when the chimes to his office rang.

"Come in," he called out.

The door opened with a hiss. She stood there, framed by the

entrance.

"Daith?" he asked, half standing in surprise. "What are you doing here?" The lights from the artwork danced across her pale face. He clenched his hands under his desk, fully aware of how much she reminded him of Brial. "Computer, lights."

The harsh, white lights hummed to life, dominating the room. Daith stepped forward and the door slid closed behind her. Her emerald eyes flickered around the room, resting momentarily on the sphere above them.

"Nice artwork."

"Thank you. It was a gift." He gestured for her to take the metal seat across from him. She plunked down onto it, its frame creaking.

"How are things going?" she asked, her voice jagged—void of its usual melodic quality.

"Fine." He paused. "Is there something I can help you with?"

She twisted her fingers through her long, brown hair. "No. I'm just..."

"Bored?"

"Frustrated," she countered.

"With what?"

"I don't know. Everything. Lack of progress. Lack of knowledge. I mean, I want to help you all deal with the Controllers, but what good am I going to be when we reach them? Unless they want a bunch of melty datapads."

Cenjo shifted in his chair. "I can't say I know what Trey expects you to do. Truth is, he may simply be happy you're on our side."

"But I want to *do* something," she said, pushing away from his desk. "They killed my family. They are responsible for my memory loss. And they murdered Dru. I can't be useless. Not with all this power."

"Tell you what," he said. "Why don't you do some sparring with me later this afternoon in Simulation Room Two?"

Daith snorted. "Sparring?"

"You never continued classes after that one time you joined us."

"That's because I broke someone's nose using my mind before you'd even finished telling us what the warm-up routine would be."

"True...but she did kind of deserve it."

"No one deserves that. My power got out of control."

"Then start with what you can control—your body. Your determination is great and all, but I still think there's benefit in using your body physically, too. Getting a little exercise and learning to defend yourself could also help you get out of your brain for a while."

Daith sat back in the chair, her face thoughtful. "I will, but only if no one else is there. I don't want to hurt anyone." Her eyes darkened. "At least not on this ship."

CHAPTER 5

TORRAK LEFT VALENDRA'S house as fast as his not-yet-healed body would let him. Once home, he rushed inside and came up behind Kalil. Startled, the morsel of klaad in his friend's mouth dropped to the floor. Kalil eyed the spicy, expensive meat-flavored substance and turned, annoyed at the intrusion. His face turned inquisitive at the earnest look on Torrak's face.

"What happened?" he asked.

"I need to use your computer system again," Torrak said after he caught his breath.

"Why? Was Daith home?" Kalil asked.

"No, Daith wasn't there. And Valendra didn't remember again. I need to find Opute."

"Opute?"

Torrak nodded as he gulped in more air.

"Wait, you don't mean *Ness* Opute, do you? Isn't he that

criminal you sent to jail back on C-Nine?"

Torrak nodded again.

"And what didn't Valendra remember?"

"Her sister. She forgot her and then forgot her again. It was like something in her mind wouldn't let her remember."

Kalil sat quiet for a moment. "Did I miss something? I must have missed something," he finally said. "Why would her sister not remember her twice and how could anything relating to Daith's kidnapping have to do with Opute?"

"I think Valendra may have gotten a full dose of whatever memory modification stuff was used on me. I think it doesn't let her make any new memories of Daith."

"And Opute? Why would he help you?"

"He owes me a favor. So can I use your computer again? Or are you going to go back to eating your disgusting klaad?"

Kalil looked longingly at his half-eaten meal on the table. "Sure. Why not?" he muttered. "None of this makes any sense anyway. Might as well find some crazy criminal to help you find a kidnapped girl no one can remember."

They walked into Kalil's room, resumed the search program, and typed in the request to find Ness Opute. After several standard minutes, the computer flashed the words REQUESTED ITEM NOT FOUND.

"Of course. He's not exactly the type to be listed." Torrak racked his brain for a way to find Opute. "Maybe Lang still knows what he's up to."

"Lang?"

"Pierze Lang. He owns a package delivery store on C-Nine."

Kalil narrowed the search to citizens of the city Ponsunila on the planet C-sector 9, or C-9 for short, and typed in Lang's name. As they waited for the results, Kalil asked about Lang.

"When I used to work for Central Authority on C-Nine, we used Lang's delivery store, Zzeress PhthRee, as a courier service. I got to know him pretty well. We kept in contact, but we sort of lost touch this past year."

"Zee-ress Fifth-what? What language is that?"

"PhthRee." Torrak repeated. "It's Fillaniss. It's Lang's home language."

"Oh." Kalil looked back at the screen, still searching. "Why would he know where Opute is?"

"Because Opute *also* used Lang's store for deliveries."

Kalil's eyebrows crinkled. "Huh?"

"Remember I told you I got Opute thrown into jail? Well when he got out, he came looking for me. I mean there I was, barely over eighteen standard years old, and the notorious Ness Opute learned I'd found the crucial piece of evidence to prove his guilt. You can imagine how happy he was to see me."

Kalil smirked at the sarcasm. "What happened?"

"I'd been on my way home from work, rounded the corner of a building and next thing I know, I'm being thrown into a wall. He jammed his elbow into my throat and cut off my air. I thought I was dead. But then, ironically enough, criminals saved my life."

"Some criminals came to help you?"

"Nope. They were looking for Opute. Three jumped him, knocking him away from me. They rambled on about a bad deal, something about selling them a weaker version of an expensive metal. While they held him down, one of them pried open Opute's mouth to try to pour the imitation liquid metal down his throat."

Kalil shivered. "What a terrible way to die. What did you do?"

"I took out my weapon and shot the guy above Opute. It blasted a hole through his head big enough for me to see through. The first time I'd ever killed someone." Torrak winced at the memory. "The other two scattered, but I called it in to Central Authority on my communications radio. They were tracked down within a few standard hours."

"What happened to Opute?"

"He said he owed me for saving his life and if I ever needed him he'd back me up. Then he walked away."

Kalil nodded toward the picture of Lang that had popped up. "How is *he* involved then?"

"Lang also dealt with Opute. The Zzeress PhthRee handled transactions with discretion. That's why the government and anyone who wanted to remain anonymous, including Opute, used it."

"Well let's hope this Lang guy can help."

* * *

Daith lay on her bed, her long, brown hair hanging over its edges, spread out around her head like a chestnut-colored halo. She meant to sleep until her time reader beeped, which would indicate she should leave to meet Cenjo, but rest didn't come. Not surprising since she slept so rarely lately. Every time she tried to relax, her brain buzzed with thoughts. Whether images of Dru's death flashing through her mind or self-berating thoughts telling her she would be useless against the Controllers, the inside of her skull seemed to remain a constant torrent of negativity.

Her gaze rested on the smooth, grey ceiling. The lights, dimmed seventy-five percent, glowed softly in their snug sockets. Flicking her eyes in another direction, she took in the bare, grey walls. Three weeks she'd been on the *Horizon*, and her room could have been anyone's. No personal effects reflecting herself or her life on the ship. Not that she had anything personal. Or at least not that she could remember.

Beeps filled the silence.

"Computer, time reader off." The noise quieted and Daith swung her legs off the bed to stand. She left her quarters and made her way through the hushed corridors toward the simulation rooms—a path quite familiar to her now. The smooth grey walls and worn carpeting made the area feel lived-in, cozier than if it had been completely sterile and new. It may not be her real home, but she couldn't remember her real home anyway. The thought both soothed her and pricked her with guilt.

She entered simulation room 2 and found Cenjo inside, his training program already running.

"Glad you could make it," he said, his tone light.

"Not like I have much else to do." Daith pressed the heels of her hands into her face for a moment and let out a sigh. "I'm sorry about earlier," she said.

"Sorry?"

She nodded and joined him on the floor. A squishy, yellow mat deflated slightly under her weight. The walls looked like pale strips of wood. Even though the images weren't real and Daith knew the room changed to fit the needs of the programmer, she appreciated the beauty and detail of the environment.

"I know I've been cross lately."

"It's understandable. You have good reason to be upset."

Daith stretched out across her legs. Her quads groaned in protest, but she pressed herself down further until her muscles twitched with pain. Daith could feel Cenjo's gaze on the back of her neck, watching to see what kind of reaction she might have. She didn't really want to talk about Dru's death.

His murder.

Heat bubbled inside her stomach. The energy built up fast lately. She knew anger made her more powerful, but she feared it at the same time. To have something so strong inside her without being under her control, like it had a mind of its own. She knew she needed to embrace her abilities to use them to their full extent, but what if she hurt someone again by mistake?

"I don't want to be a useless lump." She sat up straight, reaching above her. "But I don't know if I'm of use to anyone right now, much less when we find the Controllers."

"Daith."

She looked over at him, surprised by the firmness in his voice. His brown eyes narrowed, his eyebrows pulled together.

"Do you want to stop the Controllers?" he asked.

"Well, yes, I mean—"

"Then you will."

Taken aback by the finality of his tone, Daith sat silent for a few moments.

"It's not that simple..." she began.

Cenjo stood. "Yes, it is. I'm not trying to belittle you or diminish what you're going through, but you are *more* than your abilities. You are an intelligent, creative, clever woman who has come very far in a short period of time. You started three weeks ago with nothing, literally. No memories, no family, no sense of purpose. Now look at you. You've discovered a unique world of abilities the rest of us can only dream about. You've opened yourself up to possibilities that would terrify others. That's nothing to scoff at."

"But Trey—"

"Commander Xiven has been pursuing his quest for a long time. He'd like you to be able to help, but I think he'd continue on, even if you weren't here."

"You can't tell me you don't want my help just as much as Trey does," she said, shaking her legs one at a time.

"No, but I joined this cause before I knew about you. We might be more successful with your abilities, but I plan on being successful regardless. The Controllers need to be stopped."

Daith stood, bouncing on the balls of her feet. "Can I ask why you joined the Aleet Army?"

Cenjo hesitated. "My homeworld, Katala, needed help. The man who ran this army came and helped us."

"So like Trey's homeworld, Sintaur? He helped stop a war or something?"

Cenjo's eyebrows pinched together. "Or something."

Daith felt an ache in her chest, reminiscent of how she felt when she thought about Dru. Cenjo had lost someone close to him. She knew it. She *felt* it.

"I'm sorry. I shouldn't have brought it up."

"There's no need to apologize. We've all had hard times in our past. It's what brings us together." Cenjo's lip curled into a slight grin. "But right now, none of that matters. Focus on me. And defend yourself."

CHAPTER 6

PIERZE LANG UNLOCKED the front door of his small store and wiggled his heavyset body through the entrance. *Zzeress PhthRee,* a shipping and packaging supply house on C-Sector 9, sat on the outskirts of the central promenade in the middle of the capital, Ponsunila, and had been in business for over 300 standard years.

Lang sat down behind a green hardened-jelly desk, a gift from his father who had owned the store before him, and entered his access code into the computer system. To his surprise, nothing happened.

Lang entered his access code again and a small black message box appeared on the screen: ACCESS DENIED: SERVICE TO NETWORK TERMINATED. Lang gawked at the screen in disbelief. He hadn't missed a payment his whole life. There was no reason his computer system shouldn't be connected to the city's mainframe network. He started to punch in his access code again when a bass voice behind him stopped him cold.

"Pierze Lang?"

"Yes," Lang said, turning. "I'm sorry if I left the door unlocked, but the store's not open yet." Lang's breath caught in his throat. A huge, brownish-green creature towered over him, silhouetted by the rays of first sunrise. The creature held a rounded metallic weapon about a fourth of a meter long, aimed directly at Lang's chest.

"Lang identification confirmed," the deep voice said. The green shadow shrugged. "Nothing personal."

Lang barely had time to think about what those words meant when a flash of blue light exploded before his eyes. His body rocked under the electric current that struck him in the chest. For a few moments, he felt himself being cooked alive, his insides overloaded with energy as bloody foam trickled from his eyes and mouth. And then, almost as soon as it had begun, the pain stopped, and the world fell away into darkness.

* * *

Kalil just finished the rest of the klaad he'd been eating earlier when an error message came up on his computer screen. "That's strange," he mumbled.

"What's strange?" asked Torrak.

"The computer is telling us the message you sent to Lang didn't go through. It says a link to Lang's store isn't possible."

"That can't be right." Torrak glanced down at his time-reader and did a conversion to C-Sector 9 time in his head. "His store should be open right now."

"I'll check again." After a moment, Kalil shook his head. "The computer says his store is no longer linked to the city's central computer network."

"Could there have been a power outage?"

"If there was, we wouldn't get a message at all from the network. Do you think Lang manually disconnected his personal computer?"

"He has no reason to."

"Well let me make a request to C-Nine's mainframe and see what happened to the connection."

Moments later the computer confirmed the manual disconnect.

"I don't understand," Torrak said. "Why would he do that?"

"All I can think of is he wants to access his computer without the city's network knowing. Maybe he's making some transactions he doesn't want anyone to know about?"

Torrak shook his head. "Lang had a coded system when dealing with illegal transactions. It would be too obvious if he shut down his system every time he did something he didn't want the authorities to know about."

"I don't know then. We can try him back later."

Torrak closed his eyes for a moment. "Something else is going on here. And I think I need to go to C-Nine and find out what's happened."

Kalil snorted a laugh. "That's crazy. For all you know he's merely changing or updating his computer system. We haven't even tried contacting him through the vidlink. I mean, it'll cost you thirty times more—"

"Let's do that."

Kalil shrugged. "It's your money." He went through another set of screens. "Hmm...."

"What is it?"

"There's no connection to his vidlink. It doesn't even connect to a recording to tell you what store you're calling."

"I knew something was wrong!"

Kalil typed in a few commands to recheck his data. The same results appeared. "Are you sure he hasn't closed down his store?"

"Maybe, but he's been running the store for over a century—took it over from his father. I know I've been out of touch with him, but I feel like he would have told me if his business had been in any trouble." Torrak stood, no longer able to contain his pent-up concern. "Something else must have happened. If there was a fire or a robbery, Lang might be hurt. Can you filter through the hospitals and see if he's listed in any of them?"

Kalil did as requested and the results came back quickly. "He's not listed anywhere."

Torrak began to pace. "I've got to go and find out what happened."

"You can't go to C-Nine."

Torrak stopped. "Why not?"

Kalil threw up his arms in frustration. "What do you mean 'why not'? You missed finals while in the hospital. You have to take your make-up finals. And it's not like you have a ton of money or even a way to get there."

Torrak put his hands on his friend's wiry shoulders. He could feel the bones poke through his thin short-sleeved shirt. "I *have* to do this."

"Why? Why not wait a few days until you know for sure if something is wrong with his computer system?"

"If something happened to Lang, he may not have a few days. Lang is my best link to Opute who may be the only one to help me find Daith."

Kalil pulled away from his friend. "Your brain must have gotten melted along with the rest of you."

"I have to find her. I have to."

"Why? I know you feel guilty about what happened, but it's not like it's your fault. Call the authorities and let them do their job. They can probably get in touch with Lang, too."

"You don't understand."

"Then explain it to me."

Torrak sat, wishing he hadn't stopped moving. Everything came flooding back to him: the painful expression on her face, her cry to him for help. The guilt he felt overwhelmed him as he sat, preparing to explain to Kalil why he had to find her, and why he couldn't wait.

"When my mother died in a vehicle collision last year, I fell into complete shock," he began. "I barely ate, hardly slept, and felt completely engulfed by emptiness. When I got back from the funeral and went back to class, everything seemed meaningless. No one knew why I'd missed classes and I didn't understand how anyone could be happy when something so terrible had happened. I started resenting everyone for being able to live their lives normally. And what was the point? Life could end so quickly and no one would even know you were gone.

"And then Daith came into class. She had spiked her long hair in all different directions, applied multicolored stripes of makeup across her eyelids and over her cheeks, and wore giant, bright blue pants with white spots all over them.

"She sat down next to me like normal, said good morning, and turned her attention back to the professor." Torrak paused, smiling at the memory. "Everyone started laughing. *I* started laughing. So hard I couldn't stop. I thought I might die because I couldn't catch my breath. But for whatever reason, that snapped me out of my despair. When I asked her about how she knew to cheer me up, she told me she knew the pain of losing a parent."

"She found out your mother died?"

"No." Torrak slapped his forehead. "And I can't believe I didn't think about it then. I never told her anything.

"This may not make sense to you," Torrak continued, "but this is something I have to do. You are my closest friend, like a brother, but my friendship with Daith is different. She filled holes in my life that couldn't be filled by anyone else. Not because nobody else wanted to, but because nobody else could. Daith was there for me when I needed her, whether I thought I needed her or not. And now I have to help her because she needs me, even if *she* doesn't know it. I'm the only one who saw what happened to her."

Torrak paused, deciding to tell Kalil what he'd learned from Valendra. "I know this may sound insane, but I think remnants of the Aleet Army may be behind Daith's kidnapping. Her sister told me some things about her family's connection to them, and it makes sense. The authorities aren't going to be able to help. Even if they believed me, they wouldn't be able to find her. Not if the Aleet Army is involved."

Kalil blanched, frightened. "Torrak, what do you mean the Aleet Army is involved?"

"What I'm going to tell you doesn't leave this room, right?"

Kalil nodded.

Torrak spoke under his breath. "Daith and Valendra are Jacin Jaxx's daughters."

Kalil's jaw dropped. "Are you serious?"

"Completely. I really do think the Aleet Army are the ones who kidnapped Daith. Don't ask me how I know. I just do. And even though I don't know what I *could* do, I know I have to follow through with this. Lang is the only one I know who might be able to help me find Opute and Opute has the underground connections that may lead me to the Aleet Army.

"Most important of all, I'm on borrowed time. Sooner or later the men sent to kidnap Daith will realize they screwed up. As soon as they do, they're going to come back for me. If I stay here, there is nothing to stop them from trying again. I believe they already erased Daith's sister's memories, too. And maybe messed with Central

Authority's files."

Kalil had been quiet. Torrak knew how hard it must to digest everything he'd heard. But he'd also known Torrak long enough to realize Torrak was different. They all were. It's why they attended the Academy for Gifted Students. And Torrak's gift to correctly solve intricate puzzles when others couldn't was something Kalil couldn't dismiss.

"What do you need me to do?" Kalil asked.

CHAPTER 7

SWEAT MOISTENED DAITH'S forehead, temples, and underarms. The warmth that flared from inside her body, energy that allowed her to manipulate objects around her, would often bring perspiration. But this felt different. This she exuded from her pores, not because of her unique ability, but because she'd gotten her butt kicked.

Again.

With a wipe of the back of her hand across her brow, Daith pushed herself up off the ground for the fifth time.

"Tired yet?"

Daith's teeth ground at Cenjo's taunt.

"Not remotely," she lied, willing her ragged breathing to go unnoticed.

Cenjo's head dropped in a mock bow. "Then we'll go on." He took his stance, different than before. This time his feet planted themselves on the soft, yellow mat equally distanced apart. His arms hung loosely at his sides while his fingers fluttered.

Daith tried once again to use her gift and sense Cenjo's emotions and feelings before he attacked. She concentrated on reaching into his mind, but he made his move before she could make a connection.

Cenjo leapt, flying into the air. Both legs came at her, spread wide. She struck out instinctively at his ankles, but wasn't watching his body, which had arched backwards. In a swift motion, his legs wrapped around her head, pinning her arms to the sides of her face. His hands on the ground, he pulled her forward, over his hand-standing body, and she tumbled across him in an ungainly mess of a roll. He sat up, his back to her, and flipped around, straddling her body.

Frustrated, Daith squirmed under his hold, her muscles screaming in protest.

"Tired yet?" he prodded again.

"I'm not tired," she snapped, "I can't move. I thought you were going to teach me something, not throw me around like a limp doll!"

He leaned toward her, his olive skin dancing with beads of sweat. "You wanna get up, then get up."

"Tell me how to get out of this hold," she said through gritted teeth. Her thighs smarted from the pressure of his legs, her fingers numb from lack of blood flow.

He laughed. The noise, harsh and cold, unsettled her. It differed from his usual laid back demeanor. "I'm not holding you down. Get up. GET UP."

Tears leaked from her eyes. She wiggled in his grip, but couldn't move. The energy in the room changed. She no longer felt safe. Here she lay, pinned down, helpless. Cenjo had all the power. "I can't. I'm telling you I can't!"

"It's a good thing Dru's dead. He'd be so disappointed."

Everything went white. Blinded, Daith blinked her eyes. Her eyelids felt heavy, hot. They peeled open to reveal her standing, holding Cenjo against the wall, her hand thrust upward against his throat. Eyes bulging, mouth open in an attempt to breathe, he struggled in her grip, feet kicking limply in the air.

Daith yanked her hand away and Cenjo collapsed to the floor, sucking in large amounts of air.

"I'm so sorry!" she exclaimed, leaning down next to him. She watched in horror as red finger-marks appeared across his olive-toned neck.

"You're bl—," he rasped, coughing.

"What?" she asked.

"You're bleeding," he managed, massaging his throat. He pointed at her face.

With an impatient swipe, Daith ran the side of her arm across her face, smearing the blood.

"Never mind that," she said, "are you all right?"

Cenjo got to his feet, his breath coming more easily. "I thought it would help," he said. "I thought if I made you angry it would catapult your abilities. I remembered how you broke Sequiria's nose because she made you upset."

Daith rubbed the back of her arm against her shirt to wipe off the blood. A red slash now under her chest matched the drops that had dripped there.

"I don't know if making me angry helps," she admitted as they walked toward the center of the simulation room. "My abilities manifest completely out of my control. Like a reflex, but not one I wanted to have."

Cenjo's face fell with disappointment. "I thought for sure...."

Daith patted him on the shoulder, trying to ignore the sense of defeat radiating off him. "It's really all right. I appreciate your help.

But do me a favor? Don't. I couldn't bear it if I hurt you."

"I chose to take the risk," he said.

"Maybe. But I wouldn't want anything to happen to you. It's not like I have many friends here. Even most of the crew avoids me." A lump stuck in her throat. She felt tired of feeling alone. Tired of missing Dru. Of caring for a family that no longer existed, one she no longer remembered.

"Well I'm not sure what I can do to help, but I do think sparring will help keep you out of your head. Exercise never hurts, either. I hope you'll continue to train with me?"

Daith smiled. "As long as you actually *teach* me the moves next time."

"Deal." Cenjo motioned to her face. "You better head to medical. Commander Xiven would be furious if he knew I didn't make you check in with Doc Milastow."

"All right, all right." Daith trotted upstairs to the medical bay, glad the sense of failure from Cenjo had faded.

* * *

Torrak glared at the image on the screen of a small, dinged, vessel with disgust. "They call that a ship?"

"For your price and such short notice, this is the best you're going to get," Kalil replied.

Torrak groaned. He and Kalil could *build* a better ship. But unfortunately he didn't have the time or the money to do so. He had no choice. "All right, I'll take it."

Kalil checked off the appropriate box and a monotone voice told them that they could pick it up the next day. Instructions about the ship's location appeared on the screen.

"Trunza Corner?" Torrak said as he read the address. "Great. I couldn't have picked a worse place if I'd tried."

"Where did you expect to get a cheap ship like this? Batat Plaza?" Kalil asked.

"No. But Trunza Corner is so run-down. I don't know." Torrak stared at the image. "It looks like a piece of junk. I should head out there now and take a look at it. What if I have to make repairs?"

Kalil motioned outside. "Nobody goes to Trunza Corner this time of night. Besides, you still look like garbage." Kalil crinkled his nose. "And you smell, too."

"Fine, I'll take a shower."

"Great. What time should we leave tomorrow to pick up the ship? I figure we'll want to go pretty early to—"

"Hold on," Torrak interrupted. "What do you mean what time should *we* leave?"

"We, as in you and me. You don't think I'm letting you go by yourself, do you?"

"Forget it," Torrak said. "You're not coming with me. I don't care what kind of condition I'm in. You're barely over eighteen standard years old and you've never even left this city. I'm not going to hold your hand during your first space flight or show you the sights of C-Nine. This isn't a vacation." Torrak came off harsh, but he needed to deter his friend. He didn't know what to expect and he wasn't about to let Kalil come along if trouble arose.

"The safest place for me to be is with you. From what you've told me, it's only a matter of time before someone comes back for you. Do you think they're going to leave me alone when they find out I'm your roommate? I'm not going to wait around to be tortured to tell them where you are and end up with my brain a mushy memory-less mess."

"Kalil, you don't understand—"

Kalil's face flushed with anger. "No, *you* don't understand. Whether you meant to or not, I'm involved. You told me everything and now I'm a liability. I will not be the reason they find you. And I know if the situation were reversed, you would never let me go without you. So I'm coming. Period."

Torrak couldn't deny Kalil's logic. He would be in danger if he stayed here. And if things were the other way around, Torrak would have found a way to sneak aboard Kalil's ship if necessary.

"I don't know what I'm getting into. You could get hurt, or killed."

Kalil paled, but didn't waver. "I may not be the best in a fight, but there are other things I'm good at, and you know it. I've got a little bit of money, I'm a good navigator, and you are not the only genius in this house. What if something on the ship dies or you have to break in somewhere that's protected by a shield code? You might need my help."

Torrak reluctantly admitted to himself that having Kalil with him would probably be better than doing this on his own. Flying a ship alone wasn't impossible, but having someone else around would make things much easier. Plus Kalil's atypical genius when it came to machines would come in handy. Anything wrong with an object made of wires or metal or circuits, Kalil could fix, even if he didn't know anything about the machine. It was the reason he attended the Academy at such a young age.

"You're right," Torrak yielded, "I need your help. Just don't do anything to get yourself hurt, okay?"

"Trust me. It's not on my to-do list."

CHAPTER 8

THE NEXT MORNING, after a good night's sleep and thorough showers, the two roommates headed for Trunza Corner. Once they arrived and paid the *Anywhere and You're There!* driver, Torrak pulled out the address sheet and headed to his left. Kalil trailed close behind, looking around silently. They made their way through a maze of old, broken-down houses and corner shops, which took up space on the blocks like pieces of litter, until they came to a dirty cream-colored building with a small ship parked outside. They approached the building and knocked on the door. It opened slowly and a large figure crept toward them through the dimly lit doorway. A Corenthian, most likely female from her size, walked forward into the light.

"What?" she demanded.

"We're here about the ship," Torrak said, eyeing her long, sharp stinger as it swished behind her.

The Corenthian female stared, her single, green eye shifting between them.

"Mwww!" she screeched. She tromped off and a small Corenthian male came to the door.

"Please excuse her," he said. "She's had a rough day. You two are the ones who want to rent my ship?"

"Yes."

The male gazed out at his ship with his large, blue eye. He ran his fingers over the few yellow hairs on his head.

"Yeah, she may look old and tired, but she's still got spunk. I'll go and get you the contract screen to sign."

The male returned. "Pretty standard contract," he said, handing Torrak the datapad. "Your fee will automatically deduct from your account. The ship belongs to you for a standard month. If any damage occurs, you are responsible. If the ship is confiscated, impounded, etcetera, you need to pay the fines. And if you keep it longer than a month, you'll be charged each day you're overdue. If you agree to these terms, please sign."

Torrak let the datapad scan his retina.

"Have a good trip."

With the deal concluded, Torrak and Kalil headed over to the landing pad.

Torrak gripped his luggage bag tighter as he looked at the vessel. Rust spots seemed to have bred along the edges of the door and viewports while chips of paint had jumped ship.

Torrak opened the main hatch. A gust of damp, stale air blew the hair away from his face.

"Smells like it hasn't been used for quite some time," Kalil said from behind him. He stepped in front of Torrak to ascend the ramp. Torrak followed and glanced around the dimmed interior.

A goofy grin bloomed on Kalil's face.

"What?" Torrak asked.

"It's a good ship," Kalil responded, a far-off look in his eyes.

Torrak, who noticed the loose wires and bare frames, wanted to disagree, but he knew Kalil could sense something he couldn't. Torrak trusted in that.

"I'll head to the control room to start the preflight checks," he said as his friend headed toward the engine room.

Once in the control room, which consisted of two chairs and a console full of switches, touch-screens, and a nest of wires, Torrak tried to ignore the mess. He began to check each system on the ship. "Fuel is good. Cooling system for the engine is online and ready," he yelled back to Kalil.

"The engine itself will hold up," Kalil called out as he made his way to the control room. "Life support, altitude control systems, weapons systems, and defense systems are all in the green."

"Think she'll start up?" Torrak asked as he motioned toward the chaotic console.

Kalil scanned the wires. "This is nothing. Wait until you see the engine room."

Torrak swallowed. "You still think it's safe to fly this thing?"

"Of course. Nothing more than cross-wiring. Look, the fuel pump ignition moves through this console to this touch screen and the engine start-up connects from this wire to this lever here."

Torrak was suddenly very glad his friend had insisted on coming.

"Truth be told," Kalil continued, "I can't wait to get back into the engine room. Do you realize how much potential this little ship has?"

Torrak powered up the vessel. "It's not our ship. You can make it run, but can't change anything on it." The ship rumbled beneath them. "Hang on." The craft shuddered, and Torrak wondered if they had made a huge mistake. He reached over to shut it down when the ship lurched and hovered right above the ground. Kalil gave Torrak a smug smile. Frustrated at the non-verbal "I told you so," Torrak accelerated quickly. Kalil fell back into his chair as the ship flew through the cloudy sky toward the stars.

While they pulled out of the atmosphere, Kalil's face turned a sickly shade of white. "It's really amazing up here, isn't it?" he said, his voice higher than usual.

Torrak looked over at his friend, feeling a little guilty for the sudden takeoff. He forgot Kalil had never traveled off-planet before. "Yeah. How's your stomach?"

Kalil made a non-committal noise. His eyes went wide when he looked back down at Fior, now a round ball of blue and tan. "This ship sure moves fast." Some of his color returned as his focus shifted to the ship's circuitry. "Bet I could tweak it a little bit to make it go even—"

Torrak looked over and Kalil cut his sentence short.

"Right, right. It's not our ship."

Torrak, satisfied with his course, initiated the start-up sequence for infinlight. He sent a message containing their flight plan to Fior's orbiting satellite. An automated response approved their request for infinlight and wished them a happy voyage.

"You thought lift-off was exciting?" he said. "Get ready for this."

Torrak flipped a switch and the ship burst forward, propelling itself into infinlight. Kalil jerked back into his seat, his eyes so wide that Torrak thought his eyebrows might reach his hairline. The darkness of space blurred with white streaks of light as they moved past the stars at a dizzying rate.

"I can't believe I'm actually off Fior."

Torrak smiled. "Wait until we get to C-Nine."

"What's it like? I don't really remember much from my Eomix Galactic History class."

Torrak searched his memories. "C-Nine was really beautiful. I lived in Ponsunila, one of the largest cities. It has something like thirty million inhabitants—mostly families and small businesses with larger corporations and governmental buildings located on the northern side of the city.

"During my teens, the Aleet Army came. C-Nine is close to several other planets heavy in metals and fuel, so it made sense for them to use it as a military base. They declared martial law, took whatever they needed, jammed our transmissions for their own security, and crowded our air space with their ships. Some of our citizens tried to rebel, but it turned chaotic and I think it did more damage than if we would have left things alone.

"After the Aleet Army disbanded eight years ago, traders filled in the gaps, taking advantage of all we'd lost. A lot of businesses developed since then, but most of the families and communities have disappeared. Now it's a good place to find anything you want, both legally and illegally, but to be honest, I'm kind of glad to have gotten away from it. It's just not the same place I knew."

"How come you never talked about it before?"

"Easier to forget about it that way."

CHAPTER 9

"YOU NEED TO deal with your grief."

Daith's hands clenched into fists under the doctor's desk. Black and white pictures of graphs covered the walls, keeping the place void of much color. "You already said that."

"Well it's still true." Dr. Milastow tapped some notes on a datapad. Her third appendage, void of joints, lay relaxed around her own neck. "There's nothing I can do for you. You aren't sick. You aren't hurt, except for pushing yourself too hard without proper training and supervision. The reason, in my professional opinion, for your lack of progress revolves around your state of mourning. Besides, I'm tired of treating you for nosebleeds. Blood clotting agents aren't easy to get a hold of and I don't like the rate you are using them up."

Daith glared at the new doctor, angry she held the position at all. She missed Dr. Ludd. She missed the pictures from his children hung on his walls, his accredited documents propped on his desk. He'd been so proud to be a doctor—something she learned he'd been destined for since birth.

She still couldn't believe he'd betrayed them to the Controllers.

Doctor Milastow meant well, but her demeanor lacked individuality. Instead of being talked to, Daith felt Milastow talked *at* her. Another patient on the doctor's list.

The heated energy curled inside Daith's stomach, tempting her to release it and relieve her anger. "There has to be something else I can do," she said, gritting her teeth. She hated feeling so helpless. She wanted to do something immediately to get rid of her unwanted emotions.

Milastow studied her with her diamond-shaped eyes. "Grief takes time. You need to let it run its course."

Daith shoved her chair away from the desk. "I don't have time to take time. We meet with the Controllers in less than two standard weeks. I need to feel this stupid pain about Dru's death and get over it." Daith could feel the doctor's fear, afraid she'd pushed the ticking timebomb too far.

"Ugh. How can you help me when you're terrified solely because I'm in the room?"

"I'm not afraid of you."

"Liar. I don't even have to try. You're like an audio file with the volume turned up. You're practically screaming at me."

Daith felt the doctor's fear intensify to the point of panic.

"I can't deal with this right now. I can't deal with you. You can't help me. I'll figure it out myself."

Daith stood and strode out, knocking over the chair as she left.

"Miss Tocc, wait!" Milastow called out.

Daith ignored her. She hated everyone avoiding her and scurrying away at the sight of her. She needed to prove to them she could handle herself and help them. To do that she needed to get over what happened to Dru. And she didn't have time to wait for it to happen naturally.

She needed to force the change, confront it head-on.

* * *

Ness Opute strolled through the city of Ponsunila early in the morning, the first of the two sunrises breaking through the clouds. He flipped a small package around and through his fingers, feeling the silky texture against his rough and callused knuckles. He headed across town, away from the local package delivery service, which could have easily delivered the small item in his hands. But this item needed special care. Opute only trusted one man to help him with this: Pierze Lang.

About a block from Lang's store, Opute saw a Manach emerge from the front door. Opute slowed his pace—his steely grey eyes focused on the new addition to the scarcely populated street. The Manach stood huge, well over two meters, and his reptilian eyes squinted in the erupting sunlight. The Manach stomped away, its cloven feet pounding on the ground.

As soon as the Manach strode out of sight, Opute rushed to the store. He pushed through the front door and halted. A figure, slumped in a chair, had an electric-volt ring scorched into his chest. His eyes had rolled back into his head. Foam dribbled from his eyes and mouth. The stench of burnt flesh filled the air.

It was Lang.

Opute strode over to the chair and took a pulse.

Nothing.

He could still hear the crackling of flesh burning underneath Lang's shirt.

He could still see smoke rising from the smoldering cloth.

Blood rushed to Opute's head, his heartbeat drowning out any other noise. He didn't react by turning away, gagging, or vomiting at the gruesome site. Only one thought rushed through his mind like an oncoming wave.

Vengeance.

Gathering Lang into his arms, he pulled the heavy man across the room and stashed the body in the back utility closet. He didn't want anyone to see the body through the windows. Opute wrestled the keys away from Lang's belt loop and left, locking the door behind him.

He stood for a moment as the second sun crested over the planet's edge, bathing the plaza in golden light.

He'd known Lang for years. Lang worked with everyone—a neutral party. Totally harmless.

So why kill him?

Rage consumed him. His hands tightened into fists. His arm arced through the air and smashed into the store's neon OPEN sign. The sign swung, hit the wall, and shattered. Opute walked away as the sign came off its hinges and crashed to the sidewalk below, splattering broken glass everywhere.

* * *

Daith stood in the empty corridor, her breath shallow. The thin carpet flattened beneath her slipped-on shoes. She rocked back and forth on her feet, unable yet to look at the door in front of her. She had been so determined after leaving the medical bay, but now that she'd arrived, moving forward seemed much harder. And yet it's the only thing that seemed to be keeping her abilities from progressing. She had to move past her grief.

Harsh lights hummed above her, recirculated air hissed from the vents behind.

No one walked by—the main crew's sleep cycle hadn't quite finished. The only ones awake currently worked on the bridge, in engineering, or in the infirmary.

Her heart pounded. Terror gripped her at the thought of remembering Dru—afraid it would hurt too much. His caring eyes, his patient air, the surge of energy they felt between them.

With an extended exhale, Daith looked up at the door. If she wanted to help, she needed to move on.

Trembling fingers pressed the panel to open it. The door swished to the left, the breeze blowing against her face.

Besides the standard furniture, desk, and vidlink that came in every suite, the room lay empty.

Completely cleaned out.

Daith took a step inside, her legs wobbly. She didn't know why she expected the room to be the same—strewn datapads, old food trays, clothes scattered about. Dru had been incredibly messy, but everything about that part of him had been bagged and trashed.

Daith's fingertips danced across the polished desk leaving slight trails of oily residue. She wondered if any of his things still existed or if they'd been recycled into the nutritional food tanks for the silari trees.

He was truly gone.

The tears in her eyes burned with anger. Daith looked down at her hands pressed against the surface, warm with powerful heat from her anxiety. Their tips sunk into the desk, now gooey around her nail beds. Removing them from the melted material, she closed her eyes in frustration, wiping her fingers on her pants. She *had* to get her abilities under control.

Her insides turned cold, like steel. She would simply work harder, tap into anything that would allow her to become more powerful.

She couldn't let the Controllers get away with what they'd done.

She wouldn't let them make her forget about Dru.
And they needed to pay for taking him from her.
Time to talk to Trey.
Without a glance back, Daith strode from the room, head high.

CHAPTER 10

TORRAK LEANED BACK in the ship's control room piloting seat.

He thought about all he learned concerning Daith and her connection to Jacin Jaxx. He still found it hard to believe. She'd never even hinted at the kinship. Not that he could blame her. Torrak didn't think he would have advertised that relationship either.

Torrak wondered about it. He hadn't been very upfront about his life with anyone, not even Kalil. It wasn't shame or anything, he only wanted to move on.

Before he enrolled in the Academy, he worked three years for the C-9 government, solving cases, and putting criminals in prison. But it wasn't enough for him. He felt stunted, his potential squandered on things *anyone* could do.

His mother called him selfish. His father called him immature. His friends called him egotistical. They didn't understand why he would want to leave an incredible career to go back to school. The whole point of school was to get a great job, which he already had.

Surprisingly enough, Lang suggested Torrak apply at the Academy for Gifted Students on Fior. Torrak flew to Fior for tests, which revealed a genius level in mathematics and comprehension, and the Academy offered him a full scholarship.

Torrak's departure from his family and friends hadn't been very pleasant. None of his friends came to see him leave and when he and his parents arrived at the docking port, his father stayed in the vehicle and his mother told him she couldn't believe he wanted to give up a perfectly good career with Central Authority to pursue something that may lead nowhere.

And now he was headed back to C-9 having ditched his classes, cashing out his life savings, and with no idea what he might be getting into. He could imagine his parents saying "I told you so."

Torrak jerked out of his negative thoughts when the proximity alarm beeped to signal their arrival at C-Sector 9.

Kalil strolled into the cockpit, a long, greasy smear on his left arm. "What's going on?"

"We're coming into orbit."

Kalil looked out at a planet that hung in the nothingness of space. Large, sporadic, yellow dust clouds covered the brown sphere. The neighboring stars' light reflected off the clouds, casting an eerie yellow glow around the planet. They had arrived on the night side and as their ship flew closer, pinpoints of lights from buildings peeked through the clouds.

A voice came through the communications panel and startled Torrak.

"This is C-Sector Nine Traffic Control. State your destination and purpose," the voice requested, monotone.

"Ponsunila City for business." No one responded from the other end. Kalil leaned over, flipped a switch, and rolled his eyes. Torrak ignored this and repeated his response.

"Vessel is cleared through atmospheric shielding. Please proceed to docking bay six hundred twelve. Repeat: docking bay six one two."

Torrak piloted the ship toward the planet, touching down gingerly on the landing pad. He left the cockpit, grabbing his bag on the way. He met up with Kalil and they waited until the outer hatch opened before walking off the ship into an enclosed terminal. Shaped like a huge, metal box with one end open for ships to arrive and depart, the building air hummed with the sound of engines.

Torrak stretched his arms over his head and walked toward a bright yellow, meter-high machine. The machine spit out a ticket which had the date and time on it. Once Torrak had taken the ticket, large metal clamps rose from the ground and fastened themselves onto the ship.

As they walked toward the main door, Kalil excitedly pointed out the models of ships docked near theirs, talking in detail about the special features of each one. Torrak, wanting to avoid a standard hour-long discussion on the differences between ship engines, hurried along as fast as he could.

Once outside and away from the fumes of the running ships, Torrak breathed in deeply, and immediately started to cough.

"I'd forgotten how clean the air is here," he said sarcastically. Not much cleaner than inside the polluted docking bay, the sooty air of the city came from the non-existent vehicle exhaust and environmental enforcement laws.

Kalil laughed. "That's what you get for trying to speed me out of the hangar."

"You noticed, huh?" Torrak asked, smiling despite his dying coughs. The two of them headed toward the main square of Ponsunila. While they walked, Torrak took in the sights of his old hometown. Banners of all different lengths and colors waved from each store front, advertising the store's name and its merchandise: a silver building designated as a cultural developmental center, a run-down Manach-owned store that sold spare ship parts, a busy Grassuwerian restaurant. Lang's store sat on the other side of the square. Torrak wondered if it looked the same.

"So what's this Lang guy like?" Kalil asked.

"Generous. And fat." Torrak laughed. "Well, at least when I knew him he was. The first time I met him I'd been working for the C-Nine authorities and assigned to apprehend a criminal named Hallia, who'd been connected with several illegal transactions involving shipments of twig. Hallia fled into Lang's store, taking him and several others hostage. She tried using him as a shield, but couldn't get her arm around him because he was so wide." Torrak laughed.

"How did he get out of there?"

"On the third day, our sniper had a clear shot." Torrak shrugged. "I never did care for that part of the job. I liked solving cases."

"So that's how you met Lang?"

"Uh-huh. I went back to Lang's store to talk about damages and we hit it off. He's got a great sense of humor and tells the best stories..." Torrak trailed off as they approached the main square. Tents and stands covered the square's perimeter, while portable sleeping-units littered the middle. It looked as if the entire city had crammed itself into a six-block radius. Different types of music played loudly from alternate corners as individuals walked by sampling cuisine from sellers that had erected temporary store fronts in every available space.

"Whoa. Is this usual?" Kalil asked.

"Not that I remember." Torrak tapped a nearby Garken, a lumpy grey mass whose blank face sported nothing but a very wide mouth.

"Excuse me. Could you tell me what's going on in the square?"

"Sa-Ding Festival of Moons," the Garken gurgled. "Once every three thousand glicks, moons merge. Stars crash. Rocks burst. Explosions. This is last night." The corners of its mouth curved outward in a sign of glee.

"I completely forgot that took place this year," Torrak said as the Garken waddled away.

"What is the Sa-Ding Festival?"

"It celebrates the merging of moons."

Kalil furrowed his brow.

"Let's see. How can I explain this? Okay. So C-Sector Nine's origin theory is that a gravitational rift in the middle of the galaxy pulled other planets and moons to this area. When the rift collapsed, the moons began to orbit the closest large mass. Once they settled, the planets and moons were split into sectors: the Arl's sector, the Brl's sector, and the Crl's sector. C-Sector Nine is the ninth planet in the Crl's sector, which explains how it got named." Torrak gestured to the black flags sported by many of the booths—three circles in a row, the first red, the second blue, and the third, larger, green. The green circle contained nine black dots inside the center, to indicate the ninth planet in the third sector.

"Great flag."

"I've always liked it."

Kalil watched the Garken park itself in front of a stand and order some food. "Okay, so then what's the festival all about?"

"C-Nine's orbit lasts around six hundred years. Once during that time it comes close to another planet from the Brl's sector called Ding. Ding is small, surrounded by rings made of cosmic dust and debris. The debris gets pulled by C-Nine's gravity and showers the planet for about two weeks.

"The first time this happened, the original colonizers had no idea what to expect. Meteorites pummeled the planet, killing over half the population. Afterwards, the planet's government built and installed planetary atmospheric defense systems, or PADS, which act as energy fields, blocking falling fragments and dust." Torrak pointed to a large, spherical building in the distance. Every so often an energy arc built up from the bottom of the sphere and pulsed upward toward the sky.

"Since then," Torrak continued, "C-Nine celebrates with the Sa-Ding Moon Festival—to rejoice in the beauty of chaos."

"Can we come back later and watch?"

"I'd really like to. I remember being so excited when I was little that the festival would take place during my lifetime and—"

Torrak pulled up short half a block from Lang's store. He saw its sign lying broken on the ground. He ran to the door, banging on it, but no one answered. Desperate yanks on the handle yielded no results. His throat tightened with panic. "There's a cellar entrance in the back," he said. The two of them sprinted toward the rear and found the entry to the cellar, bolted, but Torrak managed to wrench it open. Torrak and Kalil climbed inside and down the ladder into the dimness. Meter-long brown shapes ran by, scuttling away from the light.

"I don't even want to know what those were," Kalil muttered. Torrak ignored him and made his way to the stairs. Kalil followed right on his heels. Torrak pushed open the door at the top of the steps and stumbled into the well-lit room. Squinting, he heard Kalil shut the door behind them. The enclosed area, full of stocked supplies, muffled the partying outside.

"This doesn't look like he's gone out of business," Kalil said. All the boxes in the room had recent dates of delivery.

"Pierze?" Torrak called out as he entered the front of the store. No answer. Torrak looked around, identifying the surrounding clues as he slipped back into his old investigative habits. He took in the soot left over from scorch marks on a chair, the smell of burnt skin, and the ACCESS DENIED phrase that ran across the computer screen at the desk.

"Um, Torrak?" Kalil stood in front of an open closet door. "I think I found Pierze Lang."

CHAPTER 11

"ENTER."

Daith walked in, her lips pursed. "I need to know more about the Controllers." She stood tall and looked down upon Trey, who sat at his desk.

Trey tilted his head. His jaw tightened at her impudence. He knew the dream-deflector pills and circumstances made her more irritable, but she shouldn't barge in here demanding things from him. He quickly secured his mental block, so Daith couldn't access his thoughts, and forced a smile on his face. "Won't you take a seat?"

Daith sat across from him, glaring.

"I'm not sure what more I can tell you, but I'll go over it again with you. They are a faction fighting against the former leader of the Aleet Army and what he represented. They call themselves the Liberators. They feared our leader's abilities and that he used them to help change the course of history for the better. Most of them are war mongrels or profiteers from governmental conflict and wanted to reinstate those conditions across the Eomix Galaxy. That's when we started calling them the Controllers, since it became clear they only wanted to reestablish their former power.

"When our leader died," Trey continued, "they went after anyone else with abilities like his, which includes you. They wanted to make sure no one could follow in his footsteps. I'm not sure what else there is for you to know."

"I don't know either, but there must be something: news articles, statements, communications. I'd like access to the ship's communications so I can research the group." She crossed her legs and arms in the chair.

"That's not possible."

Her eyes narrowed. "No? Why not? I've agreed to help you with your mission. Clearly I'm on your side. So why can't I have the same privileges as any other crewmember?"

"You misunderstand," he said, keeping his tone light. "Even crewmembers can't access information about the Controllers."

Daith's voice rose in pitch as her foot tapped the floor. "I can't believe that. They must want to know things. How do they know what's going on outside this ship?"

Daith's anxiety manifested itself in the room—the air shimmered with ill ease. "Please, let me show you what I mean." Trey booted up his computer system. The cursor blinked as he punched in his access code. When the system became alert, he turned the screen toward her. "The ship's systems deal only with matters of the ship." A schematic came up of each of the five ship's levels. "Crew members can check their shift arrangements, menu specials in the mess hall, simulation room activities, and so forth." With each of these statements a new screen emerged with the pertinent information. "That's all. Outside access could be traced or penetrated."

Daith's tongue darted out of the corner of her mouth while she watched the images.

"You don't believe me," Trey stated. With quick movements, he flipped his data entry panel over to her side of the desk. "Feel free to type in anything you want."

Her eyebrows raised. "Seriously?"

Trey nodded. "You are a part of this crew and everything that comes with it. Our computer system is limited, but open to you if you wish. As for contact outside the ship, we do have vidlink communications panels, but communication is limited to prevent detection of any outgoing signals. However, calls *can* be approved by me, and then transmitted when we are in a safe enough area. Unfortunately, I don't know when the next safe point might be, not on this current flight path."

Daith took the datapad and for a moment seemed subdued, but then her lips pursed. Smacking the device on the table, she let out an exasperated breath. "I can't accept this. I need information outside of this ship. History. Facts. Politics. You can't expect me to help you fight against this group empty-handed."

Trey clenched his jaw in irritation. His patience dribbled away. She needed to remember who ran this ship. "You said you made your choice."

"Yes, but—"

"You chose to stay on this ship rather than leave it and search for answers about your past."

"I know, but—"

"I rescued you from the assassination attempt that killed your family." Trey's clipped accent accentuated in his anger. "I gave you a safe place to stay. I introduced you to a doctor who could help get your memories back. I offered you friendship. And what has happened since I've done all that?" Trey ticked off his fingers. "My brother was murdered, Dr. Ludd betrayed us, and you still don't trust me."

Daith's eyes blazed with anger, though the droop in her shoulders told Trey she felt guilty. "I'm trying to help. I didn't ask to be shot at. I didn't ask to be brought on board."

"Maybe not. But it's better than being dead." Trey felt tempted to soften, but he needed her to follow his leadership. On the other hand, she probably had the power to blow up the ship if she wanted.

Trey closed his eyes. He had to get hold of himself. He had to turn this into a connection with her. He continued, his words softened. "I'm sorry to lash out. I know this has all happened quickly and with Dru gone...," he let out a long sigh, "it's a little bleaker on this ship."

He felt a warm touch on his fisted hand as Daith's slender fingers offered their comfort. He bit his tongue to keep the smirk from his face.

"I'm sorry, Trey. You had to take a chance that the Controller was telling the truth about defecting. Any information he had would have been invaluable. But I know Dru's murder must be hard on you, too..."

An unexpected lump caught in Trey's throat.

"It's fine," he said. The sting of threatening tears burned his eyes. He turned his face toward hers. "I don't blame you for wanting to know more. I'll tell you everything I can, about the Controllers, about their missions and tactics, anything I can to help."

"Thank you." She squeezed his forearm, the warmth of it raising his heart beat. "I don't want to let you and the crew down."

"I don't believe you will." Trey's communications indicator lit up. "Can we schedule a time later to meet? Perhaps tomorrow?"

Daith nodded and exited.

Trey cleared his throat. What was his problem? He didn't miss his brother. He always knew Dru wouldn't want to be involved with his plan and would have to be killed. Having it happen sooner rather than later was the only problem.

Perhaps Daith's grief oozed out into him. Yes, that must be it.

"Yes?" he answered the communication.

"It's Kircla for you."

Trey instantly perked up. "Patch her through." He smoothed the front of his immaculate uniform as the vidlink system connected the call. The screen filled with a seated Orcla female, her aquamarine skin tone a sharp contrast to the greys and black of the cockpit of her ship.

"It's good to hear from you, Kircla. I assume you have been successful on your mission?"

Kircla sucked at her pointed teeth. "You assume wrong. However, do not be afraid. Though poor, the information you gave me allowed me to narrow down the list to twenty-nine suspects. They will all be eliminated."

Trey's breath caught in his throat. "*All* of them? Is that really necessary?"

Kircla's head cricked to one side, like a flying birna cocking its head. "You provided me with limited intel: male, medium-brown skin, pale yellow hair, attends the Academy for Gifted Students on the planet Fior. As I am not allowed to ask for any other information concerning him or others that may know him, I have reduced the list to twenty-nine candidates. In order to be sure of success, they all must be targeted. Unless there is some other information you can give me?"

Trey slowly shook his head. "I'm afraid not." His stomach clenched like hard stone. "Do what you must. Let me know when the assignment is complete."

The conversation ended.

Trey sat rigid in his chair, his gut heavy. Twenty-nine dead so he could make sure to kill one. Trey wasn't a stranger to killing, he'd seen plenty of death during the civil war on his planet, but he tried to avoid unnecessary casualties. He always felt justified when he had someone eliminated. Their death had purpose, whether it be to protect himself or keep his plan moving forward. But never random innocents.

Sometimes you have to sacrifice the few to save the many. An old mantra, one he adopted years ago when he worked for Jacin Jaxx. He believed it then, as he did now, but it didn't undo the knot of guilt inside him. The witness who'd seen Daith kidnapped couldn't be allowed to live. His own crew had already bungled the recovery mission.

Kircla was his last chance.

CHAPTER 12

THE ASSASSIN WAS GOOD.

Ness Opute was better.

Sunk low behind a bush, Opute watched the Manach enter its lodgings for the night. Treading softly, Opute made his way behind the building. He slipped a bit as he climbed over slime-covered rocks and cursed when he knelt onto a sharp stone. A light sheen of sweat coated his body while the planet continued to radiate heat, even though second sunset had taken place over a standard hour ago. He pulled on his night-vision goggles. They squeaked against his moistened forehead and he adjusted them to detect thermal signatures. After he located his target on the second floor, Opute pushed the goggles onto the top of his head and analyzed the situation. He would wait until the Manach entered its sleep cycle.

Three standard hours later, Opute crept toward the building. He hoisted himself up by a large tree branch and swung himself onto the balcony attached to the room next to the Manach's. Opute rubbed his sweaty hands on his pants before he jumped to the Manach's balcony. One hand slipped on the metal railing and he nearly fell into a thick bush of prickly plants below. He secured his grip and pulled himself up, his arms throbbing from the strain. A brief pause on the balcony to catch his breath before he moved toward the plate-glass doors. He slid down, laying on his belly, and peered through.

Two iridescent yellow eyes stared back.

Opute bit back a gasp. Terror gripped him. He tried not to blink. A tail whipped around behind the eyes.

A Nikana.

Vicious guard animals, the 12-kilogram felines were quite rare, costing more money than Opute made in a year, and were thought to be so quick they could dodge direct attacks from most hand-held energy weapons.

The fact that the Manach assassin had one proved his high-quality.

Unbeknownst to his target, Opute *had* seen a Nikana before. Well, the Nikana had seen him. The creature had been set loose on Opute when a client decided not to pay.

Three weeks later, after intensive surgery to repair the chunks of flesh that had been sheared from his body, Opute's boss at the time came to visit him in the hospital.

The first words spoken confirmed the death of the client. Then she told Opute, having raised a Nikana, she knew a technique to put the feline in a trance-like state, a state that kept it from responding to any noise or movement for a short period of time. Three rapid flashes of light directly in the Nikana's eyes.

Simple.

Except at the present moment Opute's portable light unit sat snug inside its holster, strapped to his thigh and not pointed at the Nikana.

Opute held his breath. He reached back, slowly, and took hold of the light. With a quick flick of his wrist, he flipped the unit around and pointed it toward the Nikana. A low growl came from the feline, loud enough to be heard through the glass, but it still hadn't moved. Opute's nerves superseded his concern about the Manach hearing the beast. The Nikana could break through the glass and rip Opute's throat out before the Manach would even know it had happened.

Opute brought the portable light unit slowly to the center of the Nikana's face, hoping with each movement the Nikana wouldn't react. A bead of sweat dripped into his eye. The eye closed. The feline picked up on the movement.

Its fur rose.

Opute flashed the light three times. The Nikana's fur settled. Its round eyes narrowed to crescent moon shapes.

Opute let the pent up air out of his lungs and drew in a shuddering breath, aware he'd almost passed out. He crawled to the middle of the balcony where the two glass doors met and pulled out a small electromagnetic device. He began to counter the magnetically-sealed, motion-sensitive alarm rigged on the doors. A click signaled it had worked. Opute slipped his specialized knife between the two doors and made a clean slit downwards, cutting the locking mechanism in half. He opened the right door, away from the Nikana, and slipped inside. Opute pulled his night-vision goggles back over his eyes and scoured the pitch-black room.

Through his goggles, he saw the room with a greenish glow. Sparsely furnished, the space gave the impression it was for short, cheap visits. The Manach stood next to the bed; its eyes wide open, but sound asleep.

Even though Opute knew it wasn't awake, the sight still unnerved him.

Not about to take any chances, Opute quietly approached the upright body. At the moment before his attack, a loud crash sounded outside the lodge. Opute watched through his green-tinted vision as the Manach woke and moved its eyes, searching for the disturbance. Opute lunged. The Manach, having excellent night vision, ducked under Opute's outstretched arms, rolled across the bed, and landed in a crouched position on the floor. The Manach dove for the open glass door, but Opute cut it off.

The Manach let out a low growl. "Who are you?" it demanded.

Opute's knife glinted in a brief moment of moonlight. "I'll ask the questions."

The Manach's eyes flicked to the side of his bed where its own weapon lay, out of reach.

Opute saw the look and raised his knife, bringing the Manach's attention back to him. "What's your connection to Pierze Lang?"

"You're asking about the fat man?"

Opute almost sliced the Manach's throat right then and there. "Why the kill? What did you need?"

The Manach's eyes twitched back and forth, looking for an escape route. It licked its scaly lips. "I don't have to tell you anything."

Opute's hand struck out. The Manach pulled back, but not fast enough. The knife slid cleanly from its shoulder to its elbow, exposing bone.

"Let's try this again. Why the hit?"

The Manach's eyes bulged in their sockets and he stumbled backwards, toward the bed. Black blood poured down its lifeless arm and pooled onto the floor.

It cried out in pain.

Opute closed the distance between them. "Don't make me repeat myself."

"Exarth ordered the kill," it said, its hand wrapped around its wounded limb. It sat on the bed. "It was just a job."

Opute's teeth ground. "Exarth," he snarled. "What did she want from him?"

"Some computer disk."

"What's on the disk?"

"How should I know? Why don't you ask Exarth?" The Manach moved for his weapon. Opute anticipated the move and slashed out with his knife. A clean slice appeared across the Manach's throat.

"Maybe I will," Opute muttered.

As black fluid oozed into a thick puddle around the body, Opute searched the room. He found a small, silver disk under the bed, stuck it into his pocket, and exited the scene. While he climbed down the drainage pipe, he noticed the Nikana watch him from the balcony. It had come out of its trance.

"No hard feelings, right?" Opute told it.

The Nikana blinked. It jumped to the limb of the tree next to the building and scaled down the side of its trunk, landing softly on the ground as Opute dropped off the drainage pipe.

"Oh, no. You can't follow me."

The Nikana growled softly.

Opute pulled off his goggles. He didn't want to draw attention. "Fine, do whatever you want. But I'm not taking care of you."

The Nikana followed him at an equal pace, its large white paws silent as they treaded over the slimy rocks.

On the way back to Lang's store, Opute wondered what information could possibly be on the disk to warrant Lang's murder.

CHAPTER 13

KALIL STOOD HUNCHED over the entire contents of his stomach.

Torrak peered into the utility closet. There lay Lang's body with a large blackened hole where his chest used to be, the edges peeling and flaking off. The smell of burnt flesh filled the small, enclosed space and Torrak swallowed hard so he didn't also vomit.

Kalil moaned weakly, his face pinched and red from the strain of puking. "I've seen a lot of corpses in anatomy class before, but they never smelled."

Torrak clenched his fists at the sight of his friend's dead body. His anger boiled near the surface. He wanted to throw something or punch the wall, but he knew he could better help Lang by figuring out what happened. With a click, he closed the closet door and peered around the store.

Torrak put the scene together in his head, reading the clues he saw, throwing out impossible outcomes. "I think a third party was involved."

"What do you mean?"

"There seemed to be no struggle between Lang and his attacker. Lang was sitting in his chair when he got shot," Torrak remarked, pointing to the scorch marks. "Why would the killer then drag a hundred and twenty-five kilo man into a closet and smash the sign on the front of the store? The first would take a while and broken glass would attract interest. No...someone came afterwards, moved the body to the closet, and proceeded to smash the sign."

"Why would anyone do that after seeing a dead body?" Kalil asked. He wiped a hand across his mouth.

Torrak thought about his own anger and how he had wanted to break something. "Someone who cared about Lang."

"Who?"

"I think it was Opute since he'd also be strong enough to move Lang's body."

"Opute?"

Torrak nodded. "The immediate question now becomes what do we do with him?"

"What do you mean 'what do we do?' We call the city's authorities and file a Fatality Claims Report."

"That may not be the best course of action," Torrak said. "Think about it. If we get the city's authorities involved we'll end up –"

An explosion from outside the shop rocked them both. They raced outside and skidded to a halt at the spectacle.

The entire sky had turned crimson except for a thin line of black, which lay where the edge of the sky met the ground. Small pinpoints of light from individual stars looked larger than normal as their edges trickled white into the deep red around them. The source of the explosion, which now filled the sky with silver dust, came from a meteorite having been pulverized in space and its debris settling onto the PADS.

Torrak and Kalil watched the scene with awe. The sky changed to silver. Music blared all around them. Crimson banners lowered and silver banners took their place to match the sky. The whole square sparkled. Beings made their way through different tents set up all around. Tents were decorated with flowing drapes, flashing lights, and vibrant colors to attract the public's eye. Some contained food from areas all around the galaxy, others featured arts and crafts or theatrical shows. One tent had Slithes, long, reptilian-like female dancers. Their clothing shimmered while it changed colors with the banners around them. Torrak nudged his friend. Kalil's mouth snapped shut and he blushed as he pulled his gaze away from the undulating figures.

Torrak and Kalil stayed motionless for a few moments, adjusting to the stimulation around them. Kalil's eyes shined with the reflected silver light and he looked at Torrak, quickly bringing himself back to the problem at hand.

"I still think we should go to the authorities," Kalil said.

"I don't know. There's something off about all this." Without Lang, he had no way of locating Opute, without Opute he had no way to learn about the Aleet Army, and without the Aleet Army, he would never find Daith.

Torrak's shoulders sagged in defeat.

"Let's clear our heads," Kalil suggested. "No offense to your friend, but I don't feel like sitting around with a dead body while we think things over. Besides, my stomach needs a break."

The two of them walked around the square, watching the shifting colors of the sky, as they figured out exactly what to do.

* * *

Gold-colored dust settled on the planet's energy shield above Opute. He ignored the partiers in the square as he reached Lang's store. About to unlock the door, Opute frowned when it opened. He crept in, cautious, and relocked the door right after the Nikana slunk through. Everything seemed in order. Perhaps, in his haste, he had merely thought he had locked the door. He went back to Lang's body, wrapped it in a blanket, and lugged it down into the cellar. He opened one of the large freezers and pulled out enough shelves so the body would fit. He would eventually return the body to Lang's family, but he didn't want to leave it out in the open while he worked.

Opute returned upstairs and sat down in front of the computer, twirling the disk he'd taken from the Manach's room.

"Let's see your secrets."

As he worked, the sky outside changed into violet.

* * *

The violet sky above them changed to green as Torrak and Kalil approached Lang's store. The two of them decided, with much reluctance on Torrak's part, to call Central Authority and report Lang's body anonymously. Torrak wanted to do more, but what else could he do? He didn't know if Opute had found Lang, and even so, who knew if he'd return.

As they came up to the store, disappointment weighed on Torrak like a wet blanket. He'd come all this way and for what? A dead friend and a dead end.

Torrak approached the door and pushed. It didn't open.

Torrak's mood flipped instantly to irritation. "Why'd you lock the door?" he accused Kalil.

"What are you talking about?"

"The door. Why'd you lock it?"

Kalil frowned. "I didn't."

Torrak couldn't see anyone through the windows.

"Something's not right." He motioned for Kalil to follow and kept alert as they moved back to the cellar entrance.

"Keep quiet." Once inside, they tiptoed toward the stairs. Torrak winced at a loud crash behind him.

"Sorry," Kalil said. "I tripped."

* * *

The Nikana growled moments before Opute heard a crash from downstairs. A glimmer of silver reflected the lights as he slid his knife from his pocket.

* * *

Torrak reached the top of the stairs. He hesitated for a moment before opening the door.

* * *

Opute gripped the knife in his hand. The cellar door opened. When the intruder emerged, Opute grabbed him by the arm and twisted it behind his back. He held the knife against the intruder's throat.

Opute saw another individual creeping up the stairs. He kicked a large box, which collided with the second intruder, knocking him back down into the cellar. Opute pressed the knife harder against the first man's throat, drawing blood.

"You picked the wrong store to loot," Opute snarled.

CHAPTER 14

DAITH SHOOK HER hand in pain. "I'm sorry," she exclaimed. Rubbing her throbbing knuckles, she looked down at Cenjo, who she just punched in the jaw.

Patting his face tenderly, he smiled at her, and got back up to his feet. The squishy, yellow mat underneath him had protected his fall, but his face already swelled.

"No worries. You did exactly what you were supposed to do. I should've seen it coming. Very nicely done."

Squeezing and releasing her tender hand, Daith's shoulders relaxed now that she knew he wouldn't be mad. She'd held back during their second sparring session. Ever since she lost control and hurt him, she worried about doing it again. But this time, it had been a solid punch. She'd squared her shoulders, moved in with her hips, and hit him with full force.

"I've never hit anyone before. Well, at least not on purpose. As far as I remember." She grinned, the pain in her hand subsiding.

"We should probably put a chiller pack on your hand so it doesn't swell."

Daith waved him off. "My hand is fine, now."

"What?" he asked, moving his jaw around.

"My hand. It's fine. It doesn't hurt anymore." She held it out for him to see. The redness had faded and the swelling had stopped.

Cenjo took her hand in his, his rough, calloused fingertips sliding over her knuckles. "Incredible. How can you do that?"

"I'm not sure on the specifics. I can heal quickly. There's something inside me, like a warmth, and I can move it to parts of my body. Once it's there, it just fixes me somehow."

He dropped her hand and tapped his injured jaw. "Could you heal this?"

Daith hesitated. "I-I'm not sure. Probably not." Her stomach twisted in fear. "I'd probably make it worse or blow up your head or something." She meant the words to sound like a joke, but her fingers trembled while she spoke. What was wrong with her?

"Wouldn't want that." Cenjo smiled. "Are you ready to continue?"

Daith opened her mouth to say yes. "I think we'd better stop for today."

"Are you sure? You asked for a second session."

Bile crept into the back of her throat. She swallowed it back down. "I know. I needed something to do—to keep my mind off of everything I can't do."

"All right. Well if you want to meet up in the mess hall later for a bite, feel free to show up or stop back here later. I'm going to be running through some stances with the newbies—it wouldn't hurt for you to listen in."

"Sounds great," Daith lied. She gave a curt nod and forced herself to move at a normal speed from the room. Once outside, her breath quickened and she briskly walked to her quarters. She entered, face warm, stomach rolling. In one quick motion she flung herself through the washroom's door and dry heaved into the sink.

After catching her breath, she took a seat on her bed, shaking. What was wrong with her? Why did she feel totally terrified? Cenjo had only asked if she could heal him. And in truth, she probably could.

She remembered it being one of the things she and Dru never worked on. The only test they performed involving healing required her to *not* heal him. Dru made her watch him die to prove that even with all her power, she couldn't do everything. It turned out to only be a simulation, but they never got a chance to pursue her ability to heal any further.

Then Dru had been taken from her, killed by the same group that murdered her family.

Losing the truest friend she could remember hurt enough, but she'd been so close to him emotionally that she even "saw" his death—an echo of the event filled her mind at the moment it happened. The memory still hung in front of her when she closed her eyes to sleep—a sharp crackling noise, an arc of blue electricity, the scent of burnt flesh as she looked down to see a gaping hole in his abdomen where he'd been shot.

Daith reached automatically for a small vial next to the head of her bed. She popped one of the pills inside, a dream-deflector, designed to keep her from dreaming. Even though she knew she wouldn't fall asleep for hours, just knowing the terrifying images would be kept at bay were enough to sate her for the moment.

Daith pulled her knees to her chest and wrapped her arms around them. Holding herself tightly, she forced herself to take long, slow breaths. She hadn't felt this scared since one of her first days aboard the *Horizon*. She remembered how terrified she'd felt when she would wake up, afraid she'd be trapped once again in a room with no memories. But after Dru came on board, reassuring her they would work on her restoring her memories, she became calmer, felt safer.

And here she was without him.

She hated feeling like this. Maybe she could do it on her own, but she didn't know how. How could she ever feel at peace again without someone to help her find her way?

* * *

Cenjo watched Daith leave, noticing her tense body. He hoped she was all right.

With a few words he ended the simulation program and left the room, heading for his own quarters. Silent corridors greeted him. Sparseness infected the crew like a virus. With Trey's temper, many crewmembers were dismissed for simple mistakes.

Cenjo sauntered down another flight of stairs, the recirculating air hissing louder in the confined space. He'd been keeping an eye on Daith since her arrival. At first, he thought she joined on like the rest of the crew, but when the rumors spread about her abilities—he couldn't help but notice their similarities to the crew's former leader, Jacin Jaxx. When he first saw her, he knew why.

She *was* Jaxx's daughter. He'd met her once before, on a mission to retrieve her. She'd immobilized his entire squad in moments.

A swish of a door and Cenjo entered his quarters. The soft light of his sister's art sculpture permeated the room. He'd forgotten to turn it off. His chest tightened at the sight of his homeworld, Katala—or what it used to be. Now it floated in space as a dead object, a ball of useless rock and dried-up riverbeds.

All because of a senseless mistake by another Katalan.

The chemical reaction created to destroy pesticides went horribly wrong and snaked through the planet's water system. The contaminated water killed every living thing it encountered. Millions died before the world government realized the source and evacuated civilians onto space vessels—removing them from the toxic surface.

Cenjo had been off-world, competing in a combat tournament, when news of the phenomenon hit the vidlink reports. He couldn't get home—spacecraft weren't allowed to return to the planet, as it had been quarantined. He could only watch news reports, hoping they'd reveal names of the survivors, furious at himself that he hadn't been there to help.

Reports of Jacin Jaxx flooded in. He landed on the planet. He healed survivors on the surface who had been infected and weren't allowed to leave. One of them was Cenjo's sister, Brial.

Cenjo had cried—the first time he remembered crying since childhood.

And then the unthinkable happened. Protesters—the Controllers—began firing upon ships containing the citizens cured by Jacin Jaxx. Thousands of saved lives were extinguished in minutes.

Brial was gone.

Cenjo, spurred on with nothing but thoughts of revenge, joined Jaxx's army the following week and dedicated himself to stopping the Controllers. Once his rage settled, he began to notice some things that didn't add up. Jaxx's isolation, the ever-growing power Commander Xiven assumed, and the less-than-tolerant means their army used to subdue protesters.

Cenjo stood idly by while their army lost control—while Jaxx lost control. Suicide ended Jaxx's life, though no report ever spoke of why he'd chosen that path. Commander Xiven took over, right in time for a double-cross to hit the army's main base, killing thousands. Most of the soldiers fled, running like wounded animals, trying everything they could to disassociate themselves from the Aleet Army. The Controllers pounced on their chance to ridicule the army any way they could, using propaganda to attach a stigma to the name.

Cenjo walked back into his bedroom and lay flat on his back, staring at the black ceiling.

Eight years since Jaxx's death. It felt like a lifetime ago.

Cenjo stayed true to the cause. He'd been with Xiven when their base had been attacked. He helped Xiven re-form and recruit soldiers who wanted to restore peace.

And now Daith roamed the same ship, a direct descendant, and Commander Xiven didn't want the crew to know.

So many illusions. So many secrets.

But he wasn't sitting idly by this time. He'd already begun to plant seeds—to ensure Daith discovered the truth. To prevent her from suffering the same fate as her father. He may not know Commander Xiven's true intentions, but he did know Daith wouldn't last much longer in her current condition.

With that kind of power, all of their lives depended on keeping Daith stable.

CHAPTER 16

TORRAK SWALLOWED HARD, feeling cold metal press further against his neck. Hot breath moistened his cheek.

"Who are you?" the voice asked.

"My name is Torrak Spirtz."

To his surprise, the pressure on his throat lessened.

"Torrak?"

Torrak resisted the urge to nod. "Yes. I'm a friend of Pierze Lang." Pressure lessened on his arm.

"What are the odds."

Torrak spun around. Steely grey eyes, dark, cropped hair, muscular body. "Opute?"

"In the flesh. What are you doing here?"

"It's a long story, but we were trying to find you and we—oh, no! Kalil!" Torrak rushed down the stairs. Opute followed and once he reached the bottom, leaned over Torrak to stare at a red-haired, skinny kid on the floor. A splatter of blood enmeshed into Kalil's hair and his left leg bent the wrong way at the knee. Torrak leaned over his friend and gently shook him until he woke.

"Ow," Kalil groaned. His eyes fluttered open. "What happened and why do I hurt so much?"

"You got knocked down the stairs," Torrak answered. He helped Kalil sit up. "This is Opute."

"Hey, kid."

Kalil's eyes widened and he gulped. "Uh, hi?" He tried to stand and cried out in pain. "That can't be good."

"You'll live," Opute said. He opened the nearest freezer and chipped off a chunk of ice, wrapped it in a towel draped over a nearby chair, and handed it to Kalil. "This should help. Now, brace yourself 'cause this is going to hurt." In one fluid movement, Opute swept Kalil over his shoulder. Kalil howled as Opute walked up the stairs. Once on the main level, he ungracefully dropped Kalil on top of the desk.

"Thanks," Kalil snapped sarcastically.

Opute looked at Torrak. "Who is this kid and where did he learn it's smart to mouth off to someone a lot bigger than he is?"

Kalil paled.

"Kalil is a friend of mine from Fior. He helped me try to contact Lang and when we couldn't reach him, I realized something must be wrong."

"Why are you looking for Lang?"

"We were actually trying to find you." Torrak paused. "What happened to Lang?"

"Murdered."

Torrak closed his eyes for a moment. "What can I do?"

"Nothing. His killer is dead, but there was another... *party* involved. I'll handle it."

Torrak's mind raced with a hundred questions about his dead friend, but something told him not to press the matter. "You'll make sure this gets fixed?"

Opute's eyes narrowed. "I will. It's personal."

Torrak's own anger rose. "It's personal for me, too. You weren't the only one who cared about Lang."

"There's more going on than you know. It's more than you can handle."

Torrak wanted to argue, to prove he could be an asset, but he already had his own issue to deal with. Besides, he couldn't think of anyone else who would make sure everyone connected to Lang's murder would pay.

Torrak started when he heard Kalil clear his throat.

"I hate to interrupt while the two of you argue over who gets to kill someone, but maybe I should go to the hospital?" Kalil motioned through his ripped pant leg to his knee, now purple and twice its normal size.

"He's right. There's an emergency clinic right past the square. Are you going to be here for a while?" Torrak asked. "I'd like to meet later to talk."

Opute looked down at his blood-splattered clothing. "Cleaning up first would probably be a good idea. I'll be here by the time you two get back."

Before he left, Torrak noticed the open closet—empty. "Where's Lang?"

"Basement freezer. Didn't want him to spoil."

Kalil's face turned a sickly shade of green.

* * *

Three standard hours later, Torrak entered Lang's store with Kalil limping behind him. The hospital reported no concussion from

Kalil's head injury, but his knee had been dislocated and he'd torn several ligaments and some cartilage. A quick surgery followed using a cell-replicating program to regenerate the damaged tissue. The new tissue needed twenty-four standard hours to adjust to Kalil's specific body chemistry. Kalil received a pain-reducing stimulant and the doctor told him to check back if the swelling hadn't gone down in a day.

Torrak walked into the store and stopped abruptly, causing Kalil to run into him.

"Why are you...?" Kalil began.

Opute balanced on the edge of a chair, leaning his body toward a large stack of shipping crates. His loosened pants were held in a desperate grip while he reached with his other hand toward the crates, on which sat the Nikana, its massive white paws protectively guarding Opute's belt.

Kalil began to giggle. Startled, Opute's hand slipped from his pants which slid down his legs. Reaching down to pull them back up, he lost his balance and crashed into the boxes next to him, sending the Nikana scrambling to the floor. Torrak rushed over to help Opute when the Nikana growled. Torrak froze. A hair-raising howl came from the feline's mouth.

"Kana, no!" Opute yelled out. The Nikana eyed Opute and reluctantly backed away from Torrak, its fur still raised.

"Sorry. Never had a Nikana before. Was washing the blood off my belt and it came out of nowhere and snatched it from me. How's the knee, kid?" he asked, nodding in Kalil's direction.

"Dislocated. Should be fine by tomorrow." Kalil's glazed eyes matched his goofy grin.

"They gave him some great painkillers," Torrak said.

Opute turned his attention to Torrak. "So why have you come back to your old stomping ground looking for me?"

"I need your help."

"You've come to collect on your favor."

Torrak nodded. "I need to know if you've heard anything about recent Aleet Army activity."

Opute's eyes widened, but he said nothing, so Torrak continued. "A friend of mine was kidnapped and I believe remnants of the Aleet Army may be involved."

"Whoa."

"I know, but I have no choice. My friend is in trouble and I have to help her."

"What do you want to know?"

"Have any of your contacts mentioned anything about the Army?"

Opute took a moment. "I heard a rumor about someone in the market for leftover scrap metal from Aleet Army ships."

"Do you have a name?"

"No. But I could send you in the direction of the dealer who talked to him."

"Well, let's go."

Opute snorted. "I don't think you want to meet my contact in the middle of the night. You should head out in the morning."

"You mean you're not coming with us?" Kalil asked, eyes still glassy, a pout on his lips.

"Running head first into something like the Aleet Army is not my idea of a good time."

"I don't know how we are going to do this without your help. You know these back streets better than anyone," Torrak said.

"Don't sell yourself short. It'll all come back to you." He paused. "You both really going to do this?"

"I'm the only one who saw what happened to her. I'll do whatever it takes."

"And you?"

Kalil looked at Opute with his large, green eyes. "I've already come this far and I can't imagine backing out now. Besides, I have a test tomorrow on black holes I really don't mind missing." The smile on Kalil's face died at Opute's stoic expression. "I'm in this," he said, his eyes clear. "Until the end."

Opute nodded. "Then let me show you where to go."

CHAPTER 16

TORRAK WOKE THE next morning with a headache. He lifted himself from the floor's cold surface and rubbed his temples. Kalil still slept, his chin pressed against his chest and his bad leg propped up on top of a box. Opute had gone.

Torrak stood and walked to the door. When he looked outside, thoughts of the night before flashed through his mind: Opute drawing a crude map to the place where the dealer, Nuis, would be, loud noises from the crowd outside as the Festival of Moons continued on through the night, and a drunken woman who'd burst through the door, followed closely by two male companions who apologized profusely while she tried to give Kalil a lap dance.

Now, in the bright light of the two suns, Torrak could see the mess from the previous night's activities. Banners, streamers, and garbage were strewn about the square as city volunteers helped to clean up. Some festival-goers who'd had too much to drink were busy being sick, while others were shoved into vehicles to be taken back to their homes.

"Why does it have to be so bright on this planet?" A voice behind him whined.

Torrak faced Kalil, whose eyes squinted in the light of the planet's two suns, one a bright yellow, the other a pale red. "You'll get used to it." Torrak looked at Kalil's knee. "How does it feel today?"

"Not too bad. Pretty stiff, but it doesn't hurt as much as yesterday."

"Think it feels good enough to meet a black-market trader at a bar?"

"Probably. As long as I don't have to run."

Torrak thought it over. He didn't know how sticky the situation might get. "Maybe I should go alone. I'm not sure how things will go with this Nuis guy, and I might have to get out of there fast." Torrak rolled up the directions Opute had written out for him.

"What do you expect me to do while you're gone all day?"

"I don't know. Train the Nikana to do some tricks?" Torrak joked. Now that he had a plan, his tension had lessened considerably.

"Very funny." Kalil paused and looked around. "Speaking of, where is the beast and its master?"

"I'm not sure. Neither were here when I got up."

"You think Opute took off?"

"Maybe." Torrak stepped outside and looked around. The air smelled of fresh dew and lingering food odors. Nobody out there, except a few cleaners and a couple of morning pedestrians. Two men who walked down the street waved in Torrak's direction. The two men, who looked vaguely familiar, came up to him at the door.

"Mornin'!" the one on the right said with a drawl, his shaggy black hair almost covering his eyes.

"Morning."

"You probably don't remember us very well," said the one on the left side, his blue eye rolling around in his head as his brown eye stayed fixed on Torrak. "We came into your store last night to retrieve our drunken, dancing friend."

Torrak placed the two men from their story. "Of course. How is she today?"

"A lil' worse fer wear, but no lastin' harm. We jus' wanted to make sure that our friend didn't do any damage to yer store during her ruckus."

"I don't think anything was disturbed."

"Well, could ya make sure? I'd hate to find out later that she did damage and we didn't pay fer it."

"Sure..." A sharp lump caught in Torrak's throat. Something felt off with the situation, but he couldn't put his finger on it. The pictures came to mind, but the connections weren't there.

Kalil looked up as they entered. "What's going on?"

"These men were the ones who came in last night to retrieve their dancing friend. They wondered if she caused any damage."

"It would be hard to tell in this place. It's a mess."

"All right," one of the men said. "I'm glad she didn't wreck anything."

Torrak gestured to the door. He couldn't wait to get these two guys out of here. His mind flitted around, trying to figure out what seemed off, but he couldn't pinpoint the problem. "Well, thanks for checking."

"Unfortunately, we can't leave yet." The one with the rolling eye locked the door while the one with the shaggy hair placed his hand on Kalil's shoulder. "We know Lang's dead. So after the big guy left this mornin', we figgered it wouldn't be too hard to take on a couple of kids, 'specially one that's already messed up."

"Besides," the man with the rolling eye chimed in, "we don't want to hurt anyone."

Torrak bit back his anger. He couldn't believe he'd let these two guys in. Why couldn't he make the connections?

"You may find I'm more trouble than you think," Torrak said, not willing to give anything up without a fight.

"Not if yer both dead, boy." The man with a drawl pulled out an electric-volt weapon from under his jacket and aimed it toward Kalil.

Kalil blanched. "Easy man, easy. There is nothing here to kill over. Take whatever inventory you want."

"We don't want any of that. We came fer this." The man with the shaggy hair went over to Lang's computer system and checked the dataport. "It ain't here," he said to his companion.

"What?" The other man came over to the desk. "What do you mean it's not here?" Frantically searching through datapads and drawers, the man stopped abruptly and turned to face Torrak. "Where is it?"

"Where's what?"

"Don't play games! You must have found it and kept it for yourself." The man lunged toward Torrak. Out of pure instinct, Torrak side-stepped and threw him to the floor, using the man's own weight to propel him.

"That's enough," the man with the shaggy hair growled. He pointed the weapon back at Kalil. "The disk was here. Where's it now?"

"I don't know what you're talking about," Kalil said, his voice catching. "I don't have anything. Maybe someone else took it."

A low voice came from behind Torrak. "The kid's right. Someone else took it." Torrak spun and saw Opute in the doorway. "You have one chance," Opute said slowly to the men, "to leave right now and I won't kill you."

The man with the shaggy hair smiled and held the electric-volt weapon up to Kalil's head. "I don't think you should be the one givin' orders. Where's the disk?"

Opute looked at Kalil. "You think I care about him? Who do you think snapped his leg?"

The man glanced down at Kalil's leg. In that moment, Opute threw his knife. It hit the man in the head right above the ear and he dropped the electric-volt weapon in Kalil's lap. Opute took two steps toward the man with the rolling eye and broke his neck. The man's body fell to the floor, his eye rolling into the back of his head. The man with the shaggy hair had time to touch the knife protruding from his skull before he fell backwards onto the desk.

Kalil slid out of his chair. The weapon rolled off his lap as he hobbled away from the dead body.

Opute went over and retrieved his knife, wiping off the man's bodily fluid. He pushed the dead body off the desk and sat down. "You two all right?"

"You—you killed them." Kalil said in shock.

Opute shrugged. "Better them than us. They weren't going to leave you two alive."

"What disk were they talking about?" Torrak asked, relieved to hear his voice sounded steady.

Opute pulled out the disk from inside his coat. "It's encrypted. I'm going to take it back to my ship and work on it. But whatever's on it must be valuable. It's the reason Lang was murdered, which means there will probably be others who come looking for it."

"Well, thanks for saving our lives." Torrak helped Kalil to his feet. "I guess we'd better head out. Maybe I'll see you around sometime."

"Who knows? It's a big universe."

CHAPTER 17

THE *HORIZON* SPED through the vastness of space, sure and steady on its course. It thought nothing of its cargo, its crew, or its past.

The Commander of the *Horizon*, wanted to do anything *but* think.

Trey paced in his office.

He remembered the captain of his army unit when he asked who would take care of eleven-year-old Dru: "You don't have time to worry about your brother! This planet is falling apart! Get out there, stop thinking, and fire!"

The judge after his mother had been killed: "We know what these two soldiers did to your family, but now that Jacin Jaxx changed their thoughts, they'll never do anything like that again."

"What a coward," Trey sneered. "Hiding behind his judge's robes. He didn't care about justice. He just wanted to pretend the war casualties had never happened, like we were an embarrassment."

And Jacin Jaxx's final words as he addressed Trey's homeworld after ending the war: "You do not need to live in fear anymore!"

Trey walked faster around his office at this last memory, his fists clenched next to his thighs.

"What a fool I was, believing in him," he said. "What a waste of skill and talent. I won't make the same mistake." Spittle formed in the corner of his mouth and he hastily wiped it away. "Your daughter will fix your mistakes!"

A beep brought him out of his rant. With a sharp tap, he opened the communications panel.

"Yes," he snapped.

"Morning, Commander," the voice on the other line said.

"Lieutenant Commander Cenjo. What do you want?"

"I thought we could meet to discuss Daith's progress."

Trey closed his eyes for a moment. "Come to my office in a standard hour."

"Yes, Commander. Cenjo out."

Trey cut the channel and rubbed his eyes, his smooth fingertips soft against his skin. He knew what the report would be. It's what all the reports indicated—Daith still wasn't progressing with her abilities.

Trey's anger left a nasty taste in his mouth. He hated this place. He hated this crew.

He couldn't wait anymore. He needed to move ahead with his plan. It was time to push Daith forward and if she burned out, he would continue anyway.

Trey placed an outgoing vidlink call and left a message for the recipient on the other end:

"Kyla, it's Xiven. We are a go in two standard weeks. Implement our chain vidlink calls to our next planetary members. Make sure those worlds hate the Aleet Army."

CHAPTER 18

DAITH SAT IN the mess hall. Usually she avoided the place, hating that most of the crew evaded her, like she was some sort of monster. But she couldn't stay in her quarters. Alone in her room, her stomach clenched every time she thought about using her abilities. After Cenjo had asked her to heal him, she felt terrified. Even the thought of practicing her powers by melting datapads scared her. Within moments, she'd broken out in a sweat. Her quarters seemed to shrink, pressing in on her from all sides. She bolted from the room and headed to the mess hall.

After being on board the past few weeks, Daith knew the crew's schedule well enough, and when the mess hall would be empty. At the moment, only two cadets sat in the room that could hold 200.

Her kilari root soup turned cold while she sat. The huge knot inside made eating impossible.

The door to the hall slid open and out of reflex, Daith looked up.

A young woman, one of the pilots, entered the room. Her bronze skin shimmered under the harsh lights, giving her a sickly glow.

Ishia had been one of the first in the crew to avoid Daith, so when she veered straight toward her, Daith's eyebrows skyrocketed.

"Miss Tocc."

"Yes?"

"May I sit?"

Daith's gaze flittered around the room. The two other cadets both stared, turning their glances away hastily.

"Of course."

Ishia took a seat across from her, her posture rigid, her amber eyes wide. She looked terrified.

A struggled smile wiggled on Daith's face. "What can I do for you?"

"I heard a rumor you can fix machines. Is that true?"

"I'm not sure what you mean...."

Ishia gripped her hands tightly to stop them trembling. "I have a problem. With one of the piloting consoles. On the bridge." Each phrase came out short and punctuated. "It's my duty to repair it, but I'm having difficulty. Can you assist?"

Daith's body rippled. Part of her constricted with horror at the thought of using her abilities. But another part of her tingled with excitement. A crewmember was asking her for help.

"What do you expect me to do?"

Ishia's words came out rushed. "I don't know. Will you come look at it? I'm supposed to have it ready in a few standard hours for Commander Xiven, but I don't think I can get it fixed by then. I don't want him to dismiss me if the console isn't working in time."

Daith's stomach churned. *Come on, Daith! You can do this. Start by saying yes.*

"Okay. I can't promise anything, but I'll come take a look."

Ishia's shoulders relaxed. "My gratitude," she gushed. "When are you available?"

Daith glanced at her cold soup. Her lip curled at the sight of the slimy coagulated layer on its surface. "I'm free right now."

"Wonderful," she said, standing. "Please follow me."

The two of them left the mess hall and wove their way down the bridge. Four crewmembers staffed the area—all sitting at consoles that faced the chair in the center of the room. Ishia led them to the second station on the left. A blank screen reflected Daith's pale face.

"I believe the navigation system is malfunctioning, but I can't determine how. When I insert a command, an alternate result occurs."

Daith took a seat on the floor, ignoring the looks from the other crewmembers. "Why didn't you ask someone from engineering to help?"

Ishia squatted next to her. "They have no one to spare at the moment. Preparations keep everyone busy and time is limited." She unscrewed a panel and opened up the console. Wires, conduits, and lights filled the space.

Daith felt her chest tighten. What did she think she was doing? She wasn't ready for this. What if she did more damage? What if she blew the whole thing up?

Daith closed her eyes. *One step at a time.* She let the warmth build inside her, pushing her mind forward, looking into the circuitry.

A snicker sounded behind her.

Daith opened her eyes and swiveled toward the sound. Ishia stood, hands on her hips.

"What's your problem, Poka?" she demanded.

The culprit leaned forward over his console, his flat, featureless, purple face covered in fungi-like shapes. A slit on his forehead opened. "You called *her* to the bridge to help you? Don't tell me you actually believe she can do anything. Her so-called powers are fancy lighting and cheap tricks. A telepath projecting lies."

Daith's face burned. "Excuse me?"

Purple drool hung on the corner of his slit. "You heard me. We are wasting time on a joke. We don't need your help. We can do this mission without you."

Shame and anger hit her.

Ishia spoke up in defense. "What about Sequiria's nose? She broke it last week in the simulation room during training. How do you explain that?"

Poka waved his four arms and pincered hands. "Who knows? Maybe Sequiria hit herself and shifted the blame? No one saw the medical report. That traitor Doctor Ludd erased everything when he left."

Ishia's face fell.

Daith had enough. The reminder that Dr. Ludd had left her, the constant apprehensive energy she felt from the rest of the crew, and her anger at her own lack of progress shifted totally and completely onto Poka. "You make me sick," she said. She pushed herself to her feet and strode over to Poka's console. He puffed up, preparing to defend himself.

"You keep away from me, you liar. I don't care if you're Commander Xiven's prize—you do anything to me and I'll paralyze you." He held his slit open, wide. The purple saliva pooled in his mouth, bubbling and hissing.

"Please." Daith allowed the heat inside her to well up and flow into her hand. With a dramatic slam, she plunged it onto the console. The surface bubbled and crackled. Her hand submerged itself into a hot goo. Pulling back, she showed him a blistering palm, which smoothed out into healed skin while he watched.

With a smirk, Daith whirled away from Poka and returned to the console. Still hot with anger, her energy narrowed into a tight beam. She quickly located the problem within the console, a faulty wire, something Ishia wouldn't have discovered without testing each one. Allowing the heat to fill inside her, she directed it toward the wire, mended its weak points, and felt the energy surge back through it.

"All fixed," she told Ishia.

Ishia sputtered a thank you.

"Don't worry about it," Daith said, wiping her runny nose. Her sleeve came away with a crimson splotch. "See you around." She hurried off the bridge, sleeve pressed against her face. When she reached her quarters, her legs buckled. She tumbled onto the bed, exhausted, but giggling uncontrollably.

The look on Poka's face. She'd never felt such satisfaction.

Spurts of laughter barked out of her. She could barely breathe, her eyes brimmed with tears.

Get a hold of yourself!

With harsh gasps she calmed down.

The door chimes rang.

Daith sat up abruptly. "Just a moment," she called. With a quick wipe her tears were gone. Two flips rolled up her sleeves, hiding the blood stains. "Enter."

Ishia stood in the doorway. "May I come in?"

"Of course." The words came quick and eager. Daith willed herself to slow down. "Is there something wrong with the bridge console?"

Ishia stepped inside. Daith opened up her senses to feel the woman's emotions. Fear, yes, but also curiosity and gratitude.

"The console works perfectly."

"Then why are you here?" Daith winced at the harshness of the words.

Ishia frowned at Daith's tone. "I don't mean to intrude."

"You're not. I'm sorry. I'm just not used to anyone on the crew being friendly."

Ishia gingerly sat on the edge of the bed. "I want to tell you I don't agree with Poka's opinion, but I understand his viewpoint. Most of us felt strange when Commander Xiven brought aboard an outsider to help. When we heard what you could do, we feared he merely meant to replace his old leader."

"Don't you mean *your* old leader?"

Ishia shook her head and swiveled her body toward Daith. "I did not belong to his crew during that time. In fact, very few of us did. I believe Commander Xiven and Lieutenant Commander Cenjo are the only ones left. I only joined a standard year ago."

Daith hesitated. "Can I ask why you joined?"

Ishia smiled and the pressure in Daith's chest eased.

"I was a small fledgling when the Aleet Army came to help my planet. Until that time, I had only known terror. Our world fought others for generations because of a mistake from decades earlier. But Jacin Jaxx met with all the governments and in that one day, the officials called a truce. No one at the time really knew how he did it."

Daith felt an inkling of despair creep into her belly. "And then he died."

Ishia nodded, the smile gone from her face. "Whatever hold he had on my planet disappeared in an instant. The Controllers, or Liberators as they called themselves, reignited our passion for revenge. Within a few standard months, our peace dissolved. When I grew old enough, I left my planet. I heard a rumor of others who did not agree with Controller actions. These rumors led me to Commander Xiven."

Daith thought for a moment, cycling through Ishia's words. "What does Trey think he can accomplish against the Controllers with one ship and such a small crew?"

Ishia straightened. "Commander Xiven is a man of many talents and I have seen him accomplish much against heavy odds. He knows

Sintaur is the Controllers' base and so that is where we must begin to change things."

"Sintaur? Isn't that Trey's... I mean Commander Xiven's homeworld?"

Daith's door chimes interrupted Ishia's answer. Ishia raised an eyebrow.

"Come in," Daith called out.

The door slid open and Trey stepped into the room. A flicker of surprise crossed his face.

Ishia jumped to her feet. "Commander!"

"No need for alarm, Cadet Ikar." He paused. "Weren't you supposed to be working on the bridge's piloting console?"

"It's fixed, Commander."

Daith could sense fear emanating from Ishia.

"She came from repairing it when we bumped into each other in the corridor," Daith lied. "I invited her in since her next shift doesn't start for a standard hour. Thought I could get to know someone from the crew a little better."

Relief swept through Ishia so hard it nearly knocked Daith over.

Trey gave a sharp nod. "An excellent idea. In fact, it's about time you met everyone on board, don't you think?"

"Um...sure?"

"Perfect. We'll meet tomorrow before main shift starts in the mess hall." He directed his next words toward Ishia. "Finished, Cadet?"

Ishia gulped. "Yes, Commander."

"On your way, then. You can see Daith tomorrow with the rest of the crew."

Ishia gave Daith a quick glance. Daith felt a warmth emanate from her—it made her feel safe and content. A feeling of friendship.

Ishia slid around the Commander and out of the room.

Trey stared at the closed door for a moment before returning his attention to Daith. "It's nice to see you interacting with some of the crew. I'm sorry I didn't think about introducing you to everyone sooner. So much has happened. It hasn't really sunk in that you are now a part of this crew."

"It's understandable."

"I also heard you've been making progress in your sparring sessions with Lieutenant Commander Cenjo?"

Daith laughed. "Well, I hit him once, if that counts."

"It most certainly does. The Lieutenant Commander is a highly regarded physical combatant. He used to be a master champion for his nation, he competed all across his world and others."

Daith couldn't believe it. "I didn't know that."

"In fact, he's never been bested by anyone on this vessel. It's not surprising though, with abilities like yours."

"That's the funny part—I didn't use my abilities. I mean, I tried, but he was too fast."

Trey raised an eyebrow. "Really?"

Daith nodded. "It seemed like he wasn't thinking about what he planned next, so there wasn't anything I could grab hold of with my mind. His body responded before he made a move."

Trey clasped his hands in front of him and took a more relaxed stance. "That's fascinating, Daith. I wonder if—"

Bang! Bang! Bang!

Daith jumped at the pounding. Trey whipped his head toward the door.

"Open up in there, you freak!" Words poured through the door like oily acid. "I know who you are. I found you."

A fury pressed upon Daith. Rage swelled in her chest though her heartbeat remained steady, her breathing normal. She didn't understand what was going on inside her.

Then she realized it wasn't her anger, but Trey's. For the first time, she could fully feel his emotions. His being shook with white-hot energy, tinged red with wrath.

Trey slammed his hand on the button to open the door. "TRAITOR!"

There stood Poka, his purple face contorted with hatred. In a moment it slid into a greyish, puckered oval. Terror pulsed off him in waves. The emotional energy battered against Trey's as Daith watched, stunned into stillness.

Trey removed something from the front pocket of his uniform and slapped it onto Poka's cheek. A yelp escaped his lips. He clawed at a small circle.

Too late.

The circle erupted tiny claws which sunk into his cheek. With a hiss, toxins inside the chip released.

Poka gurgled. His skin swelled and turned pale yellow. A gasp escaped him before he crumpled to the floor, deflated like a thick rubber suit.

Daith screamed. Trey whirled around and struck her across the face.

Blackness engulfed her.

CHAPTER 19

TORRAK AND KALIL checked into a hotel. Kalil's drowsiness from his pain medication overtook him and he fell asleep the moment he sat on the couch. Torrak propped up his friend's injured leg before he headed out to find Nuis.

Their hotel sat south of Lang's store in a cheap part of the city. Before he left, Torrak took a last look at the crude map Opute had drawn out for him and headed toward a bar called *The Fishbowl*. It would take Torrak little less than a standard hour if he went on foot, and he thought it wiser to save any money he could. He wasn't sure if Nuis would require a bribe to answer his questions. Opute had told Torrak money wouldn't impress Nuis, but Torrak didn't know of anyone in the smuggling business who couldn't be bought.

Heading out of town, he walked past the Central Authority building, tall with tinted windows, and Torrak's mind swirled with thoughts of the past. He knew from childhood he wanted to be a detective. From early on, he had a gift for figuring out answers to puzzles and problems when no one else could. It seemed sometimes the less he thought about trying to solve a case, the faster he did.

Right before his sixteenth birthday, his father talked to the chief of C-9's governmental authority. He told them about Torrak's interests and analytical abilities and asked if his son could follow an officer around for awhile during his school's heat-season break to check out the job. Torrak trained with Teph Slaphen, a female officer who worked in homicide. Toward the end of the heat-season, he started speaking up about cases Teph had been assigned, telling her who he thought were the guilty parties. Teph humored him, listening attentively as one would a small child, until she realized almost every case ended the way he predicted. Over ninety-three percent, in fact. The remaining unsolved cases were either changed due to bargains or had too little evidence. When Torrak turned seventeen the following year, he took the offer to work part-time while still enrolled in class, motivated by Teph's generous recommendation.

When school finished, he worked for another three years before deciding to continue his education. Torrak looked into academies for advanced students. He read about Fior Accelerated Academy and started there the following year on a full scholarship.

Cackles from overhead birds brought him out of his thoughts. Crimson and orange bled into the edges of the sky as *The Fishbowl* came into view. With quickened steps, Torrak approached the bar while the first of the two suns began to set.

Torrak entered the small, dank establishment. The mixed smell of body odor and fruity drinks hit him like a wall. With a glance around, he noticed a booth to his left in which two massive Trairs sat, a species with unusually large sweat glands over most of their bodies. Their scent nauseated him, so Torrak quickly headed in the other direction.

The single room consisted of a bar, some stools, and a few moldy booths. There were two doors, one marked as an exit and the other do not enter. Torrak knew most patrons wouldn't come until after second sunset, so he ordered a glass of local ale and waited at the end of the bar.

Three drinks after second sunset, Nuis arrived. Torrak's eyes flicked up briefly, long enough for identification, and dropped back to his watered-down ale. The man's curly, tawny hair fell to his broad shoulders. He had auburn skin, tinged redder from the sun, and a large, dazzling white smile. Torrak realized quite quickly, from the neatly pressed and tailored clothes and the clean, shined shoes that Nuis may not be the bully his reputation suggested. His companions, however....

Two huge, bulky men followed close behind Nuis. They sat at the bar and Nuis ordered a round of drinks for himself and his friends. At first, Torrak looked for a place he could move to overhear their conversation, but realized it wouldn't be necessary. Nuis spoke loudly and from the sound of it he had no problem with everyone hearing his story.

"There I was, face to face with a Wict, and he challenges me over some parts I sold him." Nuis imitated the over-sized, muscled Wict with a series of snarls and grunts. Torrak noticed that many of the listeners smiled at this imitation.

"Apparently," Nuis continued, "this Wict didn't know who he was dealing with and thought there'd be no contest. So I fake defeat, telling him I'd talk to my supplier again and find out why he sent faulty parts. Right when the Wict thought he'd won, I punched him in the chest and he crumpled to the ground, gasping for breath!" At this, Nuis started to laugh. Infectious, soon his captive audience around him laughed as well.

Above the laughter, a voice spoke up. "Quite a story. Too bad it isn't true."

The whole bar quieted. "Excuse me?"

Torrak spoke again. "Your story. You tell it with such conviction, but it's a complete lie." ͺ

Nuis put down his drink and walked over to Torrak's booth, his hands clenched. "Would you like a re-enactment?"

Torrak smiled. "Anyone who's ever met a Wict knows they don't breathe. It would be impossible for him to gasp for breath since there isn't any air in him to begin with. They exchange gases through their skin." Torrak sat back in his booth. "Perhaps you should do more research about the imaginary beings you beat up before you tell your stories."

Several patrons in the bar laughed at Nuis's flushed face. "Perhaps *you* should do more research before you insult someone you don't know." Nuis's two companions started to close in on Torrak.

"Have to send your muscle after me instead of getting your own hands dirty, Nuis?" Torrak internally cringed at how stupid the words sounded. He hoped he sounded like a tough guy.

Nuis held up his hand and the two attackers stopped. "How do you know who I am?"

"I *did* my research. But I'm not here to fight. I came to talk."

Nuis remained silent in thought. He then gestured toward the door behind them.

Torrak slipped out of the booth to follow him.

"They stay out," Torrak said, in reference to Nuis's thugs after they checked him for weapons.

Nuis dismissed them. Torrak shut the door. The room, not much larger than a closet, had dull, brown walls and faded cyan carpeting. A broom with a chipped handle stood in one corner, the other held a stack of yellowed papers. A small desk sat in the middle of the room with two chairs on either side of it. Nuis took a seat in one and waited until Torrak followed suit.

Nuis leaned back in his chair and picked delicately at his neatly trimmed nails. "I don't know who you are, but you'd better have something good to talk to me about before I smash your face in."

Like you'd ever risk wrecking your perfect manicure, Torrak thought to himself. "I'm looking for information."

"Information, huh? Information isn't free, you know."

"I know. How much do you want?"

"Depends on what you need."

"I'm interested in finding a client of yours."

"I've got lots of clients. Some are worth more than others." Nuis smiled.

"Alright. It's about a client who wanted to buy scrap metal from Aleet Army ships."

The smile on Nuis's face melted away. "You do seem to know quite a bit. I'd be interested in who directed you to me."

Torrak smiled. "We all want to know something."

"True." Nuis leaned forward. "Meet me here," he said as he scribbled on a piece of yellow-stained paper, "in four days."

CHAPTER 20

"DAITH? DAITH CAN you hear me?"

Daith's head pounded. Her eyelids fluttered open to see Trey leaning over her.

"Trey?" Dried saliva cracked in the corner of her mouth. "What's going on?"

"You were screaming and I came into your quarters. You were thrashing around. I called for medical to come help." He nodded over at Doctor Milastow.

Daith's head felt heavy when she lifted it. She caught Trey's eyes, full of worry, but she remembered them being filled with malice.

"No," she muttered, pulling away from him. The blanket under her bunched up at her feet. "Stay away."

"Lie still for a moment." Milastow's cool fingers pressed against her forehead.

"You killed him," Daith said, drawing her legs into her chest. "I saw you." The images of Poka's deflated body filled her mind. And then Trey had turned his rage onto her....

Trey raised his eyebrows, bewildered. "What are you talking about? I haven't killed anyone."

Daith nodded, her head swimming in pain. "Poka came to my quarters. You killed him out in the corridor." She touched the side of her face where Trey had struck her, but it felt fine. No swelling, no pain.

"What?" Trey turned his confused stare to the doctor. "Poka? Who's Poka? We don't have a cadet by that name, do we?"

Milastow shook her head. "I-I don't know, Commander. I'm not familiar with all the cadets by name." She moved over to the computer wall console and activated it. "Computer, is there a Cadet Poka on board?"

"There is no record of a crewmember with that name on board."

Daith slid her fingers into her hair, pressing on her throbbing skull. "I don't understand."

"Could it have been a nightmare?" Trey asked, his voice gentle.

Daith grimaced. It seemed so real. "I suppose..."

Milastow stepped back over. "Have you been taking your dream-deflector pills?"

Daith could sense the doctor's nervous energy.

"I think so? I've kind of been sleeping here and there, though."

Milastow's shoulders drooped, her third limb wrapped loosely around her neck. "Commander, I wouldn't be surprised if these were images implanted in her mind while she slept. We are approaching the Fracc system, which is densely populated."

Trey rubbed his chin. "True. After Doctor Ludd left the ship, he may have alerted members of the Controllers about our current plan. They may know we are closer, and proximity does make telepathic connections stronger." His jaw muscles clenched. "I don't know what to do anymore, who to trust. I keep so many of the crew from knowing all the details of the plan for precisely this reason." He sighed. "Daith, would you like to tell me about your dream? Maybe there is a clue as to who is behind this?

Daith's headache worsened. She didn't want to be around him. He'd been terrifying and the images felt so vivid—Poka's vindictive jeers, Trey's wrath, the pain when he slapped her. She couldn't think straight. "Can we talk later? I don't feel very well."

Milastow leaned over and injected Daith with a syringe. "This is a sedative to help you sleep. I've added a dose of dream-deflectors to it. You should be out until tomorrow."

"Please make sure I'm awake in time to meet the rest of the crew in the morning, Trey," she mumbled, her eyelids heavy.

"Oh, of course, Daith."

Through the haze, Daith heard Trey whisper to Milastow.

"What meeting is she talking about?"

* * *

Trey paced across the slick, black glass floor.

So close. So close to ruining everything. All his years of waiting, planning, training. Almost gone in a moment.

All because of that idiotic crewmember, Poka.

Trey stopped, arms rigid at his side. He forced a breath through his teeth. It whistled in the large room, evaporating into the sound-proof walls.

He couldn't believe he lost control like that. And he'd struck Daith!

Trey's fists whitened. Another breath out—this one longer, slower.

He and Doctor Milastow had quickly removed Poka's body from

the corridor and stashed it in medical. Doctor Milastow would eventually disintegrate it and reprocess it into the ship's recycling systems. Then Trey examined the bridge—he replaced the console she melted with her hand, told them Poka had been dismissed from service, and warned that any mention of him to other crewmembers would result in immediate dismissal.

After, he returned to his office and wiped any trace of Poka from the ship's logs and memory banks. So simple—search for a name and remove it. But what to do about Cadet Ishia Ikar? Daith would certainly go to her to ask what she remembered. Trey believed Daith was strong enough to sense if Ishia lied.

Trey's muscles relaxed through his breathing. His anger abated. Control returned once more. He walked to the center of the room, located on the top floor underneath the ship's observation lounge, void of any other crew. The massive space dwarfed him and the only other item that occupied it—a Memory Machine.

He found it long after Jacin's death, broken and rusted, a warped shell of a device on a trash planet. Everyone who ever took Eomix Galaxy History knew about Memory Machines—used by the Chears to erase and implant memories in others. The Chears had nearly conquered the galaxy, but after their downfall, the M.M.'s were deconstructed and deemed illegal to use. The law was one of the first unanimously passed by every planet through the Eomix United Front.

Trey approached the gleaming, white machine. With a large helmet that hung over a flat bed, the contraption looked as welcoming as a dissection table. In a sense, it could be considered that. Except instead of a scalpel to the body, it focused its energy on the mind, targeting a patient's memories.

He ran his hand over the smooth helmet and initiated the startup sequence. The machine hummed to life as lights around the helmet glowed magenta. Without this contraption, his plan would never have gone into play. It removed Daith's memories when they first brought her on board. Now she believed anything Trey told her.

He feared to use it on her again to erase the memory of Trey killing Poka, in case it damaged her mind, so creativity had taken over. A quick search and destroy of Ikar's memories, like a file search and delete on the ship's computer, would take care of the problem.

The door to the room slid open. Doctor Milastow entered, guiding a wide-eyed Cadet Ikar in front of her.

"You wanted to see me, Commander?" the cadet asked, her voice betraying her awe and fear. She tucked her short hair behind her ears, her gaze drawn to the contraption in the middle of the room.

"Yes, Cadet," Trey said, patting the table. "This will only take a moment."

CHAPTER 21

FOUR DAYS AFTER the encounter at *The Fishbowl,* Torrak and Kalil set off to meet Nuis. Kalil's knee felt better, although the faded yellowish bruises made it look otherwise.

Their destination lay on the other side of the city, so they rented an *Anywhere and You're There!* vehicle. The driver steered them into a wealthy suburb. Towering houses sat next to each other, intricately designed with elaborate yards.

The car drove up the winding white path of a silver and black mansion, which towered over them. The front of the house featured a huge garden full of plants and flowers, all different colors and types. Exotic and rare, Torrak knew it must have cost a small fortune to have them delivered from their native worlds. Kalil's mouth hung open at the sight.

The building consisted of three parts—a large, rounded center dome with two smaller wings on either side. The grounds showcased a spacious patio spread out on the left side of the house and a nah-tsu courtyard sat on the right. The silver color etched into the black walls created a fluid pattern on the house. Only when Torrak got closer did he realize silver liquid actually flowed under a clear cover.

They exited the vehicle, walked up the wide staircase that led to the main door, and rang the bell. A gong sounded from somewhere inside.

"Torrak, if this is Nuis's place, we are in trouble. What could we possibly offer someone who obviously has no problem buying anything he wants?"

"I don't know, but this is our only lead so somehow we have to get this information." The door opened. Torrak wasn't sure what to make of the being that stood there.

The being stood almost three meters tall with bright gold skin. Twisted sections of rusty-golden hair lay loosely on top of her head. Long tresses hung down to the being's waist, and the very tips were a bright yellow. Her garment, a copper colored gauzy material, wrapped around her neck, shoulders, waist, and right leg. A dark, golden pattern swirled across the being's skin in circular and curved figures.

"Welcome", the being said over her purr. Her feline nose twitched. "My name is Preeaht. Nuis is expecting you. Please, come in."

The foyer opened up to a wide white marble staircase. The stairs were accentuated by golden handrails and covered with a lush, mauve carpet. A huge chandelier hung from above and emitted a gold-tinted light that set off the specks of gold engraved in the white tile. Violet-red curtains hung from large windows, creating shadowed patterns that stretched across the floor and spilled onto the walls.

"Don't worry," she said, the words vibrating. "Everyone stares the first time." The being turned and winked at Kalil. His eyes widened, but he remained silent.

A strong scent of incense enveloped them once they entered the room to the left of the main door. Multi-colored woven drapes hung from the center of the ceiling and swooped outward toward each corner, casting shadows from the smoky lights. Creatures and beings, most of them unrecognizable species to Torrak, lounged upon huge cushions and lavish rugs strewn about the floor. Several lay entwined, limbs wrapped around each other, absorbed in murmured conversation or more intimate physical contact. Nuis sat in the middle of the room on a large, plush pillow with a companion on either side of him. One fed him food, the other massaged his hand.

"Welcome to my humble abode, gentlemen. Could I offer you any refreshments before we get started?" Nuis asked.

"No, thank you." Torrak replied. He expected some seedy dive, surrounded by a large number of back-up thugs. This new atmosphere unnerved him. "We really would like to get down to business."

Nuis eyed Torrak up and down. "Pity," he mumbled. "As you wish. Shall we move to my office?"

Both Torrak and Kalil moved to follow him.

"No, my dear," Nuis said to Kalil, "You will have to remain here. But don't worry, Preeaht will take excellent care of you." At this remark, Kalil turned toward Preeaht, whose grin widened on her golden face.

"This way," Preeaht cooed.

Kalil followed her out of the room, throwing a look of alarm in Torrak's direction while Nuis guided Torrak to his office. Nuis took a seat behind his desk.

Black carpet spread across the floor, complimented by shiny, ebony walls. A crimson ceiling contrasted the dark, lit by a sole, pale, golden bulb hanging from the center. The light cast a red glow in the creases of Nuis's face, giving him a fiendish look.

Torrak felt like he'd entered some sort of circus house.

"Please, sit."

Torrak sat in the large, black chair facing Nuis.

"Since you are now a guest in my home," Nuis continued, "I wonder if you'd let me know who told you about me?"

Torrak hesitated. He wondered if dropping Opute's name would improve his chances. At this point, he guessed it really didn't matter. "Ness Opute told me about you."

Nuis's left eyebrow rose. "Interesting." He paused. "So you've come for information. What do you have to offer me in return?"

"How much do you want?"

Nuis laughed. "Have you looked around? Money is not a concern for me."

Torrak clenched his teeth. He was tired of the strange settings, the false pretenses, and the doubletalk. "No more games. Tell me what you want."

"Games, huh? What an interesting notion." Nuis considered for a moment. He stared at Torrak, his gaze lingering on his young body and lean physique. "Did you see my nah-tsu court outside?"

"Yes. I noticed it."

"Have you ever played before?"

"A bit, back in school."

"Good." Nuis declared. "I have thought of what you can do for your payment. I have played against everyone in my house and no one has ever beaten me. They may be afraid if they won I would kill them, which may be true, but it takes away from the sport when the other side isn't playing its best."

"You want me to play you in a game of nah-tsu?"

"Yes, but there are conditions." Nuis paused as a devious smile spread across his face. "If you win, I will tell you everything I can about this client of mine."

"And if I lose?"

"If you lose, you work for me for one rotation of suns."

"Doing what?"

"Whatever I need you to do."

Torrak suddenly felt very uncomfortable at the idea.

"Do we have a deal?" Nuis asked.

Torrak thought about it. He used to be captain of the nah-tsu team in school, but he hadn't played in several years. The idea of losing and being Nuis's "worker" for the next rotation of suns was not appealing, but he needed to get that information. If he lost, he'd figure something out. He hoped.

"Okay. I agree to your terms."

"How exciting!" Nuis said. "I can't wait. In fact, I won't. We'll set up now and play after dinner."

Torrak followed Nuis out of the office, through the room filled with pillows, down a short hallway, and into a lavishly furnished dining room. Mounds of food spread across an intricately carved stone table, decorated with cream and silver scarves. Most everyone had already sat down, although Torrak noticed that Kalil wasn't there. Silver, twinkling lights chimed quietly above them.

"Where's my friend?"

"Oh, I'm sure he'll be around shortly. He's a little...busy at the moment." Nuis nodded to the table. "Please, sit and enjoy yourself."

Even though Torrak's stomach rumbled with hunger, the ball of nerves clenched inside made it impossible to eat. If he lost at nah-tsu, he would never find out what happened to Daith. And he hated the idea of wearing some sort of ridiculous costume while prancing around the estate for Nuis's pleasure.

A short while later, Kalil entered—hair mussed, clothes askew. A lopsided grin accompanied his disheveled appearance.

"What happened to you?" Torrak asked in alarm.

"Huh?" Kalil looked at him, dazed.

"I asked what happened. You look like you fell down twelve flights of stairs."

"Uh-huh."

"What?"

"It was the most amazing experience of my life."

Torrak realized Kalil wasn't listening to him. He reached over and tugged him down into a chair. "What *happened?*"

Kalil came out of his stupor. "She did." With these words, Kalil glanced up at Preeaht.

"Her?"

"Yup."

Torrak shook his head. "Here we are in some strange place where I may end up a dancing slave and you go off and let Miss Golden Purr 'take care' of you."

"I'm simply enjoying their hospitality." Kalil stuffed a chunk of food in his mouth. "Wait... a danshing shave?"

CHAPTER 22

HEAVY EYELIDS PROTESTED opening. Daith's head felt stuffy while she lifted it from the pillow. Saliva streaked across her hand as she wiped her face. With measured movements she pushed aside the grey blanket and swung her legs over the side of her bed. Her timereader read oh-nine hundred hours. She'd slept solidly through the night.

Memories of the day before seeped into her mind. The situation had been so real—Poka on the bridge, Trey's raging temper. How could it have all been a dream? Were the Controllers really so powerful they could reach into her thoughts from across the cosmos?

Or were they closer than everyone thought?

The idea wedged into Daith's mind. What if the Controllers were closing in?

Daith changed and left her quarters, her stomach rolling with hunger, too famished to think straight. She made her way down one floor to the mess hall. She didn't even realize she'd gone there instead of ordering something from the chute in her quarters until she walked through the door.

Once inside, she spotted Ishia sitting at one of the tables.

Relief flooded her. Someone she could talk to. Smiling, Daith strolled over. She signaled to one of the mess hall attendants to come take her order. With an air of ease, she pulled up a seat.

"Morning, Ishia!"

Ishia's amber eyes widened. "Hello, Miss Tocc." She paused, putting down her utensil. "Is there something I can help you with?"

"No. Just wanted to say hi. Any more problems with the piloting console?"

Ishia's brow furrowed. "No. Is there a reason there should be?"

Daith placed her order. The little server scurried away on its three legs. Daith watched the bright blue being return behind the counter, its white bumps reflecting the harsh light. "I suppose not," she answered Ishia. "I guess I wanted to make sure. I'm still pretty new at my abilities. I worried maybe my fixing it didn't work."

"I don't understand what you mean. You fixed my console? When?"

Daith stared at her. "Uh, yesterday? You asked me to fix it. Remember? I got into that fight with Poka?"

Ishia's squinted her face. "Yesterday? I don't recall. And who is Poka?"

Daith sat, stunned. Two long, flexible arms from the server placed her mosana meat dish in front of her, removing the dish from its flattened top. The server squeaked before toddling away. The large lump of meat steamed, but Daith ignored it.

Ishia didn't remember Poka? Impossible. Except... except Trey said Poka wasn't a crew member. That Daith had been dreaming—controlled by a Controller. Had the whole incident been a set-up?

The conversation with Ishia? The console incident on the bridge?

She needed to be sure. Tentatively, she let the warmth inside her surge forward and she propelled the energy toward Ishia, searching her mind for thoughts tied to the bridge incident, to Poka, any of it.

Nothing. The memories didn't exist. Ishia wasn't lying. Their meeting had never happened.

An embarrassed flush warmed Daith's face.

"Are you all right, Miss Tocc?"

Concern mixed with fear flooded out of the young cadet. Daith retracted her connection, severing the bond.

"I'm fine," she lied. "I guess...I must have been thinking of something else." She stood. "I'm sorry for interrupting your lunch." With a quick turn, Daith left the table, her mosana untouched. She strode to her quarters, willing her eyes to stay dry until she could reach its confines.

Once inside, she brushed away the falling tears, ashamed at crying over something so stupid. But her body didn't listen and the tears came anyway. Daith genuinely liked Ishia and the Controllers had planted an entire dream to get Daith to open up—to talk about the mission.

Anger swelled inside her chest. These monsters created something inside her—a friendship, a belittling, a murder—simply to get into her mind. Would they stop at nothing to get her? And how much did they really know? Obviously they had knowledge about the crew and her insecurities. Or had they learned about her through her subconscious?

Daith's head spun, tired of feeling all these conflicting emotions. The only one she wanted to talk to had been killed by the same individuals trying to invade her mind.

Daith sat on the bed and rubbed her temples.

Her door chime rang.

"Come in."

The door slid open to reveal Trey. He entered, hands laced in front of him.

"I see you're awake."

Daith nodded.

"May I sit?"

"Sure."

Trey took a seat on the edge of the bed, his back rigid, his feet flat.

"Do you think you're able to talk about your dream?"

"I think so." Daith paused, her gaze meandering around the room. "The whole thing must have started before I left my quarters. I felt trapped, panicked, and made my way to the mess hall. Guess that should have been a sign it was a dream—I usually don't go to the mess hall. I'm not really comfortable around the crew.

"I met Cadet Ikar and she told me her piloting console on the bridge didn't work. I went to fix it, using my abilities. While on the bridge, Cadet Poka called me a fraud and I-I lost my temper."

"Go on," Trey encouraged.

"Anyway, I came back to my quarters and Ishia showed up. We talked for a bit and then you came in. Ishia left, then Poka arrived, yelling for me to come out. You opened the door and threw...I don't know, some sort of small device that attached to his face and killed him."

Trey kept silent for a few moments. "Do you remember what you and Cadet Ikar spoke about? Did you reveal anything about our destination or plan?"

"We spoke about what happened on her homeworld and why she'd chosen to join the Aleet Army. Then she said the Controller's main base is on Sintaur."

Trey's eyebrows rose. "*She* said that?"

"I'm sure of it."

Trey stood and paced the small room. His face had paled and looked chalky under the harsh lights. Daith reached out to sense what he felt, but she couldn't read him.

"Does this mean our mission is over?"

Trey stopped. "No. Try as I might, I knew there'd be a chance they might find out we're coming to Sintaur. After Doctor Ludd betrayed us, I assumed they would know everything he did. But he didn't know our exact arrival date. We still have that element of surprise. I believe we will be there sooner than they can mobilize a counter-attack. The fact that they are trying to search your mind for clues tells me they still need more information."

Her skin prickled at the idea of giving away vital information. "This is all my fault."

Trey placed a hand on her shoulder. It lacked the warm energy of his brother's, but the pressure reassured her.

"It isn't your fault. You've been running yourself ragged trying to help us with your gifts. You've over-extended yourself and the stress of everything has caused erratic sleep patterns. You fell asleep without a dose of dream-deflectors by accident. I only wish the Controllers had revealed something to you about their plans." He squeezed her shoulder. "For now, let's concentrate on keeping you strong and healthy." He gave her a smile and left her quarters.

Daith drew her knees into her chest. If only she *had* learned some of their plan. It wasn't fair they could infiltrate her mind and she couldn't theirs.

Or could she?

CHAPTER 23

AFTER DINNER, EVERYONE moved outside. Torrak went to his side of the nah-tsu court and picked up the equipment provided for him. He swung his racket back and forth, listening as the breeze rustled the tightly wound springs screwed in a crisscross shape across a square metal frame.

Torrak saw Kalil lean over toward Preeaht. They'd both chosen to watch from his side of the court.

"What's this game again? Gnat zoo?" Kalil asked, eyeing the two courts with two nets and a slab of flat material hanging above it.

"Nah-tsu," she corrected him.

"Oh." Kalil said. He waited a moment before awkwardly asking what that meant.

She smiled. "Nah-tsu originated on Nuis's home world. Each opponent has a ball and the goal is to hit the ball over the first net with their rackets, bounce it off the net stretched above them," she said, gesturing above the court, "and then get the ball over the second net on their opponent's side. The opponent then hits the ball back in the same manner.

"The point system is a little tricky," Preeaht continued. "If your opponent misses the ball, you gain a point. You lose points if you hit your own net, miss bouncing the ball off the upper net, or fail to get the ball over your opponent's net."

Kalil scrunched his face in confusion. "If you are able to lose and gain points, how do you know when someone has won?"

"Each player starts with twenty-five points. If you reach zero you lose, fifty you win." She entwined her hand with his.

Kalil's cheeks flamed.

Torrak fought off a grin and focused on the game.

A ball appeared from a small hole below each player. The balls hovered for a moment on a jet of air—a golden one in front of Torrak and a silver one in front of Nuis. A projection of their scores set at 25-25, floated above the court.

Torrak grabbed the golden ball at the same moment Nuis grabbed the silver one and the game began. Nuis served right away. Torrak counter-served, deciding to get the feel for the court and his racket before he tried any tricks. The silver ball shot over Torrak's net in a fast, low arc, a tricky shot, but worth it for the difficulty in the return. Torrak swung and missed. The sign changed as Nuis's score increased by one. Torrak didn't have time to think about it before his own ball came back at him on the return. Torrak made contact this time, but the ball went flying in the wrong direction, nearly hitting someone on the sidelines.

Nuis smiled as Torrak's score lowered by one point. Torrak had barely grabbed his ball when the silver one came flying over his net. Torrak swung and missed again, unprepared.

"I thought you would be some good competition, but if you lose,

I will still be satisfied," Nuis said with a wink.

Torrak's stomach dropped. *Don't think about that! Focus!*

Nuis smirked. Torrak's golden ball approached him and, right after hitting it, he served his own ball.

With a quick calculation, Torrak switched the racket to his left hand. He hit the golden ball, spun to gain momentum, and whacked the silver ball with greater force. They ricocheted off the hanging net in opposite directions. Nuis flung himself to the right and narrowly missed the golden ball as the silver one flew past him on his left. Torrak's score increased by two points, making the score 27-26, in favor of Nuis. Cursing, Nuis threw down his racket.

"I thought you would be some good competition," Torrak mocked.

A few snickers rose from the crowd, but quieted at Nuis's glare.

"Now," he said, turning toward Torrak, "we play."

Torrak's muscles ached. The racket's grip slid in his hands and he had a stitch in his side. His body protested, but with the score at 5-3 in favor of Nuis, Torrak knew the end neared.

Torrak returned the silver ball when a strange feeling passed through him. He felt like his mind was pulled through his skull. He stumbled. Words wanted to come, but before they did, he blacked out.

Torrak stood in a surgical room. The room reeked of sterility. A body lay strapped on a table surrounded by silhouetted figures. Torrak spoke to the figures, but they took no notice of him. He felt jagged, out of place. Like a spectator watching from outside a room.

He looked up and saw someone floating above the table. Daith!

She looked different than the other figures—more solid. And she noticed him.

Daith stared, puzzled. She spoke, but the words came slow and thick. He couldn't understand her.

"Tell me where you are!" he yelled. The words bubbled out like air pockets popping in mud. "I'm coming to find you. I can help you. I can find you if you tell me where you are!" The words rang through the air, misshapen. Torrak felt dread rising inside as the look of confusion deepened on her face.

A yank pulled him away from the scene. His panic grew. He struggled to stay, desperate to make her understand, but the more he struggled, the faster the darkness grew around him.

Torrak's eyes flickered open. They blinked several times.

"Torrak, can you hear me? Are you all right?"

"I think so," Torrak replied. His eyesight cleared and he could see Kalil and Nuis hovering over him.

Kalil helped Torrak stand and the three of them moved off the court.

"What happened?" Torrak asked, his steps unsteady.

"I'm not sure. You sort of seized up and then your eyes rolled into the back of your head and down you went."

Nuis stood subdued in the background. "You really worried us."

Torrak turned toward Kalil. "I dreamt—Daith, but—but it wasn't mine—I mean it was hers—and I was watching...."

Kalil patted his back. "Deep breath. Start again."

Torrak inhaled and exhaled loudly. "I dreamt about Daith, but it wasn't my dream. More like she dreamt and I happened to be there, watching. I found her in a room, floating over a body strapped to a table. I called out for her to tell me where I could find her, but the dream ended before she answered. I think... I think she wanted to contact me."

Kalil's forehead creased. "Maybe you've been pushing yourself too hard to find her."

"No," Torrak said roughly. "I know it sounds strange, but it wasn't a simple dream. I saw her. I spoke to her. I'm not crazy." Torrak said this more to convince himself than them. "She's out there and I have to find her, before it's too late."

Everyone moved into the dining room. Nuis told the rest of the spectators to retire and told one of his servers to fetch some tea. The four of them sat at the end of the long table. The server brought in a large steaming bowl and four cups, all meticulously carved out of black stone. He ladled a large dollop of pale green liquid into each cup.

"Drink this," Nuis said. "It will help you relax."

"What is it?" Torrak asked.

Nuis smiled. "I have no wish to harm you or your friend. It's an herbal drink, a bit bitter perhaps at first. My mother taught me how to make it years ago, to help me relax." Nuis proved the contents were safe by taking a sip from his own cup.

The four of them sat and drank, Preeaht's hand resting gently on Kalil's knee. Torrak's stress did seem to melt away. It felt good to sit after such a strenuous game, too.

At that thought, Torrak's anxiety spiked. "What about our game?"

"Although I would have liked to see how it ended, I now realize you are on a quest that is more important than satisfying my ego. I have decided to tell you the information you wish to know, even though it will sadden me to lose your presence here."

Torrak eyed him with curiosity. So far, Nuis seemed like a spoiled rich kid pretending to be a thug. He knew there would be a catch, but until he found out what that was, he decided not to press his luck.

"The buyer who talked to me is Faan Kaano," Nuis told them. "I can give you directions in the morning."

Torrak gulped down the rest of his drink. "I don't want to wait until morning."

Nuis let out a chuckle. "You don't have much choice."

Torrak's head spun. "Thank you for telling me what I need to know so I can go and not be so tired becauseIhavetoleaveand…" Torrak fell backwards out of his chair onto the floor, asleep before he hit the lavish carpet.

CHAPTER 24

DAITH'S VISION BLURRED.

Where am I?

She blinked slowly and the scene cleared.

She floated over a long table with a body strapped to it. Daith tried to see the face on the body, but a large metallic helmet covered it. Figures entered the room, oblivious to Daith's presence. They circled the table, tightening straps and adjusting the helmet. One figure injected the body with a bright yellow liquid and the body bolted upright. Its head slammed into the metallic covering, moving it aside.

The figures rushed around trying to restrain the individual. But Daith had already seen enough. The face on the body belonged to her.

An injection of cloudy liquid caused the Daith below her to stop struggling. The helmet repositioned over her head. It glowed magenta.

The scene mesmerized her. But something caught her attention. A figure, clear and sharp in the darkness. A young, blond, darker-

skinned man. The man spoke, but his words came slow and garbled. She could only make out bits and pieces.

Daith remembered her original intent—to search for a Controller. And here he was, in her dream again, sending her confusing images. She screamed at him, ordering him to tell her his plan. The words sounded trapped, like yelling into a glass.

The scene dimmed. The blond man stared at her, his eyes full or sorrow.

"Tell...me...coming...find...where...you...are..."

An invisible source sucked her upwards and she rocketed out of the room, into complete darkness....

Daith awoke with a start. Flinging her grey blanket aside, she jumped out of bed. Terror manifested itself and streaked across her skin in ripples of goosebumps. Her breath came in short gasps.

What was that?

Daith grasped onto the images of the dream. Had she been in someone else's mind? The Controller's? Or her own? And that huge machine? Was that real? Had that really happened to her?

Too many unknowns. She'd been foolish to try to reach out to the Controller in a dream. What experience did she have with this concept? She never worked on it with Dru. Another thing she wouldn't get to learn from him.

Daith dressed and made her way through the corridors, shooting suspicious glances at other crewmembers. If Poka had only been a dream, what if no one else here was real? What secrets might she reveal through harmless conversations? The Controllers may be in her mind right now!

Daith's chest tightened. She felt like she couldn't breathe. She slowed, putting a hand on the wall for balance. With a quick look, she found herself on the third floor, standing outside Dru's old quarters.

Desperate for some privacy, she entered into the empty room.

Daith sank onto the carpeted floor and rested her back against the wall. She wished more than anything Dru would walk in from the back room and talk to her. He felt so far away—as if years instead of days since his death. The bare surroundings taunted her, teased her into thinking he hadn't been real either.

Daith's heart thumped in her chest. A film of sweat prickled her brow and under her arms. Ragged breaths filled her lungs. What if he had been fake? She had nothing of him to prove he'd been real. Not one thing.

Daith jumped up and strode through the room, searching for something she'd missed before, anything to make his existence a reality. The room, starkly clean, gave the impression it had never been used. But Dru had been messy and disorganized. Surely a food stain or a crumpled piece of clothing lingered somewhere.

She marched into the back of the suite. Bed made. Closet empty. Table clear.

Daith's body shook with panic. He couldn't have been fake. He *couldn't*. She remembered his scent, earthy and safe. His grey eyes like a soft storm. His tousled brown hair, which he constantly flicked from his eyes.

Daith plopped onto the bed. She recalled when they went out to dinner and laughed at stories of his childhood. How the warmth of energy surged between them without her having to try. How he arranged a game for her to find him on the ship, leaving datapad clues all around....

Daith held her breath. The datapads. She still had them in her quarters.

Hurrying, she left the room and raced back to her own, flying past a few crewmembers who gave her a wide berth. Pushing aside her clothes on the floor, she reached under her bed and retrieved the stack of datapads. Firing the first one up, her muscles melted with relief as the words from the first clue appeared on the screen. Now she had proof. He'd programmed these datapads himself.

Laughter fell from her lips. He'd been real.

Daith lovingly read through each datapad, sealing the memories of the game in her mind. When she turned on the fifth and final clue, her breath caught in her throat.

She had forgotten.

Different words once filled the screen. Someone else left her a message.

She struggled to remember what it said.

"Nothing is what it appears to be//you've realized this through your time here. There are many who lie, deceive, and trick// preying on doubt and fear. You're being betrayed, it's all a lie// your life is just an illusion. In your mind is the truth //to break through your confusion."

Daith lowered the datapad to her lap. Who could have sent this to her? And why? Another trick? A Controller spy on board?

Daith pulled the datapads into her chest, squeezing them as if she could squeeze energy from them to comfort her. She had no control over her own destiny. Now she didn't even know the truth from the lies.

But perhaps there was a way. With her abilities, she could sense others' emotions and thoughts. Maybe through practice, the traitors would be revealed.

Daith let the datapads slide to the floor. Adrenaline drained out of her. She yawned, but ignored the inviting bed. Feet tucked under her butt, she closed her eyes. Slowing her breath, she concentrated, letting the warm energy fill her, stretching out with her mind into her surroundings, into the minds of the crew.

* * *

Cenjo ran through his routine again. Breathe in, punch, kick, roundhouse, breathe out. Switch sides. Over and over until his muscles seared in protest. Finally he stopped, wiping his face with a towel that lay on the floor next to him.

So many changes in the past two standard weeks. Daith on the ship, dismissal of multiple crew members, Dr. Ludd's betrayal and departure. Things were getting out of control.

Cenjo ended the program and left the simulation room. He also couldn't believe Daith never asked anyone about her past. He thought his datapad message would have made her ask questions, but she seemed more confused and closed off than ever.

And that will just put her more out of control.

Cenjo couldn't let that happen. He wouldn't watch everything the Aleet Army worked for fall apart.

A quick detour brought him to the above deck. He rang Daith's chimes.

"Who is it?" Daith called out from inside.

"It's Cenjo. I thought maybe we could meet for dinner later?"

"Oh, I'm sorry Cenjo. I'm pretty busy at the moment. Maybe tomorrow." Daith's voice sounded high and tense.

"Are you sure? We all have to eat."

No answer.

"Daith?"

"I'm really busy."

Cenjo ignored the knot in his chest. "Alright. I'll check back tomorrow." He strode away. What else could he do?

CHAPTER 25

TORRAK WOKE THE next morning on a large, soft bed. Flowers petals covered his blanket, giving off a fresh, floral scent. Once he regained his bearings, he went in search for someone to give him an explanation.

Torrak found Kalil and Nuis sitting at a small table in an elaborate room of midnight blue and peach. Upset, he barely noticed the flowing drapes and crystal blue fountain that circled the table, and marched straight up to Nuis.

"Why did you drug me last night?" he demanded.

Nuis calmly put down his embossed napkin. "The thought of you leaving unprepared concerned me. You were obviously exhausted by our game, weakened by your blackout, and yet determined to leave that very instant. I couldn't allow that. So I had my server, Bewetru, add something to your drink to help you sleep."

"But I saw you drink some, too. Why weren't you affected?"

"I was. I fell asleep soon after you did, and I must say I haven't slept that well in weeks."

"Neither have I," Kalil chimed in, hurriedly stuffing his mouth full of food during Torrak's piercing glare.

"I don't appreciate being lied to," Torrak said.

"I didn't lie to you. I told you the drink would help you relax and it did. I wanted you rested and restored before running off on some wild chase."

"Why do you care so much about what we do? Before Torrak's blackout, you weren't willing to help us at all," Kalil pointed out.

"True enough, but I thought about how your situation could benefit me as well." Nuis motioned for Bewetru to clear his plate from the table.

Here's the catch. "What do you want?" Torrak asked.

"I need to get off this planet—today. I want you two to take me."

"Why should we? You already told us what we need to know."

"True. However, Faan is quite dangerous and deceptive—and isn't fond of talking to strangers."

"That's what we heard about you," Kalil sputtered through his full mouth.

"A lot of that is reputation, I admit. Who would take me seriously if I didn't have a little bit of a dark side? My fun is in gambling and games, not pain and torture. But make no mistake, Faan falls into the latter category."

"What do you want from us *exactly*?" Torrak asked.

"I will accompany you to Juha and introduce you to Faan. From there, you can work things out on your own. In return, you will take me, Preeaht, and Bewetru to Jetur, which is the planet next to Juha, and leave us there. Silence about our whereabouts is required, of course."

"Why the sudden need to get off this planet?"

Nuis sipped from a silver goblet. "I suppose I can tell you. When you fell unconscious on the court, one of my servants informed me that a bounty hunter, Kircla, had sent out a request for any information pertaining to my whereabouts, probably over some silly debt I owe. Although I'm surprised she'd come after me."

"Why is that?" Kalil asked.

"Kircla," Nuis explained, "is one of the most ruthless, animalistic assassins in the galaxy. Business must be slow for her to take me as a contract. Still, if she's sent messages ahead, it gives me time to leave."

Torrak thought about Nuis's deal. "I agree to your terms, Nuis."

Nuis smiled. "Excellent! Preeaht is already packing my bags. As soon as we've finished breakfast, we'll head out."

Torrak rubbed his forehead. *I hope this doesn't come back to bite me later.*

Torrak, Kalil, Preeaht, Nuis, and Bewetru, arrived at Torrak's rented ship in late afternoon. The five of them departed for their two-day trek to the planet Juha.

They arrived at the planet's night side, but much to the discontent of the sleep-deprived passengers, Torrak orbited around to the day side.

"I can't function on only a standard hour of sleep," Nuis complained. "How do you expect me to stay awake? I have so many forms to fill out, not to mention—"

Torrak cut him off. "Sorry, but the city of Jenma is in daylight right now. We'll sleep during the day and look for Faan at night. Or would you prefer I take you back to C-Nine?"

Nuis opened his mouth then shook his head. "Until I'm safely on Jetur, I'm part of your group. Sleep during the day it is."

As the sun set underneath stacks of layered colors, four of them set out, leaving Bewetru behind at the hotel. They all obtained separate rooms, but Kalil rigged the electronic keys to open any door in the hotel, in case they needed to make a quick exit.

Since only Nuis knew Faan, he and Torrak would look for her. Preeaht and Kalil went to collect supplies and refuel the ship.

Torrak let Nuis take the lead. He could tell, however, Nuis had only been to Jenma a few times because more than once they hiked to a tavern he half-remembered or a gaming hall he'd once patronized. No one really seemed interested in divulging any information about Faan, although Nuis dropped a few monetary credits here and there.

"We're getting nowhere," Torrak murmured, after the two of them exited a rather seedy bar. "I thought you knew this guy. Got any other ideas?"

"I might, but it will have to wait."

"Why's that?"

"Because ever since we left that tavern, we've been followed."

Torrak casually looked around at the buildings and caught a glimpse of a hooded figure about ten meters behind them. He mentally cursed himself for not noticing. *Why are my instincts still so off?*

"Should we worry?" Nuis asked, his reddish face mottled under the harsh streetlights.

"I don't think we have time. Whoever it is, they're coming up fast."

Torrak grabbed Nuis and they slipped between two of the buildings. He clenched his hands, wishing he had a weapon of some sort, but couldn't find anything useful.

Torrak crouched, alert, until the pursuer came around the corner. He dove as feet came into view.

Their follower went down, but somehow twisted out of Torrak's grip and ended up on top of him, pinning him to the ground. A sharp, cold piece of metal stuck into his chin. Torrak lay still.

"All right, Faan. You've had your fun. Now, let him up," Nuis said through a chuckle.

Torrak saw the flash of a smile from Faan's shrouded face, before rising.

"That was an incredible move," Torrak told Faan. Torrak turned his attention to Nuis. "You knew it was him, didn't you? You could have warned me!"

"I suppose," Nuis said with a grin. "But life is more fun this way. Besides, I didn't know at first she was the one following us."

"*She?*" Torrak gaped.

Faan removed her hood. "You say that like it's a bad thing."

Torrak's heart skipped. Faan's short platinum hair hung to her chin, perfectly straight. Her ice-blue eyes sparkled with specks of silver, which seemed to accent the iridescent tone of her pale skin. How could he have not seen that face underneath her hood?

Nuis came over and put a hand on Faan's shoulder. "I never stand a chance when you're around."

Faan's gaze shifted to Nuis. "I believe your own blue eyes stole away a few of my prospects in the past. Let's not forget about Quilaan, shall we?"

"How could I forget about him?" Nuis sighed dramatically and then laughed out loud. "But we can talk about old times later. We are here to discuss business. Would you like to come back to our hotel to talk? Bewetru's there, too. I'm sure he'd love to see you again."

"Lead the way." Faan hooked her arm inside Nuis'.

"Hold on a second," Torrak cried out.

The pair turned.

"What's wrong?" Nuis asked.

"You two are friends?" Torrak turned toward Faan. "I thought you were a ruthless killer. Some big, creepy guy. You pinned me like a rag doll and, *poof*, now you're this...well... look at you!"

Faan paused for a moment. "Didn't mean to disappoint."

Torrak stuttered in embarrassment.

Nuis winked at Faan. "Quit teasing. Let's get out of here. It's starting to get cold."

* * *

Once he reached the hotel, Torrak felt like he might burst. Nuis had insisted they split up to look less 'conspicuous' before whisking Faan away on his arm.

Torrak waited awkwardly at the foot of Bewetru's bed in his room, where they agreed to meet, until Nuis and Faan sauntered in several standard minutes later.

Ignoring Nuis, Torrak directed his words toward Faan. "Nuis told me you're interested in buying scrap metal of Aleet Army ships."

"Yes," Faan said, noticing Bewetru on the bed. "Hello, Bewetru. Long time."

Bewetru lifted his head from his reading material. "Miss Kaano. A pleasure as always."

Torrak's fingers tapped impatiently against his thighs. "So you are aware of recent Aleet Army activity?"

Faan returned her attention to Torrak. "Why would buying scrap metal make you think I would know anything about that? It's a collector's hobby."

Torrak felt his hope sink into a black hole. She was right. Why did he assume that? He shouldn't trust his instincts with how shaky they've been lately. "Now I'm never going to find her."

"Find who?"

Torrak hesitated. He barely trusted himself. He didn't want to reveal more than he had to. "Someone kidnapped my friend. I believe remnants of the Aleet Army may have been involved." Anger swelled inside him. "Now this is just another dead end."

Faan put her hand on Torrak's arm, which tingled at her touch. "It's not *quite* a dead end."

A flicker of hopeful warmth lit inside his chest. "You know something?"

"Perhaps. But there's something you have to do for me first."

"I don't have a lot of money, if that's what you want."

"No, nothing like that. I need you to join me at an auction tomorrow evening. My identity in this city is that of a married woman, and it would be...better for me to show up with my husband at my side."

"An auction?" he said. He glared at Nuis. "What is this, some sort of joke with you two? Nah-tsu games and a shopping spree? My friend is in danger."

"I'm sorry for your friend, but this is business. At the auction , we will connect with someone who knows about the Aleet Army," Faan said.

Nuis placed a hand lightly on Torrak's arm. "Give this a chance."

Torrak's anger abated slowly. He hated depending on others, but he really didn't know what else he could do. Any delays searching for other leads would waste more time.

"Fine. I'll go to the auction with you."

Nuis clapped his hands, letting out a nervous laugh. "We have all been too tense. I bet Preeaht and Kalil are enjoying themselves and not letting serious matters ruin their time together. Speaking of, where are they?"

Bewetru lifted up his head from his reading material. "My apologies. I forgot to tell you they called about a standard hour ago.

They said they finished collecting the supplies needed and were going to see a Voltag show. If interested, they said to meet them at a restaurant called the *Rewin*."

"I could never pass up a good show," Nuis said. "Would you care to join us, my lady?" he said, half-bowing to Faan.

"Normally I wouldn't be able to resist your charms, but I have other business to attend to this evening." Torrak saw Faan deftly twirl a small blade and slip it under her black cloak. She turned and looked at him. "I will see you tomorrow."

Faan left quickly. Torrak ran to the door to ask what time, but she'd already moved out of sight.

Nuis's eyes twinkled. "Faan's a fast one. You'll get used to it."

Torrak edged toward his room.

"Oh, no. We are going out."

"I don't want to," Torrak said.

"Yes, I understand that. You made it quite clear with your tantrum back there."

"My *what*?"

"Oh relax. There's nothing you can do tonight except worry. Might as well distract yourself. You coming Bewetru?"

"I prefer the realm of imagination."

"Always the dreamer."

They left the hotel and headed toward the *Rewin*. Fire pits glowed around them, lighting the busy walkways, reminding Torrak of the artificial fires lit in the libraries of Fior Accelerated Academy. He and Daith spent many an hour sifting through their class notes, studying for exams. A pang of homesickness hit his stomach. "How long have you known Faan?" Torrak asked, forcing himself away from the past.

"I met her about two standard years ago through a business endeavor. We had similar interests at the time."

"Why is she interested in the Aleet Army?"

"Nine years ago, her parents were killed in a vehicle collision while driving to their hotel. Faan believes the Aleet Army arranged the 'accident.'"

"Why?"

"Her parents were two leaders of the Liberators. They'd gone to the city of Cand to meet with the government about the unfair treatment of workers in factories. At the time, the Aleet Army exterminated anyone connected to the Liberators. Although the Army denied involvement, Faan is convinced her parents were targeted because of their political affiliations."

"Do you really think she can help me?"

"It's not like her to strike a deal if she can't. She's been tracking the Aleet Army for a long time."

"If you knew she had information, why did you tell me she only buys scrap metal?"

Nuis pushed open the thick fabric door to the *Rewin*. "Faan's business is her own and her choice if she wants to divulge it. During our walk back to the hotel, I asked if she minded if you knew about her parents—she didn't. She's just as interested in gaining information about the Aleet Army as you are. I think you two will be good for each other."

Torrak spent the rest of the walk thinking about how "good" they could be together.

The two of them entered the *Rewin* and found Kalil and Preeaht sitting close together at a table in the corner, facing a large stage. Kalil waved them over while the server cleared their dinner plates. Torrak quickly filled Kalil in on what happened before the lights dimmed and the stage lit up.

On the platform stood a very tall, bony woman with deep brown skin. Barely covered in cream veils, her hair floated all around her, as if suspended underwater. Three mouths located along her jaw line stretched from her ear to her chin. The other side of her face had three slits, like gills. Each mouth sang a different line of music, creating an intertwining three-line harmony.

Though he didn't understand the language, the singer evoked the feeling of a lost love and heartache.

When the Voltag finished her performance, the four companions made their way back to the hotel in silence. After climbing into bed, Torrak fell asleep with the haunting music still floating through his mind.

CHAPTER 26

"TWO DAYS," CENJO said while he strode back and forth across Trey's office. "She hasn't come out of her quarters in two days."

Trey watched the man's movements with growing impatience. "I'm well aware of that, Lieutenant Commander."

"Well you need to do something about it. It's not healthy. It's not safe."

Trey's jaw twitched. "I'm open to any suggestions."

Cenjo stopped. "Apologies, Commander. It's...frustrating. She shouldn't be on her own at a time like this."

"She is grieving. I've spoken with Doctor Milastow. She assures me that it's perfectly reasonable for Daith to take some time for herself. The death of my brother has been hard on all of us." Trey swallowed the bitter taste in his mouth.

"We will be in the Fracc system in a little less than one standard week," Cenjo said. "I know you want Daith to help us in our mission against the Controllers on Sintaur, but I'm not sure she'll be of any use to us by then."

"No need to worry about Daith. I've been monitoring her closely. I believe this time is therapeutic for her and she will emerge all the stronger."

Cenjo's shoulders drooped. "Commander, do you really think we need her? Most of the crew is terrified of her. And none of them really remember what Jacin Jaxx was like, except you and I. She seems more out of control than him. Do you think she'll be any more stable by the time we arrive?"

"I can assure you she will be ready for what she needs to do once we arrive. The destabilization of the Controller base will not take long. We will finally show the galaxy their true nature." Trey nodded a dismissal and Cenjo exited the office.

Moments later Trey's communications console beeped.

"Yes?"

"Commander Xiven, you have an incoming transmission from Kircla."

"Send it through."

"Commander Xiven." The vidlink monitor filled with her aquamarine face. "You have provided me with a worthy target."

Trey's tension trickled away. "I'm glad to hear it. Are you ready for your final payment?"

The Orcla female hissed through her pointed teeth. "No. I believe the target lives."

Trey's jaw tightened. "What? How?"

"I disposed of the other twenty-eight possible candidates. When I searched for the twenty-ninth, I could not locate him in the target city. Upon further search, I discovered he recently purchased a ship, using a retinal scan. I retrieved his records—his name is Torrak Spirtz and he left Fior with a secondary passenger."

Trey couldn't breathe. "He's off planet?" he wheezed. This couldn't be happening. If word somehow got out that Daith had been kidnapped, it could jeopardize everything. "We'll never find him now. He could be anywhere!"

Kircla flipped one of her blue twisted chunks of hair over her shoulder. "Do not panic, Commander Xiven. It is unbecoming."

Trey recoiled at her scold. Fury broke through the surface. His teeth ground.

"If you think—"

"I know where he is," she interrupted.

Trey snapped his mouth closed, his anger ebbing. "You do?"

"Yes. I tracked his flight path. The craft docked on C-Sector Nine. I contacted an associate of mine to locate him since it would be a few standard days until I could arrive. Torrak Spirtz contacted a low-level gambler, Nuis Weir and they left together. My associate placed a tracking device on their ship before they departed. They left one day ago and docked in the city of Jenma on the planet Juha. I am en route to intercept."

"Very well. Call me *only* when the job has been completed. And Kircla, dispose of anyone else Torrak has contacted. I don't want this to reflect poorly on your hiring status." Trey ended the call. He slammed his fist onto the desk, wincing at the pain.

So close. He'd calculated everything down to the last detail. But he couldn't have known a witness would have been left behind. Or that his brother needed to be killed sooner rather than later, Cenjo would ask questions, and Dr. Ludd would develop a conscience and leave the ship.

The level of lies he weaved was getting harder to maintain, but he had no choice. He knew Daith had tried to invade his mind during her time in her quarters. She'd probably done the same with the rest of the crew.

Luckily for Trey, no one else knew the whole plan except him. The crew believed their only mission was to sabotage the Controller base to destabilize the organization. No one knew about the space fleet reinforcements he'd hired, headed by Exarth, to meet him at Sintaur. Or about the rogue witness to Daith's abduction and the hundreds of others he had in play on dozens of planets. And especially Daith's true role in everything.

If Trey could keep his mind sealed from her until they reached Sintaur, no one in the galaxy besides himself would know his true plan.

* * *

Daith's mind whirled with thoughts—thoughts that weren't her own. She decided to mentally probe the crewmembers to see if they were lying. She knew so many things now about them: rivalries, jealousies, affections, fears. But each member seemed completely loyal to the cause. To Trey.

Other images passed through Daith's mind while she concentrated, while she focused on the minds around her. Images from those who were no longer on board—echoes of memories.

Bits and pieces from Dr. Ludd before he left.

And a moment of Dru.

She hadn't been prepared and broke into sobs, her tears mingling with the blood from her runny nose.

She remembered Dru had once described telepathic connections as "energy fingerprints", an impression left behind by all living things. Somehow she tapped into those residual traces.

A quick flash—like an electric spark during a storm. He'd been looking at her during one of their sessions, when Daith first learned about her abilities. They'd been in one of the simulation rooms and the program had them sitting in chairs on a small patch of sand, surrounded by ocean. Dru looked at her with her eyes closed, the breeze ruffling her hair, her brow furrowed in concentration, and he thought he could truly be happy with her. He could open up and let her in.

The feeling had been so warm and inviting it pierced through her veil of focus and tore at her heart. To have been so close, to never know, to almost have something unique and beautiful in such a tumultuous galaxy.

And it had been ripped away before she could ever know what might have been.

Daith composed herself and returned to searching through others' thoughts, but her mind wouldn't focus and fatigue beat down on her. She didn't know if she had the strength to fight the upcoming battle against the Controllers, those who'd murdered her family and killed Dru.

She wondered what her life would be like if she could spend time with her family. If she could find solace in Dru's voice again.

Then the image came she feared so much—Dru's death. Usually it came to her during her sleep, but this time she saw the image while awake, projected before her eyes like a broadcast, and she couldn't look away. The burst of light, the sizzling flesh, the blackened hole in his abdomen.

Daith vomited. She looked around her. The lights above her blurred in and out of focus. Her blood splattered the floor, most of it dried. Sweat-soaked clothing clung to her body. Her heart raced. Her body shook.

Daith gasped for breath, spasming into a fetal position on the floor. She knew she was dying. This is what it felt like to die.

CHAPTER 27

THE NEXT EVENING, Torrak paced while he waited for Faan. Someone knocked on his door. Disappointment flooded him at the sight of the hotel employee on the other side.

"Yes?" Torrak asked.

"A package has arrived for you. The woman who dropped it off asks that you meet her downstairs in the lobby in one standard hour."

"Thank you." Torrak unwrapped the package. He gawked at the outfit, easily worth more than his tuition to the Academy. He slid into a midnight blue jacket accented by a pair of sparkling silver cuff links, a silky ivory-colored shirt that fit snugly over his toned body, and charcoal gray pants which hung from his waist like flowing drapes. A carved bone cane, flecked with swirls of a midnight blue stone, completed the ensemble. The note attached to the cane read "Lean on Left."

"You clean up nicely."

Torrak spun around to find Nuis in the doorway. "Maybe it wasn't such a good idea for us to have access to every room in the hotel."

"I'll knock next time," Nuis said with a smile.

"I feel ridiculous."

"Well you look great. Let's say I'm sorry you're not in my market."

Torrak grinned. "I've got to get going. You headed out tonight?"

"No. I have some paperwork to take care of. Who knew there were so many forms to fill out when changing addresses—and names for that matter!"

"What about the bounty hunter, what's her name...Kircla? Aren't you worried she'll find you here?"

"Not really. No one knew I planned to leave. Besides, we're only going to be here for another night. After that, I'm a new man. At least on paper."

"I'll see you later then."

"By the way," Nuis added, "Bewetru wondered if the two of you could switch rooms. He had a terrible allergic reaction to the carpet. Since your room has marbled floors...?"

"No problem," Torrak called over his shoulder. He walked downstairs to the lobby and felt a tap on his shoulder. He looked up and hoped his eyes hadn't actually fallen out of his head. Faan, no longer dressed in black pants and a hooded cloak, wore a satiny pale blue dress, which matched her eyes. The dress, formfitting and ankle-length, hugged her body, leaving little to the imagination. The square-cut bodice showed off her curves and iridescent skin. An off-white fur lay across her shoulders. The final piece, an off-white ribbon studded with a pale blue stone lay across her throat.

"I'll take that as a compliment," Faan said.

Torrak felt heat rise in his cheeks. He composed himself and held out his arm. "Shall we go, my dear," Torrak said, cringing as his voice cracked.

"Of course." Faan took his arm and the two of them left. Once inside their transportation, Torrak asked about their fake personas.

"We are Lord and Lady Merr. We own a large house in the northern outskirts of the city of B'kri on Jetur. You are a local businessman who owns several banks. I head the Museum of Antiquities in downtown B'kiri. I warranted an invitation to this auction to see if the Museum wanted to acquire any new pieces."

"And this couple we're pretending to be? What if they show up?"

"They are...unable to attend."

Torrak arched an eyebrow.

"Don't worry," she reassured him. "I didn't do anything permanent."

Her remark reminded him of her ruthless reputation. While they quietly sped through the streets, he hoped he wasn't in over his head.

When they arrived at the auction house, Torrak caught a glimpse of himself in the vehicle's window and was impressed at the change in his appearance. During the ride, Faan had darkened and added streaks of grey to his hair. A full beard accompanied bushy eyebrows. Faan also applied makeup to fill in some of Torrak's natural creases, giving the effect of deepened wrinkles. Torrak easily looked ten years older.

"You know, you don't look half bad for an old guy," Faan teased.

When they entered, Torrak's eyes widened. Paintings and sculptures lined the back wall, while glass cases containing jewelry, stones, and fragile artifacts ran along the front. The side walls were covered with rugs, urns, vases, and other large items. The two of them circled the room, eyeing the beautiful artwork and stunning crafts-manship.

"What are you bidding on?" Torrak asked.

"This piece coming up." The two of them approached a painting that hung in the back. Blue and purple swirls jumped from the canvas in a three-dimensional projection. "It's a very old style called Mimicked Three-Dee Art. The artist goes through the motions of painting in the air, and a computer program records the movements and transfers them into a simulated program," Faan explained. "It's exactly the kind of piece that Lady Merr would be interested in for her museum."

They found the chairs reserved for Lord and Lady Merr about four rows from the front. Torrak nervously tugged at his fake beard.

"You look fine," Faan reassured him. "Now leave it alone before it falls off."

A standard hour later, their lot came up on the block.

The auctioneer, a short, pudgy man with a long mustache and small, beady eyes, grasped the painting delicately with his sixteen fingers. The bids rose quickly. Torrak watched as Faan repeatedly pressed the button in front of them to indicate her interest.

At a seemingly random number, Faan stopped. She nodded to the two remaining bidders. Torrak began to rise to leave, but Faan placed her hand on his arm to hold him back.

"Wait," she told him.

Torrak turned his attention to the other two bidders.

The first bidder was a male Aq, an aggressive species from the Kowsa sector. His red skin gleamed with a special oil mixture. The Aqs lived on a moist planet, and since Juha lacked the level of humidity needed, their skin dehydrated very quickly. A container of oil hung from his neck, nestled against his bare, red chest.

The other bidder was a member of a species Torrak had never seen before. The being towered over those around it. It had very dark, almost black skin, which continually flaked off its body, and huge pale brown eyes. It had no body hair and periodically snapped its mouth open and closed. It reminded Torrak of a reanimated, charred corpse.

The darkened being outbid the Aq, who noisily left the room in disgust. When the auctioneer announced the end of the bidding, Faan turned toward the purchaser and bowed her head.

Torrak and Faan left the auction house and entered their vehicle, but didn't drive away. Several standard minutes passed before the door opened and the darker being who won the bid climbed in.

"Good evening, Ha're," Faan said. "I'm glad you could come."

Ha're clicked a response and nodded toward Torrak.

"He's clear." Faan leaned in. "Now, what can you tell me?"

Their conversation went quickly—undecipherable to Torrak. Faan finally thanked Ha're, handed him a monetary amount, and the being left the vehicle.

On the short ride back, Faan filled Torrak in.

"I hired Ha're to find out everything he could about the Aleet Army, but all our previous transactions involved a third party. To know my identity, we decided I'd bid on the painting until a predetermined amount. After he won, I'd pay him one third of the final cost."

"You mean you didn't have any information for me before all this?" Torrak asked.

"I never promised I knew anything. I said *perhaps*."

Torrak tried to control his temper. "You used me."

"No. I told you I might be able to help you, but you had to help me first. And it's a good thing you did."

Relief crashed over him. "What did you find out?"

"Apparently, a few remnant soldiers from the Aleet Army have regrouped. They are now led by a man named Trey Xiven who wants the same status of power and control Jaxx had." Faan paused. "But without Jaxx's abilities, I don't think they'll be much of a threat."

"He may not have Jaxx's abilities, but...."

"But what?"

Torrak bit his tongue. He didn't know how much he should say. "Let's just say you might not want to underestimate this Xiven guy."

"Are you saying he has powers like Jaxx?"

"Not exactly."

Patches of moonlight filtered through the windows, lighting up her face. "Then what, *exactly*?"

"Just... don't mess with him, okay?"

"I can take care of myself."

Torrak expelled a breath, frustrated. "I'm not saying you can't. It's just—"

"Don't worry about me. I'll be fine. I know who I need to go after to get answers." She crossed her arms.

Torrak rubbed his forehead. He didn't want her to get hurt, but he didn't want to expose her to danger if she knew the truth. Except the truth was probably the only way she wouldn't go after Xiven. "You don't know what you're getting into. You should leave this whole Aleet Army thing alone."

Faan craned her neck to glare at him. "Excuse me?"

"I didn't mean that either. This isn't coming out right!"

"Then tell me what you mean."

Torrak stared into her ice blue eyes. "Fine, you want to know? The girl I'm searching for is Jacin Jaxx's daughter. The Aleet Army kidnapped her which means they have her on board."

Faan blinked her eyes in disbelief. "What?"

"And she may have his abilities."

"What do you mean *may* have his abilities?"

"We attended the same school, for gifted students, but she never told me she had any abilities. She might not even know if she has them. Or she may have been keeping them a secret."

"This is bad."

"I don't think she would ever help the Aleet Army. She knows how much damage her father did. I just wanted you to know how ruthless Xiven is, so you know what you might be up against."

"Are you sure she wouldn't help him? Because the woman Ha're works for, his source for information, is meeting Xiven in five standard days for a demonstration of his power."

"What kind of demonstration?"

"I don't know. Ha're simply said it would 'rival the Aleet Army's previous leader'."

"Where is this supposed to take place?"

"A planet called Sintaur, in the Fracc system."

"The Fracc system in five days? We have to leave now. We have to stop them," Torrak exclaimed. The sense of urgency that had ebbed away throughout the evening returned full force.

Faan smiled at him as if he were a foolish child. "And how do you plan to do that?"

"I don't know," he said, flapping his hands through the air. "I've made it this far, farther than you can imagine, with nothing but a few monetary credits and a busted-up ship. I will figure out a way."

Faan pursed her lips, silent for several moments. "The odds still aren't very good. There are six of us, three of whom are leaving tomorrow, one ship with limited weaponry, and no plan."

"Six of us?" Torrak raised his eyebrows.

"You're not the only one who has business with the Aleet Army. A deal perhaps—let's say a free ride in exchange for my help. Unless you don't want me to come?"

"Of course I want you," Torrak told her.

Faan smiled.

"I mean, I want you to come with me—us. With us."

"Well, then it's settled."

The vehicle arrived at the hotel and Torrak got out.

"We'll leave right away in the morning."

Faan nodded. "I'll be here."

Torrak turned toward the hotel when he thought of something he wanted to ask Faan. To his surprise, the vehicle was empty.

"The woman in the back," Torrak asked the driver, "where did she go?"

"Sorry?"

"Lady Merr. Did she get out of the vehicle?"

The driver looked around and then back at Torrak. "I don't see anyone, so I assume so, sir. Is there anywhere else you'd like to go tonight?"

"No. Thank you, anyway." Torrak walked into the hotel, puzzled. He trudged upstairs, exhausted from the late evening and lost in thought over his conversation with Faan. He knew he probably shouldn't have told her everything, but it felt good to tell someone. And Faan wanting to join with him stroked his ego.

Once back in his room, Torrak didn't even bother to turn on the lights. His head tried to keep him awake by filtering through ideas about what to do next, but his body wouldn't comply. Even though he still had on all his makeup and fake facial hair, the thought of a shower seemed like too much work, so he stripped off his shoes and shirt and crawled into bed.

CHAPTER 28

DAITH STUMBLED THROUGH the corridor, up one level, and entered through the medical wing's door. Doctor Milastow looked up from her desk, her eyes wide with shock.

"Miss Tocc!" She rushed over and helped Daith to take a seat. With deft movements, the doctor began to take Daith's vitals. "What under the stars have you done to yourself?"

"I've been trying to help," Daith croaked, the corners of her mouth dry. The ceiling flipped with the floor and Daith closed her eyes until the room righted itself.

Doctor Milastow brought her some water. Metallic tinges danced across her taste buds as Daith washed down remnants of the blood she'd vomited up minutes earlier.

"Well whatever you've been doing you need to stop." A chilled sterile cloth passed over Daith's face, coming away smeared red. "You are as pale as an elosi cub at birth. What happened?"

"So many thoughts. So many images."

"You need bedrest. And monitoring. I'll not have you drop dead when I've only been the doctor on this ship for a standard week."

The doctor's smooth hands felt so good against Daith's skin she didn't argue.

Doctor Milastow pulled up a chair and sat across from Daith. "Now tell me what you've been doing. I may not have all the answers, but you are under my care on this ship, and I take that responsibility very seriously."

Tears sprung into Daith's eyes. She liked Dr. Milastow well enough, but she missed Dr. Ludd dreadfully. And he'd betrayed them. She should have read his thoughts and his emotions more—seen the betrayal before it had happened.

With great effort, Daith felt the warmth rise up inside her and she focused on Dr. Milastow's thoughts. Was she hiding something? What information did she want from Daith to sell to the enemy?

"Daith?"

Daith's body shook. The warmth inside her dropped away and left nothing but emptiness.

"Daith!"

Daith's eyes rolled toward the ceiling. She felt herself falling. Falling....

* * *

When Torrak awoke the next morning, his face itched fiercely. He scratched his chin and his fingers entwined with his fake beard. Throwing back the covers, Torrak entered the washroom. While he waited for the water to heat up, he looked in the reflector unit. Dried blood caked his face and chest. Torrak rubbed his hands against the flaking substance, checking for a wound. Once he realized he wasn't hurt, he raced back into his sleeping quarters.

This time, he threw up.

Bewetru's body hung upside down over the bed, sliced vertically up his abdomen. Blood clung to the wall in coarse ropes, settling into large pools on the mattress. Torrak wiped his mouth as he stared at Bewetru's swollen, purple face—his eyes were rolled back, his mouth open. He tried not to think about the fact that his face and chest were covered with the sticky liquid now clotted on the tangled sheets.

Torrak raced next door to check on Kalil and Preeaht. After getting no answer to his vigorous knock, he used his key and burst inside, but Kalil and Preeaht weren't there. Nothing seemed out of order, so he continued to Nuis's room. He rushed inside without knocking.

Nuis dropped the glass he held and put his hands above his head. His eyes widened in fear as he choked on his drink. "Please don't kill me," he wheezed to Torrak. "I don't know anything!"

"What? Oh. It's me," Torrak told him. He ripped the fake beard off his face.

"Torrak?" Nuis lowered his hands. "What happened? You're covered in blood!"

"Bewetru's been murdered," Torrak rubbed at the pain on his chin from pulling off the beard. "This is his blood, not mine."

Nuis' legs gave way and he sat quickly on the bed. He stepped on the glass, not even flinching when it broke under his foot. "Why?" he asked, looking up at Torrak. "Why did you kill him?"

CHAPTER 29

"What? No, I didn't kill him." Torrak explained how he'd woken up next to the body.

Nuis's gaze flittered toward the door.

"Trust me. You don't want to look," Torrak said.

"Why would someone do that?" Nuis winced as he pulled his bare foot onto his lap, the jagged piece of glass sticking out.

"I don't know, but maybe he wasn't the target. The room was still registered under my name. I'd forgotten we switched." Torrak shuddered at the thought of being the one hung up on the wall.

"You? Why would someone want to kill you?"

"It has to be about Daith." Torrak stopped for a moment to think. His brain swirled with all the potential possibilities. "It couldn't have been Faan—she was with me all night. Maybe it was Preeaht and she took Kalil somewhere after? But why wouldn't the place look out of sorts?" He walked into Nuis's washroom and began to wash his face and chest. "Maybe someone who works for the Aleet Army, or they hired an assassin to kill me." Torrak thought of the open arrangement he had to rent the ship. He'd used his own name and a retina scan— he hadn't bothered trying to cover his tracks. "They must have followed me here." A cold feeling of unease settled into his stomach at the thought of someone knowing his every move.

Nuis called out from the other room. "You never said we might get killed."

Torrak dried his face and chest, annoyed at Nuis attempt to shift blame. "I never told you to come with me either." He brought a clean towel into the other room and threw it at Nuis. "You should take care of that foot. I'll go downstairs and see if Kalil and Preeaht are having breakfast since they aren't in their room and nothing seemed out of place."

"Wait," Nuis said, pulling out the piece of glass and wrapping his foot with the towel. "I'm sorry, it's just... I don't understand what's going on. My closest friend was just killed. All we wanted was a ride."

Torrak paused at the door, anger and guilt mingling inside his chest. "This whole thing has gotten completely out of control. As soon as we get out of here, I'll drop you and Preeaht off and you'll never have to think about us again."

"If you want us to get out of here quickly, we need cover stories. They'll hold us for days if they think we are suspects."

A knot formed in Torrak's stomach at the thought of lying to the authorities. "We didn't do anything wrong."

"No, but they won't care. We need to use this situation to our advantage. I've dealt with Central Authority before. They're pushovers if you know the right thing to say."

"Oh, really?" Torrak huffed.

"Calm down and listen. You can't go walking around the hotel half naked and still splattered with dried...blood. Go shower and change and I'll go downstairs and look for them. We'll meet in my room after. I'll tell the hotel manager about Bewetru so they can contact the authorities. I'll say you and I were on our way to breakfast and saw the door open. When we looked inside, we saw the body and I ran downstairs to tell someone while you went in to check on him." Nuis's words rushed through his trembling lips.

Torrak gaped. "Are you joking? They will never believe that."

"They will. I've gotten out of messier situations." Nuis stood. "Go. I'll meet you later. Make sure you don't tell the hotel manager you and Bewetru switched rooms. In fact, it might be best if we keep up the pretense you died, in case the killer hasn't left the city yet. By the time they run their tests and find out Bewetru isn't you, we should be long gone."

Torrak went into the room he should have been in the previous night. Bewetru had thoughtfully moved all his things, folded them, and put them away. He picked out a clean set of clothes and plopped them on the sink's counter. He hopped into the shower to clean up, knowing he should be quick, but once under the hot water, he didn't want to leave. He couldn't get the picture of Bewetru's mutilated body out of his head. *That could have been me. That should have been me. I shouldn't have dragged any of them into this in the first place. And now one of them is dead. Because of me.* He tried to let the water wash away the gruesome image and the guilt-infused emotions that went with it, but neither would fade. No amount of hot water in the galaxy could wash away what had happened.

Vidlink snapshots. Reporters. City authorities. Hotel staff held for questioning.

Torrak and his group wanted nothing more than to get off the planet, but no one else seemed to care. The hotel manager, hotel security, and several city authorities interrogated them repeatedly.

After several standard hours, the city authorities were convinced none of them knew Torrak Spirtz and the body had been seen through the open door, upon which they notified the hotel manager.

When the five of them finally boarded their ship, Torrak realized Faan never showed up at the hotel.

Once back on their ship, Torrak rushed through the lift-off safety sequences. He didn't want to stay on the planet any longer than necessary. He knew at any moment the authorities could realize Bewetru wasn't him. While he worked, he filled everyone in on what Faan had told him about the Aleet Army. Nuis's face became stony and Preeaht growled.

"Faan said she wanted to come with us," Torrak continued, "but I guess she decided to go her own way instead." Disappointment dripped from his words. Torrak motioned to Nuis and Preeaht. "We should get the two of you to Jetur."

"Um, Torrak?" Kalil asked.

"What?" Torrak stopped checking the fuel levels when he realized no one answered. He turned and faced Kalil, whose hand tightened inside Preeaht's grip.

Preeaht stepped forward. "You and Kalil fight for a noble cause, but you are entering into dangerous territory. With the skills I have acquired while being Nuis's bodyguard, I believe I could be of some help."

Torrak hesitated. "I appreciate your offer, but I don't think it would be a good idea for you to get involved. I can't describe the kind of power Daith might have, and if someone else is controlling her, the result could be disastrous. I can't guarantee your safety or—"

"Wait... what power?" Nuis asked.

Torrak cursed and continued his final checks. "I forgot I haven't told you. It doesn't matter. It has to do with us and the Aleet Army.

You two will be gone shortly, and the less you know, the better."

"It makes no difference to me what sort of power this girl has," Preeaht said. "I have found someone who means a great deal to me. I could never forgive myself if something happened to him and I could have prevented it." Preeaht turned toward Kalil and purred.

"You don't know all the facts."

"The facts don't matter. I would like to help, unless you don't want me to accompany you."

"Torrak, please," Kalil asked.

Torrak smiled at his friend. "Fill her in on what's happening. If she still wants to stay, she can stay." Torrak turned toward Nuis. "I guess it's just you."

"Well, wait. Maybe I want to stay, too."

"What for?"

"I have my reasons."

Torrak let out an impatient sigh. "Okay, look, both of you. This is very nice, but really, you don't know what's involved here."

"It sounds to me like the Aleet Army could be a player again and getting your friend out of there will help stop them. You'll need financial support and I want in. We both win."

Torrak raised an eyebrow. "I can't guarantee your safety."

Nuis clucked his tongue against the roof of his mouth. "I get it. So do you want my help or not?"

Torrak thought about it. Financially, he needed the help, but he didn't know why he should trust Nuis. Except that some part of him felt like Nuis belonged with this group. "As long as you're sure, the more help we can get, the better," he said. He finished the lift-off sequence.

"It's a four and a half day trip to the Fracc system and we'll have to stop about halfway there to refuel and make repairs. So," Torrak said, loading a star systems map, "we'll head toward the Horju system.

It's a day out of our way, but it's the only place we can stop that will still get us to Sintaur on time."

"The Horju system?" Nuis asked. "I know someone who lives on Dansu that can help us out. Dansu is the second planet from the outer rim of the system."

"Great. I'll set a course."

Torrak pulled out of Jenma's docking port. Once out of the atmosphere and surrounded by the immense vacuum of space, he set a course for the Horju system. Everyone went to their rooms to unpack while he sat back and closed his eyes, letting the vibrations of the ship rumble through his body. The adrenaline rush from the past few standard hours started to recede. And yet the stillness of space taunted him. A temporary reprieve until the next battle, the next action.

The next death because of him.

Torrak forced the thought from his head. He pictured his mind as blank as space, letting thoughts drift randomly, never lingering too long on any one concept. But try as he might, they continually wandered toward Faan and hovered there. What made her so fascinating? He supposed the fact that even with all his analytical abilities and his gifts for solving any problem or puzzle, he couldn't figure her out.

A whisper filled his ear.

"Peaceful, isn't it?"

Torrak's eyes shot open and he spun around in his chair. He couldn't believe it, even though Faan stood right in front of him.

"How...?" he sputtered.

Faan laughed and sat in the copilot seat next to Torrak. "I suppose I should have told you this from the beginning, but I didn't know if I could trust you."

"Tell me what? You have some sort of instantaneous disappearing power?"

"Sort of. I'm a Re'Ris."

"I've never heard of them."

"Re'Ris are a genetically altered species who contain an unusual mutation in their cells. We have the ability to read wavelengths of light and color through our skin and mimic them. In a sense, I can change my skin color to any shade I want." As a demonstration, Faan placed her hand upon the grey console and it immediately became the same color, blending in almost perfectly. It looked as though her hand ended at her wrist.

"So that's why you disappeared so quickly."

"Yes. It's not something I broadcast publicly. Only a few individuals know about it, including Nuis."

"I see." Torrak thought a moment. "Is that why Nuis wanted to stay on board? Because he knew you were here?"

"No. He doesn't know I'm here. I was surprised he wanted to join your group, though."

"You were listening?"

"I wanted to know the status of the situation before I revealed myself."

Torrak paused. "Did you hear about Bewetru?"

Faan's face paled. "I shimmered out of view when I got to the hotel and saw the authorities. I overheard a conversation about what happened." She paused for a moment. "Bewetru didn't deserve to die like that."

Guilt stung Torrak. "You think Nuis is coming along to get revenge for Bewetru's death?"

"I wouldn't blame him if he did."

"He certainly isn't what I thought he'd be. At least, not according to his reputation."

"Most individuals aren't."

"What about you? Your reputation is pretty scary."

"My reputation is true. Assassin training is in my blood. I have killed many times. I am a liar, a thief, a smuggler, a cheat, and a murderer." The look in Faan's eyes hardened. "Remember, I'm not coming with you to save some girl. I'm hitching a ride so I can conclude my own issues."

Torrak tilted her chin so he could look into her eyes. "I don't really care *why* you want to come."

Faan started to say something, but instead turned her head as Kalil entered the cockpit.

"Um—sorry to interrupt."

Faan stood quickly. "We weren't doing anything."

Kalil pointed a finger at Faan. "How did you...?"

"It's a long story."

"What's all the fuss about up here?" Nuis walked into the cockpit. The half-smile on his face dropped at the sight of Faan.

"Nuis," Faan said, her eyes sorrowful. "I'm sorry about Bewetru."

Nuis's face twitched and the half-smile returned, although his eyes were emotionless. "Faan! Glad you made it. I'm feeling pretty tired, though, so I think I'll just go lie down. See you later!" Nuis rushed out of the control room.

Faan started to go after him, but Torrak held her back. "Give him some space," Torrak told her. "I don't think he's ready to deal with what happened."

"I know the feeling." Faan turned away and stared out of the viewport into space.

CHAPTER 30

"WHAT HAPPENED, DOCTOR?"

"It's hard to explain, Commander."

Daith heard the words floating above her. They swirled in colors of red and brown.

"Try. I thought she had the ability to heal herself? Why has she been here for an entire day?"

Daith's eyelids opened. Blurry blobs stood on either side of her. She blinked and the beings came into focus.

"Trey?" Daith asked.

Trey's gaze turned from the doctor onto Daith. "Yes, Daith, I'm here."

White walls surrounded her. The scent of cleaning chemicals filled her nose. "Where am I?"

"You're in the medical bay. You passed out in Doctor Milastow's office yesterday, but you're doing much better now."

Daith pushed herself into a sitting position on the bed. She shoved the thick, white blanket off her.

"Take it slow, Miss Tocc," Dr. Milastow said.

"I'm alright," Daith reassured her. She stretched her arms above her. "I just needed to rest."

Trey's jaw tightened with concern. "Daith, what happened?"

"I think I overworked myself. I've been practicing my telepathy so that I'll be of more use to you once we reach Sintaur."

"But you've always recovered so quickly." Trey wrung his hands. "I don't like this. I think it's time we had a talk about exactly what you are doing. No more hiding. No more isolating yourself. Not if you are using your abilities." He nodded to the doctor to leave. With hesitation, he sat on the bed next to her. "Daith, with everything you've been through, I think it's a mistake I asked you to help us. I never would have done anything at the expense of your health."

Daith patted his hand. "Really, I'm okay. I didn't want to tell you."

"Why not? After everything we've been through, I thought we trusted each other."

"It isn't about trust. It's about embarrassment." Daith expelled a breath. "After I realized the Controller had been in my dream, I felt tainted, used. He made things seem so real—other crewmembers, conversations, even my abilities. I didn't know who to trust, who to turn to, or even if what I experienced was true.

"So I decided to probe the minds of each crewmember. I needed to make sure they were real and that they wouldn't betray us. After what happened with Doctor Ludd—I trusted him. We all did. And he abandoned this ship and the mission. He told the Controllers where we are headed. He told them how to find me. I mean, he even had me go off of the dream-deflectors so the Controllers could reach me better."

Anger clouded Trey's eyes. "I can't believe you did this. You should have told me." He stood from the bed. "I could have helped you. I could have brought each crewmember to your quarters so you wouldn't have to work so hard to find them throughout the ship. I could have had Doctor Milastow monitor your progress to make sure you weren't overstimulating yourself."

Daith's head swam. "I'm sorry...I didn't think—"

"No, you didn't," Trey snapped. He paused, unclenching his fists. "Daith, I know you want to help, but I don't want to lose you. You are an important member of this crew, but I won't have anyone harming themselves to make this mission work. The Controllers may be ruthless, but we can rise above that." He called for Milastow to return. "As soon as I'm free, I'll send you a message to come to my office and to give me a full report on your findings."

"Yes, Commander." Daith's shoulders slumped.

Trey started at the formality. He smiled and placed a hand on her shoulder. "I'd still prefer it if you call me Trey."

Daith nodded and Trey left the room. Milastow took her vitals, told Daith to take things slow, and released her.

Daith meandered through the corridors to the floor below and entered her quarters. Her room reeked of vomit. The floor, still covered with bile and blood, made her sick to her stomach. What had she been thinking? Every time she tried to help she messed things up more.

Her chest ached. She missed Dru. She wanted to talk to him so badly it hurt. Gathering a moistened, soapy towel from the washroom, she began to scrub the carpet. Dried vomit came up and the smell reduced. Red splotches lessened, but she knew the blood stains would never truly vanish.

With an exhausted sigh, Daith threw down the towel. She sat on the bed and fingered through the datapads with the clues Dru had left her, as if she could glean some sort of remnant energy from them. But they remained cold.

Her communications chime rang.

"Yes?" she answered.

"Hello, Daith, it's Trey. I have some free time if you are ready to talk about what you experienced?"

"I'll be there shortly." Daith ended the call, took one last look at the dirty room, and sighed. She grabbed a clean pair of black pants and long-sleeved blue shirt from the small closet, changed out of her soiled clothes, and left her quarters. Two floors down, she rang the chimes to Trey's office.

"Enter."

The door swished open and she entered. Trey's state of being matched his immaculate surroundings. Poised, clean, and alert.

"Please have a seat. I'm very interested to hear what you've discovered about my crew."

Daith sat. The bare walls and polished desk mocked her. Dru had been so messy.

She forced the thoughts away. She couldn't keep dwelling on Dru. She had to move forward, though how many times she'd thought that already she couldn't count.

Daith methodically recited all she learned from the crew. She left out the images she had of Dru. She wanted them only for herself.

"General tension runs throughout, but loyalty is foremost in everyone's minds. A few have their doubts, but nothing serious. They are all excited to reach Sintaur, certain that they can make a difference in stopping the Controllers."

Trey's shoulders relaxed. "That's wonderful to hear, Daith. I tried my best to choose a good crew, but after what happened with Doctor Ludd, I worried I'd overlooked something. Your insights are invaluable to me." He paused, tapping his chin. "Since you felt comfortable enough to probe the minds on this ship, how would you feel if you focused some of your efforts in the same area for when we reach Sintaur?"

"I don't understand."

"I've been thinking about how you could help us. One of the things that could be most useful would be to know what the Controllers are thinking beforehand. A way for us to have the advantage."

"Would I be going down to the planet?"

"I'm not sure. Do you think you could do it from orbit?"

Daith frowned. "I don't know. There's a lot of distance between here and a planet. I seem to do better when I'm closer to someone." Her stomach clenched at the thought of trying to read someone's mind so far away.

"Hm. Maybe that would stretch you too far. I have a better idea." Trey pressed the com panel. "Lieutenant Commander Cenjo, please report to my office." He returned his attention to Daith. "Truth be told, your skills would probably be more valuable onboard. I know you and Dru worked on reconstructing inanimate objects. How would you feel about focusing on repairs?"

"What kind of repairs?"

"We aren't sure what sort of resistance we might encounter, now that the Controllers have an idea of what we are up to, though I don't know how much Doctor Ludd told them. I'm not sure the extent of what he knew. But in case the ship is attacked, your assistance with repairing any of the systems would be very useful. We will have other ships to help, but I'd rather be prepared than not. What do you think?"

Daith's hands shook. "I'm not sure... I feel like every time I try to help, I make things worse."

"That's why we will have you practice." The door chimes rang.

"Enter."

Cenjo walked in, eyebrow raised at Daith. "Reporting as ordered, Commander."

"Lieutenant Commander, I'd like you to work with Daith. She has had a tour of the ship, but I'd like you to get her more familiar with the intricacies of some of our primary systems. You can start this evening after your scheduled class in engineering."

"Yes, Commander. Daith, I'll be at your quarters at twenty hundred hours." Cenjo exited.

Daith's chest tightened. "Are you sure, Trey? Maybe I'm just not ready."

"You are only going to be looking at the systems. You'll be supervised. Everything is going to be fine. I promise."

Daith patted her face dry, wincing at the pain in her head. She'd scrubbed her floor with some cleaning chemicals she requested from Dr. Milastow. The vomit had been cleared away and the blood stains barely noticeable. She grimaced at her reflection—pale skin, red-rimmed eyes, puffy cheeks. She wondered how much longer she could stay functional.

Her door chimes rang. With a forced smile, she answered them.

* * *

"All set!"

Cenjo stopped short at the sight of her. She looked much worse than she had just a few hours previously. "Are you okay?"

"Of course," she said, letting the door close behind her. "A little tired. I think I've been cooped up in my quarters for too long. It'll do me some good to stretch my legs."

Cenjo hated seeing her so worn out. A reminder of his sister came into his mind, when she'd stay up too late studying, pushing herself beyond her limits.

"Daith…"

"I promise, I'm alright. And I won't do anything strenuous. Just poking around the ship a little bit, right?"

"If you say so." He gestured for her to join him and the two of them strode down the hallway. They took the stairs down three floors to the lowest level and headed for the center of the ship—into engineering.

"Lieutenant Byot?" Cenjo called out.

"Over here!" Byot's voice carried across the clanging mechanical sounds. "By the engine!"

Cenjo took the lead and headed down a black walkway toward the center of the room. He held onto the rail to compensate for the ramp's steep decline. They reached the center next to a pool of amber liquid that swirled in random patterns.

"Is this a good time?"

"Definitely." Byot scurried over. "Any time for you and M-Miss Tocc." Byot's words skipped when he saw Daith. "How are you?"

"Fine. A little tired, I guess," Daith said. "I'm happy to be working in here today. The silari trees smell so nice."

"Well then today is an excellent day indeed. The trees are flowering." Podlike sacs clung to the trunks. Many of them were open, revealing crimson flowers, circular in shape, with bright orange centers. A couple crewmembers carefully collected the petals into containers.

"The seed pods will be preserved until we can deliver them to some of the planets on which we are trying to grow the trees non-natively."

"Do you think it'll work?" Daith asked.

"It hasn't so far, but we've only recently begun the process."

"Don't you find that difficult? I mean, I assume you don't stop very often between fights."

Byot wrinkled his forehead. "I'm afraid I don't understand."

Cenjo intervened. "Daith, I'm not sure what you believe goes on here, but we don't fight all the time. In fact, the Aleet Army has spent several years simply trying to survive, checking on old army members, and recruiting new ones. Since then we've mostly done intelligence gathering and cargo runs. Commander Xiven has been more patient than most of the crew before he finally decided we needed to step in and deal with the Controllers. He may be strict—sending crewmembers away if they don't stay up to speed—but he didn't rush into this confrontation lightly."

Daith chewed her nail. "I would never have thought that about him. He seems so driven. I can't imagine him waiting."

"Well it's true. I'd say we were ready over a standard year ago, but he insisted we wait. And even with all his precautions, he couldn't predict Doctor Ludd betraying us or his brother being murdered by a Controller spy." Cenjo winced. He hadn't meant to bring up Dru. Especially since Daith had recently spent several days in her quarters trying to deal with the loss.

Daith rubbed her face. "Well that's why I'm here, right? To give you guys back some of your advantage. So let's get me to know these mechanisms so I can be of some kind of use during the battle."

* * *

Daith grimaced. Her headache had not abated all day. Her work in the engineering room went quite well and she felt confident she could help with repairs if need be, but the dull ache that pressed on all sides of her skull made it difficult to concentrate.

Bidding Cenjo goodnight, Daith entered her quarters, popped a dream-deflector pill, and crawled into her bed.

Her quarters.

Her bed.

She stared at the ceiling, thinking how quickly she'd come to accept this place as her home. At least, the only home she knew.

She needed to get a grip. She couldn't let herself feel so tired and sick. And she knew Cenjo and Byot noticed. She knew they'd pull her from helping if they thought she couldn't handle the intensity.

Daith dropped her arm off the bed and scooped up the datapads on the floor. She didn't want to miss Dru anymore. She wanted to be able to do things on her own. To show she had the strength to help. But what else could she do?

Curled fingers wrapped around the cool edges of the datapads as she drifted off to sleep, her mind churning into deflected dreams.

CHAPTER 31

DAITH AWOKE AND stretched—her body arching with the movement. Her blanket, damp with sweat, tangled between her legs as she kicked it off her. With a clatter, the datapads fell to the floor.

She felt good. Very good. No ache in her head. No pain in her muscles.

Daith sprung off the bed and washed. She dressed quickly and asked the ship to send a message to Lieutenant Cenjo. She wanted to work more on different sections of the ship. She felt like she could repair anything.

The computer cut her off mid-message as an alarm blared at her from the console.

"What did I do?"

An automated message rang out. "Please report to your designated combat stations. This is not a drill. Repeat, this is not a drill."

Daith pitched sideways as the ship lurched. She hastily grabbed onto the wall, but a shudder caused her to lose her balance and she fell back on her butt.

Rubbing at the soreness, Daith stood and exited her quarters, buffeted around the corridor while she made her way to Trey's office.

"Trey?" She pounded on the door. No answer.

Of course. Why would he be here during a battle? He's probably on the bridge.

Daith trotted over to the center room and the door slid open. The eight stations that circled the center chair all faced inward toward Trey in the middle. He called out orders—the crew moved with ease, even with all the tension Daith could sense in the room.

"Trey," she called out.

Trey whipped his head around. "Daith?"

"What's going on?" The bridge shuddered.

"The Controllers have sent sentries to stop us. We barely entered the Fracc system when they started firing."

"How are we in the Fracc system already?"

"You've been asleep for two days, Daith." He glared at her. "Go back to your quarters."

"Not a chance. I can help."

"Two days ago you could barely walk!" He nodded to Lieutenant Koye.

Koye grabbed her from behind. Daith sensed his anger. She felt the warmth build inside her, but didn't want to hurt him.

Daith imagined the insides of his chest and found his breathing pumps. She squeezed slowly, enough to get his attention.

Koye wheezed.

"Let me go or I'll make you unconscious," Daith warned.

Koye relaxed his grip, fury evident in his black eyes.

"Hate me later." Daith gripped the back of Trey's chair, studying the screens in front of him. "Trey, I can help. Where are they?"

Trey hesitated before giving her a nod. "Above us." He motioned toward the top screen. "I think we'll be okay. We are faster than they are, but their weapons are doing more damage then I'd like."

Daith closed her eyes. Her chest tightened, but she ignored her fear. She could do this. She could help.

Daith reached out with her senses. Maybe she could amplify the shields. Or perhaps damage their weapons? But she couldn't connect to anything. The ships were too far away.

Daith rocked forward, butting her chin against Trey's head.

"Sorry!"

Trey rubbed his skull. "I'm fine. Cadet Ikar, adjust heading to fly between them next time they come around to shoot. Maybe some of our ricochet will hit them."

"Yes, Commander. Though I'm not sure we'll avoid the blast ourselves. Our engines are strained as it is."

The engines.

"You'll have your power," Daith called out.

"Daith—"

"Trust me!"

Daith sprinted off the bridge and flew down the stairs. She ran through the door straight toward the glowy amber pool.

"Daith? What are you doing here?" Byot emptied cooling tanks onto mechanical engine components spiraling up the trees. The whole room shimmered from the heat.

"No time." She walked over to one of the giant trees and placed her hand on it. The machinery around the trees pulsed with heat, drying out the tree and sucking sap at a frighteningly fast rate. At some point soon, the trees would either dry up or start on fire.

The trees ached. She could feel their pain as they struggled silently against the hot metal.

Daith felt her own warmth surge inside her, but though it felt hot, it did not burn. She let the energy run up the trees, fortifying their fibers, giving them a temporary hardened shell to keep the metal from burning them.

With less strain, the trees relaxed, and sap poured from them back at their normal pace. The mechanical components still chugged away, but the pool became less depleted.

The ship rocked again, but this time Daith remained steady. A few moments later, the general alarm ceased and the engine room fell silent, except for the gurgling of the machines.

Daith removed her hand, the warmth draining out of her, and her legs buckled. She hit the ground hard.

Byot rushed to her side. "Are you alright?"

Daith nodded, taking slow breaths. "Actually, yes. I feel okay. Just got unsteady for a minute." She wiped her face. Her arm sported a blood trail, minimal compared to her gushers lately.

"Maybe I should escort you to medical?"

"Really, I'm fine. I'd like to check in with Trey first on the bridge." Without waiting for an answer, Daith strode from the room. Elated, everything felt different. The lights seemed less harsh, the air less stale. She felt truly in control of what she'd done and made a difference.

Entering the bridge, Daith reported to Trey, filling him in.

Trey's eyes lit up. "That's wonderful, Daith. Truly incredible." He paused. "I know you did a lot for us, but how would you feel about helping with some repairs? It could go a lot faster with your assistance."

A grin bloomed across her face. "Tell me where you need me."

* * *

That evening, the ship returned on course, heading toward Sintaur and whatever awaited them. Trey insisted the sentinels would not have had time to warn Sintaur of their arrival, so the element of surprise would still be on their side. He thanked Daith profusely for all her help, but insisted she get some rest. They were one day away from Sintaur and he wanted her to be fully rested by the time they got there.

The tension in the air swirled with excitement, peaking with moments of anxiety. The crew hustled about—a few even nodded at her in the corridor as she made her way to her quarters. She'd waited so long to feel part of the crew and she finally did. She'd finally helped.

The door slid open and once inside, Daith kicked off her shoes. Yawning, she sat on the bed and thought about what she wanted to eat. Something heavy and warm sounded perfect—a stew perhaps? She closed her eyes, imagining the herb-filled scent, wondering if she should invite someone to join her. She hadn't eaten with anyone since Dru—he told the best stories. Sometimes her belly had hurt from laughing so hard....

Daith's head tipped backward against the wall, her breathing steady, and sleep consumed her.

CHAPTER 32

BEWETRU'S MURDER HUNG over Torrak and his group like a tainted fog. Their two-day trip to Dansu was filled with irritated moods, overly-fake smiles, and periods of isolation. A near-tangible shift in the air occurred when Torrak announced they arrived at their destination. The five of them practically fell out of the ship, happy to stretch their legs and breathe non-recycled atmosphere.

"All right everybody," Torrak said, "we'll be leaving at oh-five hundred hours. I'm going with Nuis to get fuel and restock our maintenance supplies."

The two of them made their way to Nuis' contact's shop. When they arrived, Torrak eyed the peeled paint and moldy wooden edges of the building. The greenish color that covered the old yellow paint underneath gave him the impression someone had thrown up over a urine stain. Nuis laughed at the disgusted look on Torrak's face.

"Wait until you see the inside," Nuis said.

Torrak couldn't think how the inside *could* be worse.

And yet, somehow, it was.

Cracked walls oozed with an oily liquid like a wounded animal bleeding and the stench of sweat and lubricant floated through the air in a heavy cloud. Broken-down ships being serviced let off exhaust that clogged Torrak's lungs every time he tried to breathe, and a sticky brownish substance coated the floor wherever he stepped. He expected some tough, dirty, large individual with stained clothing and greasy hair to walk up and greet them, but when he met Nuis' contact, he wasn't sure what to think.

Sa'Teh, greeted them, looking very out-of-place in the filthy environment—a clean, small, fragile-looking being, draped from head to toe in a shimmery midnight blue wrap, which only left her eyes and hands uncovered. Her hands were translucent and Torrak could see yellow globs floating around under her skin.

After a brief introduction and overview of their ship, Sa'Teh agreed to a refuel and a tune-up for a fair price. During the ship's refueling, they went across the street for a bite to eat.

Five standard hours later, everyone bustled onto the ship, although they all agreed they wanted more time before stuffing themselves back into such a small space.

After they departed, Torrak sought some solace in the control room, but he couldn't escape his own thoughts. He'd racked his brain for days, trying to come up with some kind of plan to save Daith, but felt at a loss. How could five of them take on an entire army with a tiny ship, no weapons, and no clue as to what state of mind Daith might be in?

Torrak rubbed his head as his mind raced. *What under the stars am I doing? There have already been two deaths and the friends I do have left are going to come to blows if they don't have direction soon.*

He let out a huge sigh.

"Everything all right?" a voice behind him asked.

"Hmm?" he answered. "Oh, yeah...I guess. It's hard to sit here and wait. I want to get to Daith and help her, you know?"

Faan sat down across from him. "Tell me about her."

"Daith?" Torrak paused before he answered. "She is—incredible. Intelligent, witty, stunning. She can always make you feel better, no matter how much you want to stay in a bad mood."

"Are you two...in love?"

Torrak hesitated, feeling awkward about how to answer the question, but wanting to reassure Faan at the same time. "I guess you could say I love her, but not really in a romantic way. She's my closest friend and I have never had a connection with anyone like I have with her."

"She sounds perfect."

Torrak laughed. "She's definitely not perfect. She would get really moody and secretive. When she got mad about something, she would brood on it for days. And she never liked talking about her past. We would chat about classes and tests and stuff, but not much else. I had no problem discussing my ability to analyze, but Daith would always change the subject or claim she hadn't really progressed in any of her classes.

"I always had a feeling that deep down she feared what she might be capable of. Now that I know who her father is, I'm not surprised. I mean, imagine being the daughter of one of the most loved and feared men in our time. It's no wonder she never wanted to talk about it or that she didn't push herself very hard in school to improve her abilities. Those things connected her to her father; showed everyone who she really was."

"I can't imagine what she must have gone through growing up," Faan said. "I always wanted to be exactly like my mother and father. And now she's been kidnapped and forced to retrace her father's footsteps."

"Do you see now why I have to get her out of there? She's not her father, even if she does have his powers, and if the Aleet Army manipulates her into using them, the results could be catastrophic."

"I can tell she means a lot to you. It's not every day you go out and attempt to rescue someone from an entire army." Faan smiled, but Torrak could see a sadness in her eyes.

What had he said now? He hadn't meant to upset her. His mind flooded with fragments of information about her. Nothing made sense.

"Faan," he asked, "why are you here?"

"You know why. I know Nuis told you about my parents' death."

He leaned in. "I didn't ask you why you want to take on the Aleet Army. I asked why you are *here*."

Faan looked puzzled as she answered. "I needed a ride."

"I don't believe you," Torrak pressed. "I know full well you are capable of finding your own transportation. So why us? Why this ship?"

"I-I don't know why," she stammered. "I'm not sure. I thought I only needed justice for my parents' death, but now? I don't have proof they were murdered, I don't have a plan, and I *always* have a plan. So when I met you, I saw you as an opportunity to take me where I needed to go. But now..." Her pale eyes widened.

"Now," she continued, "I don't want you all to get hurt." She threw her hands up in frustration. "But you're out of your minds. You have no idea what kind of psychopaths you're about to face."

"That's precisely why I have to get Daith out of there. Who knows what they might be doing to her? And since they've already picked their first target, it means they've gotten her or her abilities to a point where they can be used."

"So what are you going to do? Stroll in there and say 'Hey, you've got my friend and I want her back'? They've already killed Bewetru and your friend Lang. They want to kill you. Why under the stars do you think you can pull this off?"

Guilt and doubt hit him anew. "I don't know. I rushed into this with a lot of good intentions, but not a lot of thought. It's the strangest thing, too. I've always been able to figure things out. But lately, I can't seem to do anything right. I've been off my guard, missed obvious signals, trusted the wrong individuals, and screwed things up all over the place. It's not like me. It's more like..." Torrak sat up as if struck by lightning.

"It's more like how I'd be if I wasn't myself."

"What?" Faan asked.

"It's like—we are connected—and you know how hard it is to control—must be unconsciously projecting them..." Torrak stopped and swore under his breath. "I'm sorry. I have this thing where sometimes if I—well, it's more like moving too fast and—or like going too slow?" Torrak's breath quickened. "No, it's not like that—it's more like— and then if I talk...."

Faan stared, her look both concerned and confused. "Are you okay?"

Torrak let out a long, slow breath.

"I'm sorry. Sometimes my brain works too fast and my words can't come quick enough. I've had this problem my whole life. I told you before Daith and I have a unique connection, right? Well, sometimes it was almost scary. Like I could feel what she felt or she knew when I was in trouble. I think it was because her abilities would get too close to the surface. She would either pick up on stuff about me unconsciously or project her own feelings without realizing it."

"What does that have to do with how you've felt lately?"

"I think I'm still picking up on her. That's why I've been caught up in her dreams. And why I've been so unbalanced. Some of it was the memory loss, but it's more than that. I feel like I can't depend on myself or my actions and I've never felt that way before. I bet I'm picking up on how she's feeling." Torrak leaned back in his chair. "If I can't trust myself, how am I going to do this?"

"What makes you think you have to do it by yourself?"

Torrak laughed. "You know what? I never once thought of that. I assumed responsibility because I saw Daith get taken. But maybe someone else will have an idea."

"See? I'm already helping." Faan grinned.

Tension ebbed out of him and a yawn crept its way to his mouth.

"When's the last time you slept?" she asked.

Torrak shrugged, rubbing his face.

"Then get some sleep," Faan said, decisively. "I'll take care of things up here. We can all talk about a plan in the morning."

Torrak headed into the cargo room. He curled up in one of the larger storage closets, exhausted, and used a few blankets as padding. Feeling at ease for the first time in days, he slipped quickly into sleep.

Torrak sat alone in a large room on a space ship. The room felt cold, the walls thin, as if the vacuum of space pressed from the outside, trying to get in. A single light shone down where he sat and he could only see one door—a large grey slab with no apparent handle.

He stood and shouted out a hello. No answer, save his own echo. But something existed in the middle of the room. Two figures: a man's body, and a woman who crouched over it. The woman sobbed. She turned toward him, rivers of tears on her pale cheeks.

"I couldn't stop it. I couldn't save him. All these powers, for nothing. I couldn't bring him back!" she cried out. "I can't believe this is who I am. Am I really a monster? A murderer? If only I could remember who I was. Who I am."

"Daith?"

"Stay back! If you come, you'll die, too. And it will be my fault." Torrak soared away from her, even though Daith hadn't moved. He slammed into the opposite wall, his head smashing against the tough steel.

"See?" Daith shook her head. "It's too late."

"Daith, what's going on? Tell me where you are." Torrak's hand moved to his head. It came away wet with blood.

Daith saw she'd wounded him. "No!" She shrieked. She vanished into thin air. The body on the floor remained, although now it faced away from him. It appeared different than the body lying there moments ago. Torrak approached it, not wanting to know who it was, but the urge to see overpowered him. He rolled the body over with his foot and screamed. It was Daith. Cuts and bruises covered her as if she'd been tortured. Contorted, broken in many places, twisted and mangled under shredded, bloody clothes.

Torrak tried to look away, but his stare locked with hers. Her green eyes showed images of beings being hunted and killed. Cities demolished and destroyed. And mobs screaming her name.

Torrak couldn't move, couldn't stop the carnage. Desperate, he clawed at his own eyes, trying to get the image of her corpse from his mind.

Still screaming, he awoke.

CHAPTER 33

TORRAK GASPED FOR breath. Darkness enveloped him, except for a stream of light that crept underneath the door into the storage closet where he slept. When he raised his hands to shield his eyes, they cramped in pain. Dried blood darkened his fingers and palms.

Managing to sit, Torrak crawled out of the closet and stumbled to the washroom. He looked in the mirror, squinting in the brightness, and winced at the red scratches across his face. Images of his nightmare about Daith filled his head. Scenes of death. Of mass destruction.

And Daith said she was responsible for it all.

Torrak made his way to the common area, shaking. What did he think he was doing? Daith was incredibly powerful. They wouldn't stand a chance.

And he didn't even know why they all cared. Kalil was along for the ride. Preeaht only liked Kalil. Nuis's reasons were still a mystery. Only Faan's motivation made sense.

He'd already gotten Bewetru killed. He didn't want to be responsible for anyone else dying.

Everyone straggled in over the next standard hour and Torrak retold each one about what happened to his face. Dredging up the dream hurt and pulled at his nagging doubts. This was never going to work. They were in over their heads. Everyone would run the first chance they got.

"Okay. Let's start talking about a plan," Faan said, once everyone had arrived in the room.

Panic welled up in Torrak's chest. "Why are you all here?" he blurted out. "Most of you don't even know me and none of you have met Daith. This whole Aleet Army thing doesn't have to do with any of you, except maybe Faan wanting revenge. So why are you here? Bewetru is already dead. This isn't your fight. You don't have to do this."

Kalil smiled out of the corner of his mouth. "Worst pep talk ever."

Torrak opened his mouth to speak, but Kalil cut him off. "I may be young, but I remember growing up under the threat of the Aleet Army. I remember my parents being terrified to come forward about my gift with machines because they didn't know if others would connect me to Jaxx's 'abilities' and see me as dangerous. I had to keep my own genius a secret for years, scared someone would find out and turn against me."

Torrak opened his mouth to reply, but Kalil pushed forward. "If I can do something to prevent that from happening to someone else, I will. As for Daith, I won't let them dictate another being's life. Nobody should have to live like that."

Torrak sat there, stunned. He'd no idea Kalil had such a rough time growing up.

Nuis began to speak, softly at first. "You think this fight is only yours? When the Army seized systems to take over, my name attracted unwanted attention. With my money and influence, how could I not be the perfect puppet for the Aleet Army to control?

"I spent my whole life pretending to be someone I'm not to stay alive, doing whatever they wanted me to do. Things I would never have expected I could do. When they broke apart after Jacin Jaxx's death, I kept pretending, keeping up the pretense of someone not to be messed with, terrified someone would find out the truth. I'd made a lot of enemies. The only close friends I had were a smuggler who I rarely saw," he said, nodding toward Faan, "and a good man, gutted in the room next to mine while I slept." Nuis's gaze bore into Torrak. "I'm sick of pretending."

Torrak wanted to say something when Preeaht began to speak, her voice floating above a low growl. "I am the last of my kind. The Aleet Army wiped out my planet over ten standard years ago. In one hour, everyone was dead. They believed my species would be a threat to them, simply because of our influence and strength.

"I was off-planet" she continued, "having disobeyed my family to seek my own life, when I heard about the chemical weapon they deployed. Three years passed before the air was clean enough for me to go back and bury my family and friends, but nothing remained. The toxins had eaten away their flesh, leaving nothing but masses of bones and cloth for me to sort through." Kalil took Preeaht's hand. "If I can do something to keep that from happening again, I will give my life for it."

Torrak shook his head. He'd been so focused on Daith he hadn't realized there could be other reasons to stop the Aleet Army.

Faan, sensing his mood, placed her hand on his arm. "We may all have boarded this ship for different reasons, but we are *staying* on this ship to reach the same goal. We all want to keep the Aleet Army from regaining power, and it seems your friend is the key to it all."

Torrak looked around the room. The anxiety he felt before melted away. *They may not be soldiers, but they are ready to fight.*

"Okay. Let's make a plan.

Torrak took note of the skills and talents of each member of the group. Kalil excelled with computers and machines and Preeaht had an authoritative presence. Nuis's were influence and money, while Faan's fighting skills and ability to disappear made her an excellent spy. As for Torrak, he had the personal connection with Daith, so he wanted to be there when they found her. With their skills determined, the five of them devised a strategy to incorporate everyone's best talents.

Several hours later, they went over the plan.

Torrak pointed at Nuis. "Phase one?"

"I will go to Sintaur's main governmental office and warn them of the Aleet Army's approach. I will inform them the Army may launch an aerial assault and help them begin preparations for a counter-attack."

Torrak turned to Preeaht. "Phase two?"

"I will visit major city councils and tell them of the Aleet Army's arrival. I will advise them to send a general distress call to evacuate any sensitive areas, including military installations and power plants. I will then help them prepare for a ground attack."

"Phase three?"

Kalil answered. "I will be with you on Sintaur. We will get captured by the Aleet Army and be taken to the main ship for questioning. I will then wait with you until Faan lets me out of whatever interrogation room they have."

"Four?"

Faan spoke up. "I will stay close to you and Kalil and sneak aboard the main ship once you two are taken into custody. After you're restrained, I will free you."

"And five."

"Once I'm free," Kalil continued, "Faan and I will disable the ship's communication system and, if possible, the ship itself. We will then ready an escape craft and wait for you and Daith. If you don't arrive within three standard hours, we will leave the ship and join the fight on Sintaur."

The room became quiet until Faan asked the question no one wanted to voice. "What if Daith doesn't *want* to leave? We can't let her kill all those innocents on the planet below."

Torrak did not hesitate. "If I can't persuade her, and I can't take her by force, then I will do anything possible so she's not a threat. Depending on her abilities, I may not be able to do anything at all, but if I have a chance to stop her, I'll take it." He paused. He thought about the way she looked in the dream, hating herself for who she was and what she might do. Or had already done. "I know she would want it that way."

An uncomfortable silence fell over the room until Kalil timidly spoke up. "How are you going to get the Aleet Army's attention? I'm pretty sure they don't know we're coming."

"If we dock somewhere on Sintaur, throw my name around in a public place, and say we know about the Aleet Army's plan and how our allies will stop them, I have a feeling they'll hear about it. They've probably realized by now Kircla killed the wrong target, so they'll want to capture me. I'm not only a witness to Daith's kidnapping, but I evaded an assassination attempt and now I'm at the place where their secret plan is going to happen. They'll want to know how much I know—and to see who else I told. Rule number one: you can't interrogate a dead body."

Silence blanketed the room, different this time. This one felt full of resolve.

They were ready.

CHAPTER 34

DAITH AWOKE, SCREAMING. She fell off the bed, tears coursing down her face.

The door slid open.

"Daith!" Trey rushed to her side.

"I killed him. It was my fault. He's dead because of me!" Daith sobbed into Trey's shoulder as the images of her dream pounded her in waves.

"What are you talking about? Who's dead?"

"Dru!"

Trey pulled back from her and peered into her eyes. "It's just a bad dream. All of that happened days ago."

Daith took a few shuddering breaths. Her chest stayed tight as she spoke. "I dreamt that I'd killed Dru. It was my fault. I got too powerful and yet I couldn't save him once he died. I couldn't bring him back."

Trey rubbed Daith's upper arms. "You know that's not true. You merely had a dream. It wasn't real. None of that happened." His gaze snaked over to the dream-deflector pills. "Did you take one of your pills?"

Daith shook her head. "I fell asleep after the battle against the sentries. I didn't even realize I'd been so tired."

Trey helped her up and sat her on the bed. He grabbed the bottle and handed her a pill. "Daith, it's the middle of the crew's sleep cycle. You need to get some rest. Some peaceful rest. We can talk about your dream tomorrow. Come to my office when you wake up."

Daith took the medicine, her chest relaxing. The adrenaline drained from her. It had only been a dream.

She laid back down under the cover and Trey left. As her exhaustion won out she began to remember the other man in her dream. The one with the blonde hair. The Controller spy.

If he killed Dru, then why was she worried about hurting him?

* * *

A two and a half meter tall, sea-green skinned member of the Orcla species sat in the cockpit of her small, but highly efficient battle cruiser, the *Shadow*. She impatiently tapped her long blue fingernails on her ship's piloting console, allowing her disappointment in herself to escalate. She was Kircla, the pinnacle of assassins, and she had killed the wrong target.

Kircla had been a day away from Juha when she found out about her mistake. This marked the first time she ever assassinated the wrong individual and it infuriated her. Currently in her prime, her skills were unmatched by anyone in her clan, and she always, *always* got her target.

Until now.

Kircla opened her subject's file: Torrak Spirtz. Also considered to be in the prime of his lifespan for his species, he ranked near the top of his class at the academy he attended and he, too, had never failed on a case during his time with the C-9 government. Kircla traced the young man's name with her nail. Truly a worthy adversary. She would take pride in killing him.

Kircla straightened and adrenaline flushed through her. A flashing light in front of her indicated Torrak's ship had entered sensor range. Only a couple of standard hours until she could finish the job. She checked her bearings and realized she would catch up to him right outside the Fracc system.

As she crept up upon his ship, she readied the *Shadow* for combat.

* * *

Faan was awake.

Not that she couldn't sleep, she just didn't need to. She only had to sleep one night in a standard month and she did that two weeks ago.

During that time, Faan went through her exercise routine and memorized the ships access panels three nights ago. She counted the number of bolts on the ship, 30,124 to be exact, and calculated and recalculated their flight path by hand. She even organized all the cargo in the cargo rooms and cleaned every surface she could find.

Now she sat in the cockpit, idly rewiping between the knobs and levers that controlled the ship, while she stared out into the blackness of space.

And thought.

She thought about how far she'd come since her youth; trained to be an assassin, becoming the best in her class. Assigned her first target, an ambassador from the city Offkule, at the age of thirteen. Her parents had been so proud of her, following in their footsteps. She never really thought about the killings when she'd been younger—they were simply something she did—but she did them well: cleanly, efficiently, and quickly. She perfected her skills and established quite a reputation on her homeworld.

Her "career path" never allowed her to stay in one spot for very long, and hiding her true identity from others kept her from getting close to anyone. She spent most nights alone, even avoiding the company of her younger brother, and preferred it that way, especially after her parents were killed.

Murdered.

Faan's fingers stopped cleaning and curled into fists, her fingernails leaving little indentations in her palms. She remembered the loss of her parents, and even though it had been nine years ago, the pain still felt hot like fresh lashes across her heart. She sometimes woke in the middle of her sleep, panicked she had to find them, and then she would sob when she realized they were gone.

After their deaths, she closed herself off to the universe, and thought of nothing but finding their killers. It kept her going when she roamed through different cities with no money or food, surviving only on her determination. She left her brother and her mother's mother behind—painful reminders of a world that pretended her parent's death hadn't been an accident.

And yet things were different now. She still worked toward the same goal, but her reasons had changed. She really wanted to save this girl, Daith. She wanted to stop the Aleet Army from whatever plan they'd concocted. And she wanted the connection everyone on the ship had: she wanted friends.

Faan laughed at the notion. Yet once they came up with a plan, they all relaxed around each other. She began to enjoy her shipmates:

Kalil, with his quirky sense of humor and genuine, although sometimes tactless honesty, Preeaht, who shared some of her own battle stories with Faan over a meal, and of course Nuis, same as she remembered him, charming and witty. But the surprise had been Torrak. She couldn't deny her physical attraction to him, but something registered deeper than that. He made her feel comfortable, a feeling she hadn't felt in a very long time.

She didn't know if it was love but maybe....

At the moment a smile touched her lips at this thought she saw a black ship slow and pull to a stop in front of the viewport. Proximity alarms sounded, but before Faan could react, streaks of destructive energy raced from the looming craft, aimed directly at their small ship.

* * *

Cenjo's throat tightened.

He hadn't really meant to read the medical files. They'd been sitting there on the doctor's desk. He merely glanced at them when she went to retrieve a painkiller for his injured shoulder—one of his trainees caught him off guard during sparring. Dr. Milastow must have been working on the files when he arrived, updating them or something.

Her reason for leaving them accessible didn't matter to Cenjo. He'd seen Daith's name at the top of the datapad and glimpsed at the notes.

Unstable. Daily nosebleeds. Abilities progressing. Isolation a driving force. Recommend continuing anger and guilt complexes to maximize potential.

And then right underneath: *Subject will burn out as intended.*

As intended.

Cenjo forced a smile onto his face when Milastow returned.

"This should help," she said, injecting him in the shoulder. His muscles immediately unknotted and his pain diminished.

"Thanks, Doctor."

Cenjo walked out, keeping his gait relaxed. Once in the corridor, he quickened his pace. Xiven and Milastow were keeping Daith unhinged on purpose. They wanted her to use herself up. But why? Why would Xiven want Daith to be worthless after she exhausted herself? After she maximized her potential?

What did Xiven really have planned when they reached Sintaur?

Cenjo had no idea. He only knew he couldn't let Xiven's plan continue. He couldn't let him use Daith. He had to keep her on the right side of the line.

And if she strayed, then Cenjo would stop her. No matter how.

CHAPTER 35

A LARGE BOX in the cargo room fell on Torrak, jolting him awake moments before the warning alarms sounded. He moaned in pain and pushed it off his legs. He stood. The ship rocked and he crashed against the nearest wall. As soon as he regained his balance, he dashed to the control room.

Once there, he found Faan frantically racing back and forth between control panels.

"What's happening?" he hollered over the loud alarms.

"Pull down on that handle," Faan yelled, waving at one of the consoles out of her reach.

Torrak leapt forward and pulled the specified handle. His stomach lurched as the ship swerved to the left.

"We're under attack," Faan told him. "And I'll bet my life it's Kircla." Faan turned a small dial and the ship plummeted straight down.

"What can I do?" Torrak asked, catching himself against the console in front of him.

"Do you have any combat flying experience?"

"No." Another shudder rocked the ship as Kircla fired on them. Sparks flew from the electrical panel behind Torrak and showered him with hot embers.

"Do you have any weapons experience?"

"No," he told her, brushing away the fiery bits of metal with one hand while he gripped the pilot chair.

"Can you help with the ship's speed or shield intensity?"

"No," he said in a feeble voice.

Faan gave an exasperated sigh as another set of firing knocked her off her feet. "Then no, you can't help," she said while she pulled herself back up.

At that moment, Nuis stuck his head in the room, his knuckles whitened due to the death-like grip he had on the doorway. "What's going on?"

"We're under attack," Torrak answered.

"What?" Nuis screeched as he bolted to the viewport. "What are we going to do?"

Torrak grabbed him by the shoulders. "You are going to make sure Kalil and Preeaht are all right, and then see if Kalil can give us more speed." He shoved Nuis out of the control room and turned back to the front viewport where he saw the large, black ship turn and prepare for another pass.

"Faan, she's coming straight for us."

Faan's eyes widened in horror. "I can't shake her. Brace yourself!"

Torrak couldn't shift his gaze from the ship streaming toward them. Kircla closed in and everything seemed to speed up and slow down at the same time. Torrak could see every detail as the oncoming vessel powered up its weapons for the final assault. Without thinking, he flung himself toward the weapons panel, pressing any button he could reach to fire every weapon they had at the looming shadow.

Kircla's ship exploded.

Torrak barely registered Faan screaming with joy and didn't come back to reality until she planted a kiss on his lips.

"I don't know how you did it, but you did," Faan returned to the console to get a damage report, which kept her from seeing Torrak's bright, red face. His knees wobbled so hard he could barely stand. Giddy, he looked down at the weapons console in front of him.

His joyful moment deflated. The targeting computer readout indicated that all the shots fired missed the oncoming ship completely. Not only that, but apparently his frantic mashing of buttons opened the cargo bay door, vented out half their air, turned on the internal cooling system, and fried all the light panels in the back half of the ship. Right before he told Faan that he may have actually caused damage instead of helping, she pointed out a flashing light on her console.

"There's someone trying to communicate with us," she said.

"Do you think Kircla survived?"

"I hope not."

At the moment Faan hit the open communications button, Kalil, Preeaht, and Nuis entered the cockpit, all talking at once.

"Sounds like you're having a party," a gravelly voice crackled over the speaker. "Hope I'm invited after saving your butts."

Torrak's jaw dropped open at the group of six fierce-looking attack cruisers that appeared off their bow.

"Who said that?" Kalil asked.

"Kid, is that you? How's the knee?"

Kalil's eyes nearly popped out of his head. "It's Opute!"

"Opute?" Nuis asked. "Hey, man! It's me, Nuis."

"Nuis?" Opute's voice blared through the speaker. "How did you manage to get mixed up with this lot?"

"It's a long story."

"You think you could tow us in?" Torrak asked. "I'm afraid to know how much this little ship is smoking."

"I wish I could tell you it's not as bad as you think.... Hang on while I attach the docking clamps. See you in a few. Opute out."

On their way out of the control room to gather their things, Kalil turned to Torrak and whispered, "What is that Corenthian going to say when we return his ship in this condition?"

Torrak threw his arm around Kalil's bony shoulders. "Only you could come out of a near-death firefight and still be worried about returning the ship in one piece."

"I'm young. I don't want to put a bad mark on my credit."

Torrak laughed. "Well, don't worry. The ship was registered under my name."

* * *

Once everyone settled into Opute's cruiser, Torrak filled Opute in on how their group got together and their plan.

"Pretty gutsy," Opute remarked, as the Nikana jumped up onto the table and lay down in front of him, growling softly at the newcomers. "Sounds like a lot is riding on chance."

"Well, it's the best we can do with what we have. And we have to do something."

Opute paused for a moment. "This all happens tomorrow, right?"

"Right."

"And there's the five of you, with you as bait."

Torrak winced. When said straight-forward like that, the situation seemed pretty ridiculous. "That sounds about right."

"Well then it looks like today is your lucky day."

Torrak blinked in surprise. "What do you mean?"

"There's something you don't know. This Commander Xiven hired some heavy muscle to help him."

"What muscle?"

"A woman named Exarth and over half a dozen of her top battle cruisers."

"I've heard of Exarth," Faan chimed in. "But only as a rumor."

Opute's eyes narrowed. "I've had enough...experiences with her to think she's real. And lucky for you guys, I happened to intercept her ships. You are standing on the main vessel of the fleet she sent to meet up with Xiven."

"Why didn't you tell us she was helping the Aleet Army?" Kalil asked.

"I didn't know."

Kalil raised his eyebrows. "Then why did you attack her fleet?"

Opute turned and looked at Torrak. "Exarth put the hit out on Lang."

Torrak's whole body tensed. "So his death is settled?" he asked.

Opute growled. "Not yet. Exarth wasn't with her fleet or I would have introduced you to her corpse." He paused in his regret. "But I have a runner-up prize. Do you remember the disk those two men were looking for in Lang's store?"

"You decrypted it?"

Opute nodded. "It had a list of coordinates and dates. The coordinates are planets and the first date on the list is tomorrow. Want to take a guess as to which planet came in first on the list?"

"Sintaur," Torrak answered.

"Right as usual," Opute responded, while calling up the disk information from the console in front of him. A three-dimensional image flickered to life. "The more I looked at the rest of the list though, the stranger it seemed."

"How so?"

"The first planet is Sintaur, heavily populated, a good military defense system, and high up in the ranks for trading and business. But the rest of the planets..." Opute pointed them out as he scrolled down the list. "They are all small, non-influential, and minimally populated. I don't know why Exarth or the Aleet Army would have any interest in them."

Torrak's thoughts exploded like fireworks ricocheting around inside his head. His brain raced through ideas as he added together all his previous knowledge about the Aleet Army with what he had just learned. His mind analyzed the theories in microseconds, interweaving different scenarios, and finally came to the only possible conclusion.

"I've been wrong the whole time," Torrak mumbled. "Xiven's not rebuilding the Aleet Army. He's setting it up to fail."

Mirrored looks of confusion crossed their faces.

"What are you talking about?" Opute asked.

"What's the one thing the Liberator governments wouldn't want to happen again? For the Aleet Army to return with a leader who has Jacin Jaxx's powers. So why would Xiven purposefully use Daith, someone who *has* Jacin's powers, to lead his army? He would meet a ton of resistance and be constantly fighting battles."

"Then why use Daith at all?" Kali asked.

"Sintaur was one of the first planet's to establish the Liberator government. Their purpose was to remove the Aleet Army presence. After they did that, many believed they should no longer be in power. We all know a rift has occurred on multiple planets between the military division and the Liberator political party, but it's the strongest on Sintaur. So if the citizens think the Liberators are in league with the Aleet Army, they'd overthrow them, right?"

"What would make them think that?" Nuis asked.

Torrak sat. He tried to ignore the shakiness in his hands. His skin itched. His tongue felt swollen in his mouth. He was so close to figuring it all out.

"Xiven chose a large target as his first point of attack, right? So he obviously wants to make a big display of power and force. Sintaur won't be able to fight back because they won't be expecting the attack and maybe Xiven will spin it or he has a fake recorded conversation as if the Liberators are in league with or being controlled by the new and improved Aleet Army. As proof, he will show Daith, who is the daughter of Jacin Jaxx, and that she has all his powers and is controlling the governments. Once that happens, Xiven assumes the citizens will rebel against their governments and overthrow them, like the Liberators did before."

"How could he know that? Maybe the citizens wouldn't believe it."

"That's where the smaller planets come in. If I wanted to ensure a rebellion, I'd need to establish propaganda and instigate the coup. Maybe Xiven set up his own followers to take charge of the rebellion or he sent missionaries to spread rumors. Once the news gets out about the rebellion on Sintaur, other planets will begin to doubt their own governments." Torrak's breathing quickened again. He almost had it all out. A symphony playing its final notes.

"No one will pay too much attention to a couple of backwater planets, but if it spreads to five, ten, twenty planets, someone will notice. And if someone notices, they will start to ask questions and perhaps doubt their own governments, too."

"So," Faan concluded, "Daith is a prop. Xiven doesn't need her to gain control of the planet; he only needs her to demonstrate her abilities."

"Exactly. After tomorrow, there's no need to keep her around.

Or even alive. I'm sure Xiven knows he won't be able to control her forever. He will most likely kill her, or even worse, give her over to the mobs.

"And that's why Xiven can attack so soon," Torrak finished. "He doesn't *want* Daith stable. The less controlled, the better, because she will be easier to manipulate. Once he gets her to use her abilities against the planet, everyone will remember what happened under the control of the Aleet Army and join Xiven, no questions asked."

"If Xiven doesn't want to be connected with this first attack, will he even be there tomorrow?" Kalil asked.

"I'm betting he's the only one who has any control over Daith so he'll have to be there," Torrak said. "I just wish I knew why he wanted to do this."

"Does any of this change our plan?" Preeaht asked.

"No. In fact, it makes it more important that we succeed. Especially for you and Nuis," he told Preeaht. "Xiven will be counting on a lack of defense, so you two will have to make sure Sintaur fights back."

"Add my new ships," Opute said, "and Xiven will definitely have his hands full."

Torrak looked at him with surprise. "You're going to help us?"

Opute shrugged. "If it gets me closer to Exarth, I'd take on Jacin Jaxx himself."

Torrak nodded. "Another blow they won't be expecting. Xiven doesn't know you intercepted Exarth's fleet. But make sure during the fight you keep an eye out for our escape craft. I don't want you to blow us up in your enthusiasm." Torrak said with a look of gratitude. He knew having Opute there would help cut down on casualties, and hopefully force the Aleet Army to withdraw more quickly.

"No problem. I'll be watching."

Now that he'd figured everything out, Torrak's brain reset back on a fixed path, with knife-like direction. It felt good to have his doubt gone. He'd been worried that out of the whole group, he'd been the only one not prepared for what lay ahead.

But now, Torrak was ready to fight a war.

And win it.

CHAPTER 36

TREY ENTERED HIS office after he left Daith's quarters. Things were going better than he hoped, although he still wondered why he hadn't heard from Exarth that the monetary exchange went well. Even if she did double-cross him and didn't show up at Sintaur, he and his crew would still do fine. Sintaur would be fighting blind, but the larger the assault, the more terrifying it would be to the civilians. And he knew it would get great media coverage because Trey had his own planted citizens ready to tip off the news crews. Still, he would like to know...

Trey contacted the bridge. "What is the status on Exarth's fleet and her progress to Sintaur?"

"Exarth and her reinforcements have not yet entered this area. We are continuing passive scans, but are running silent so we aren't detected by Sintaur's satellite security system."

"Very well. Alert me when her ships come into range."

"Yes, Commander."

Trey paced his office. Daith still needed a stronger push against the Controllers. He didn't like that she shifted the blame of Dru's death onto herself. He knew she'd help them fight, but that wasn't the point.

He needed her to want the Controllers to die.

His door chimes rang. "Enter."

Lieutenant Koye came in, growling. "Commander, I believe the assassination attempt on Torrak Spirtz failed."

Trey's jaw muscles hardened like rocks. "What?"

"The most recent report we received from Kircla on the *Shadow* stated she had successfully tracked Torrak Spirtz's ship and would engage it. No communiqué since."

Trey immediately sent out a transmission to Kircla's ship. No response.

Trey cursed. "This can't be. Torrak Spirtz's records indicate he had no contacts in this sector and no flight combat experience. He could not have fought off and defeated the *Shadow*."

"The tracking device is still attached to the hull. His ship is docked on Sintaur, in the city of Wolina. He is with one other, a young male named Kalil, his roommate from back on Fior. They have been speaking quite... loudly about the Aleet Army returning to Sintaur."

"Send a team down immediately and retrieve them both—alive. Do it personally, Lieutenant. I want them in a holding cell on this ship today. If they made it this far, they may have told others what they know. We will need them to be questioned so do not damage them. Understood?"

"Yes, Commander." Koye hesitated.

"Was there something else?"

"I took the liberty of sending one of our ground-crew to check out the docked ship. She saw a total of five passengers: three males including Torrak and two females, one a feline species and the other a Re'Ris who disappeared shortly after exiting the ship. The ground-crewmember ran her file: she is Faan Kaano."

Trey stroked his chin. A Re'Ris. The woman's name danced around in his head. "Faan Kaano. Why does that sound familiar?"

"Her parental guardians were large protesters of the Aleet Army back on Re'Ris. They worked for the Controllers during their initial phase."

Trey remembered. It had been one of the first times he ignored Jacin Jaxx's orders and had the protesters killed. Their species came from a planet of assassins, so a false death record was easy, under the claim they'd been targeted for assassination.

Faan could spell trouble. But Trey had a few tricks up his sleeves.

"Collect as many of them as you can, but don't waste any time on anyone if they aren't with Torrak. Get this done as quickly as possible."

"It is rumored Re'Ris have unique abilities."

"True. But they are not invulnerable. Dismissed."

"Yes, Commander." Koye left the office.

Trey's tight jaw loosened with a smirk. This couldn't have come at a better time. Daith needed to shift her guilt to anger. What better way then serving up the man he told her killed Dru?

* * *

Torrak, Kalil, and a now invisible Faan were on Sintaur. They checked into a hotel and then made their way through the capital city, circulating Torrak's name. Nuis and Preeaht split off from the group, everyone wishing the other luck.

About halfway through the night Torrak watched an overly

large, fur-covered creature enter the bar where he and Kalil sat. Two men followed shortly after, wearing blue jumpsuits like the ones the men wore when Daith had first been kidnapped.

Torrak's pulse raced. The moment had come. He nodded to Kalil and the two of them left the bar through the back exit, forcing themselves to take measured steps. He hoped his instincts were right about not being killed. Their attackers seized them right before the back passageway opened to the public. Torrak and Kalil pretended to resist. They hoped to be conscious when brought aboard the ship, to perhaps remember some of the corridors in order to find their way back out. Unfortunately, their assailants didn't agree. Torrak's last thought before a dark, curved claw swiped him across the face swirled around the hope that Faan would follow them.

* * *

Trey checked Daith's vitals through his computer—she still slept. He watched her on his vidlink, her chest rising and falling, her lips parted. A twinge of guilt bit inside his stomach. He could still stop this. He didn't have to continue. He didn't have to lose her.

Trey's thoughts were interrupted by one of his lieutenants who informed him Torrak and an associate had been detained in Holding Block A.

"Confirmed. I'm on my way." He stroked the image of Daith's sleeping body with his fingertips.

"I'm sorry, Daith. But justice means everyone must be punished. And soon everyone will be."

Trey made his way to the fifth floor and strode into the holding area. Two men occupied separate cells.

Trey approached the first cell—the shielding over the doorway crackled with electricity. He looked first at Torrak and then took a few steps to see into the other cell at his associate, who looked younger than twenty standard years old. Both wore comfortable clothes and the guards who had caught them said they were unarmed. Trey snickered at such foolishness.

"So this is the elusive Torrak Spirtz," he said, returning to the first cell. "You've led us on quite a chase. But you shouldn't have pushed your luck."

"You think so?" Torrak asked. "You have no idea who you're dealing with."

Trey smiled cruelly. "Is that so?" He nodded toward one of his guards. The guard headed toward the other prisoner's cell. He released the shield, went inside, and with a sickening crack, kicked Kalil's kneecap. Kalil howled in pain and fell to the floor, his face pinched and red.

Trey's smile faded when he realized Torrak hadn't flinched. In fact, his eyes narrowed, more determined.

"You think I wasn't expecting that?" Torrak whispered as he leaned forward. "You think I don't have my own tricks?" Torrak closed his eyes and reached out with his hands. Suddenly, a cry rang out. The guard who stood behind Trey buckled, his kneecap broken. Trey stared down, dumbfounded.

Torrak grinned. "Daith isn't the only one with powers."

Trey snapped at the guard in Kalil's cell. "Reestablish the shield and take this man to medical." He whirled back around and glared at Torrak. "I know for a fact you don't have those types of abilities. I know all about you, your time at the academy, your gift for solving puzzles. You may be an analytical genius, but you're inept like the rest of us. Which means someone else is here. Could it be—Faan Kaano?"

Torrak's grin faltered for a split second, but long enough for Trey to know he'd won.

"Yes, I know about Faan," Trey said, picking at his immaculate nails. "The ship's heat sensors were activated the moment you came aboard. I know she left right now when the guards did. I've alerted my crew to track her heat signature and bring her back here."

"If you touch her, you're dead," Torrak hissed.

Trey laughed. "Not as tough when it's a pretty woman whose body is going to be broken. I'll be back soon."

CHAPTER 37

TORRAK'S KNEES BOWED and he fell to the cold floor.

He knows. How could he know about Faan? Despair washed over him. Their escape plan would never work. Xiven had probably already captured Nuis and Preeaht on the planet. He knew the plan had been a long shot, but he really believed he would be able to save Daith.

Torrak slumped against the cell wall, exhausted and beaten. Then he heard Kalil moan.

"Oh, no. Kalil, are you all right?"

"It had to be the same knee, didn't it? The one I injured when Opute knocked me down the stairs." Kalil cursed repeatedly. "I knew they might hurt us, but why couldn't it have been you?"

"It was a test. If Xiven saw weakness when you got hurt, he would have kept hurting you until I told him everything he wanted to know. It's an effective way to get information."

A female voice filled the room. "Then I guess I'm going to be in serious trouble." Faan materialized before them.

"You're still here?" Torrak asked. "I thought you were going to check out the ship."

"Change of plan. After I saw what had happened to Kalil, I knew I had to get him out of here. Besides, I wasn't unconscious when we came on board, remember? I can lead us to the shuttles."

Torrak shook his head. "They know you're here. They're going to find your heat signature and track you down."

A mischievous grin spread across Faan's face. "Didn't I mention I can control my body temperature?"

Torrak moved his face as close to the cell's shielding as he could. "Have I told you yet how amazing you are?"

Faan smiled wider and began to remove the cell's shields.

"Wait," Torrak said. "Leave me in here, but take Kalil and continue with the plan. I still have to try to see Daith."

"What makes you think they'll bring her here?"

Torrak could feel her presence. She called out to him from somewhere in the ship. Not with words, but a pull, like a thin wire tugging at him. "She'll come. I'm sure of it."

He could see Faan swallow her protest as she released Kalil from his cell. The shield in front of him shimmered away.

"No, Faan, I'm not coming with you."

"I know." Faan moved in and kissed him softly on the lips. "Stay alive." She melted into invisibility, reestablished the shield, and the door opened.

Kalil nervously exited, stealing a look back at Torrak. "Good luck."

"You, too."

* * *

Daith's door slid open. She caught Cenjo about to ring the chimes.

"Cenjo! It's good to see you. I was heading toward Trey's office." Daith's face fell when she saw Cenjo's stoic expression. "What's wrong?"

Cenjo stepped inside, his hands laced tightly together. "I don't know if I should tell you. It may not even be true. I mean, I only heard it in passing...."

"What? What is it?"

"They've caught the man who killed Dru. And apparently his accomplice."

Daith's chest tightened. "They're here? On the ship?" Fury blossomed inside her. Daith felt warmth swell in her gut like sharp bursts of flame, instead of the slow smoldering warmth she normally felt.

"Yes. They were caught on Sintaur."

"I thought the authorities already apprehended them?"

"Apparently they were mistaken."

Daith shook with anger. "That makes sense. I dreamt about him last night. Still alive and at large this whole time. Still trying to use me. Trying to make me feel guilty I killed Dru. But he killed him." Daith's gaze fell across the datapads on her floor, the words on them written by Dru. Her heart pounded. Buzzing filled her ears. The words mocked her. The universe mocked her.

Daith strode over to the communications console. "Where is Commander Xiven?" she asked the ship.

"Commander Xiven is in his office," it responded.

Daith walked toward the door, but Cenjo didn't move. "Get out of my way. I need to see Trey."

"Daith, you're not thinking straight. Take a minute and..." Cenjo's words died on his lips. His eyes bulged and he grasped for his throat.

"Get out of my way," she repeated.

He stumbled backward and she pushed past him. She could hear him gulping for air as she unrestricted his windpipe.

Daith stopped outside Trey's office and exhaled loudly. She wanted to rush inside and demand to see these murderers. She wanted to scream at Trey for allowing Dru to have met with them in the first place. She wanted to blast the door apart with her mind.

But instead, she rang the chimes.

* * *

"Daith, you look well-rested. How are you feeling?"

"I heard you have the man who killed Dru on board."

Trey swallowed hard. He hoped to have interrogated and disposed of Torrak before Daith awoke—fed her some story about how he'd still been alive and trying to rally citizens on Sintaur. "How did you hear about that?"

"Is it true?"

"Yes. We picked him up a short while ago off the planet. He and his collaborator."

"I want to see them." Daith's green-eyed stare bore into his.

"I'm not sure that's wise," Trey said, cautiously, securing his mind-block. He couldn't risk Daith having a face-to-face with Torrak. He would tell her the truth about everything. Unless....

"Don't you understand why they chose him, Daith? He's the only one who could get to you because you knew him. He will try to trick you, using this previous relationship of yours to turn you over to his side. He'll tell you they didn't mean to kill your family or even that your family is still alive. That he never met Dru or that Dru tried to kill him first. Who knows what else? I'm worried with the state of anger you're in, you won't be able to tell the truth from his concocted stories."

Trey's desk trembled. Anger poured off Daith in waves. Even without any special abilities, Trey could feel the energy in the room.

"Torrak has deceived me for the last time," Daith said, her voice full of venom. "Even last night, in my dream. He tried to make me think I'd been responsible for Dru's death.

"I need to see him," she continued. "I know how to close off my mind. I won't hear anything he tells me. I need to see the man who..." Daith choked on the words. Her hands, resting on the desk, melted the material and sunk into it.

Trey finally understood Daith's true intentions. She didn't care about the truth. She didn't want justice.

She wanted to kill Torrak.

Trey could think of nothing better than if Daith destroyed her only link to the truth. "You can see him, but only if Lieutenant Commander Cenjo and I are present."

"That's fine."

The two of them left Trey's office after Trey ordered Cenjo to meet them outside the prisoner's holding cell. Trey held tight control over his mind barrier and facial expression, even though his insides twitched with glee.

CHAPTER 38

ABOUT A STANDARD half hour after Kalil and Faan left to see if they could sabotage the communications and sensors, Torrak saw the door to the holding area open and close on its own. A few moments later, Faan materialized.

Adrenaline drained from his body, relieved to see her okay. "Back already?"

"We have to move quickly," Faan said, racing to the cell shield controls. "Kalil and I made it to the shuttle bay on the first floor. He changed the security system and he's working on the shuttle right now. They still think they are scanning for me throughout the ship. They won't know I'm in here with you."

"What do you mean?"

"Kalil fed the ship's main computer a false loop so the ship still thinks it's looking for me, but it's actually receiving old data, which shows I'm not on the ship. He also rigged it so the sensors think he is still in his cell."

"That kid is a genius."

"No argument here," Faan said. She reached for the controls to release Torrak.

"I can't leave yet. Not without Daith."

Faan clenched her fists. "We have to leave, now. If Sintaur fights back, Xiven will see his plan is going to fail. He'll pull back. We can try again for Daith another time. Kalil may be a genius, but the search teams might find him and he doesn't know how long his computer loop will hold. Plus he can't make himself invisible, remember? We have to leave, *now*."

"Short on time or not, we won't get another chance," Torrak said. "I don't think Xiven is going to keep Daith around after he's done using her. And if I can convince her to stop, we may save thousands of lives in the process."

Faan stared into Torrak's eyes, the ice blue color of her irises narrowing as her pupils dilated. "Fine," she agreed, her voice edged with resistance. "We'll do this your way. I trust you." Faan cleared her throat. "But if I feel like anything is going wrong," she continued, "I'm going to—"

Faan stopped, shushed him, and disappeared. Less than a moment later, the door to the holding room slid open. A man Torrak didn't recognize, with slicked-back black hair and olive-toned skin entered first, followed closely by Xiven.

Daith walked in behind them.

Torrak heard the sharp hiss of his inhale. He'd actually found her.

As she approached his cell, Torrak assessed her. His stomach turned with fear. She looked thinner and paler than he remembered. Her eyes, still emerald green, stared at him, bland and almost void of life.

Torrak stood there. He didn't know what to say. All this time, trying to find her, and he had no idea how to convince her of the truth. His mind blanked. He just stood there, staring.

She spoke.

"Hello, Torrak." Simple words, but Torrak felt the electricity in them.

His mouth completely dry, Torrak rasped a hello.

Daith continued, her eyes still blank. "I don't know what you thought you would accomplish with the things you did, but I'm here to tell you, you failed. In a few standard hours, all the strategic areas on this planet will be demolished, all your military bases destroyed, and the seeds of evil planted in those governments will be gone. You will no longer be able to hurt innocent lives."

Daith leaned forward so only Torrak could hear her. Her eyes flashed with light, fast and sharp like lightning.

"You are going to die for what you did to Dru."

Daith straightened and closed her eyes.

Torrak finally found his voice. "Daith, I—"

"Someone else is in the room," she interrupted.

"Yes. Torrak's accomplice, Kalil, is in the next cell," Xiven said.

"No, that cell is empty. His friend is gone."

Xiven's face flushed with embarrassment at not having looked.

"Cenjo, go find him. Now!"

Cenjo hesitated, staring at Daith, his lips pursed. Then he turned on his heel and strode from the room.

Daith cocked her head, like a flying birna. Her left arm rose slowly, her finger pointed to the corner of the room. "It's coming from over there."

Xiven spoke. "Computer, how many bodies are there in this room?"

"There are four bodies located inside Holding Block A," the

computer answered, coolly. "Correction, there are five bodies inside Holding Block—correction, there are three bodies inside—correction...."

"Useless piece of junk," Xiven muttered.

Daith turned her head to the celling where the computer's voice issued. "Clever," she said. "They put the computer on a time loop."

Torrak stared at Daith in disbelief. How could she know that?

Xiven spoke toward the corner. "Faan, you might as well show yourself. I know it's you."

Nothing happened for a moment and then Faan shimmered into view.

Daith returned her gaze to Torrak. "Do you want to know what she thinks about you?"

"W-what?" Torrak stammered.

"This woman. She thinks someday she might grow to love you. She thinks maybe she could be happy. Did you know that?"

Torrak stood there, his heart pounding inside his chest out of fear and excitement His glance flickered between the two women. "I don't—I didn't know, I guess...."

Daith's lips stretched into a hideous grin, pulled back over her teeth. "You feel the same. It pours out of you like a waterfall. You could be truly happy with her, couldn't you? The possibility. The potential. What could be. What might be."

Daith closed her eyes. A snap rang through the air. Faan fell to the floor, her neck bent at an unnatural angle. Platinum hair fanned out around her head like an askew halo.

"NO!" Torrak cried out. Without thinking, he ran toward her, but the shield held its place and Torrak bounced back to the floor by a jolt of electricity.

"Isn't it amazing how much it hurts when you see someone you care about die? Someone you trusted? Depended on?"

Torrak forced his shaking body to stand. He held Daith's gaze as he spoke. "I don't know what they told you, but you know they've lied to you. All this? It's just an illusion. The truth is in your mind. You only have to look." Torrak resisted the urge to look at Faan's face. He could see her from the corner of his eye—her mouth hung open wide, the perfect picture of a silent scream.

Daith's jaw twitched at his words.

"Daith?" Xiven said cautiously, moving toward her.

Daith's eyes blanked again. She looked at Faan's body. "You were innocent, like Dru. It's never fair to those who are innocent, is it?" Daith turned back toward Torrak. "Now you know how it feels to see love die. Now you know what you did to me. I hope you suffer as I have suffered."

Torrak's eyes burned with tears. Daith's body blurred as she turned from him and left the room, followed by Xiven.

CHAPTER 39

"I'M GOING TO die in a utility closet," Kalil muttered.

Three standard hours had passed since Faan had left him to retrieve Torrak. They should have been back by now. Kalil knew the computer's sensors couldn't find him, but he already had one close call. He'd been inside the shuttlecraft, after he disabled its alarm system he worked on overriding its lockout protocols, when he heard voices inside the shuttle bay. Three security personnel walked through the room, checking empty containers, and looking into the other shuttles.

Kalil ducked, panicked. He reestablished the alarm system on the shuttlecraft right before he heard one of them approach. The officer called out to confirm the alarm was still intact. He walked away without looking inside.

Kalil waited, trembling for several standard minutes after he heard the shuttle bay door close before he peeked through one of the viewports. Once he confirmed they'd gone, Kalil finished his preparations and left the shuttle, resetting the alarm once again. The question became where to wait until Faan and Torrak returned.

So now he lay on the floor of a utility closet, where he had a view of the room through the tiny crack beneath the door, wedged behind some spare shuttle parts. It may have been a dumb place to hide, but there wasn't anywhere else in the room he could go, and if he left, it would only take one crewmember to see him and realize his civilian clothes, busted leg, and grimy appearance didn't belong.

Where were they? Had something happened? At this point, Kalil didn't know if he could leave even if they did arrive soon. One of his legs felt numb and completely asleep, the other on fire and swollen at the knee, and his bladder screamed at him for relief. If someone caught him he'd either fall from pain and numbness or urinate on anyone who grabbed him. Kalil laughed nervously at this thought and then sobered up when he heard someone enter the room.

"I'll check in here," the voice said. "You check the other rooms."

Kalil peeked through the crack and saw a tall man with black hair and olive skin looking around. He'd been in the prison cell room. Kalil silently hoped that for some reason this man wouldn't check in the utility closet when he heard the strangest thing.

The man called out for him. By name.

"Kalil? Are you in here? I have to talk to you."

Kalil held his breath, wondering what sort of trap this was, but then his leg twitched and banged into one of the spare parts.

The man's head swung toward the utility closet.

Another soldier stuck his head into the room. "Anything in here, Lieutenant Commander?"

The Lieutenant Commander narrowed his eyes at the closet. "No," he told the other soldier. "Nothing. But I'm going to check the shuttles anyway. Apparently the assassin's accomplice is very good with machines. I suggest you do the same to the other shuttle bay."

The soldier confirmed the order and left.

The Lieutenant Commander made his way over to the utility closet and opened the door. "We have to go, now."

Kalil swallowed the lump in his throat. "Who are you?"

"My name is Cenjo. I know you're trying to stop Commander Xiven. I'm here to help. But we need to leave."

Kalil, seeing no other choice, began to crawl out. His progress stopped short as pain bolted through his injured leg. He bit his tongue to keep from crying out.

"What's wrong?" Cenjo asked.

"Already forgotten that one of your crewmates busted my kneecap?" Kalil said through clenched teeth. "And my other leg is asleep."

"I didn't know that was going to happen." Cenjo lifted him with ease and draped one of Kalil's arms over his shoulder. Kalil's terror at how little control he had vanished when fire blossomed through his wounded leg and the pins-and-needles feeling dug into every part of his other leg that was beginning to wake up.

"You look awfully young to be a Controller," Cenjo said.

"Why does everyone care how old I am?" Kalil hissed through clenched teeth. "And I'm not a Controller, whatever that is." They made their way up a flight of stairs, Cenjo huffing toward the top, and entered a dark and empty room.

"I suppose you call yourselves the Liberators."

Kalil adjusted his body the best he could on the edge of a desk. "Liberators? Nope, doesn't ring a bell."

Cenjo crossed his arms. "Then what are you doing here? Commander Xiven said you are responsible for killing his brother, Dru."

"I haven't killed anyone. We just want to help Daith."

Cenjo's brow wrinkled. "I don't have time to check out your

story, but if you want to help Daith, maybe we are on the same side. Regardless, we have to get her away from Commander Xiven. He lied to us about his plan.

"This is my office," Cenjo continued. "You'll be safe here. I'll come back to get you."

"Wait! My companions think I'm in the shuttle bay. That's where we are supposed to meet. Granted, they were supposed to be there hours ago."

Cenjo uncrossed his arms, his shoulders dropping. "Torrak Spirtz is still in his holding cell. I assume your other companion was Faan Kaano."

"What do you mean, *was.*"

"I'm sorry to tell you this, but they located her in the holding room. I had to leave on orders to find you and wasn't there when it happened. She's dead. I can't be sure what occurred, but from the look in Daith's eyes when I left…"

Kalil sat, stunned. He knew it was possible they wouldn't make it out of here alive, but knowing that one of them actually died…

"I need to continue to pretend like I'm searching for you." Cenjo continued. "I have to admit, you've led us on quite a chase. Commander Xiven is furious."

Kalil felt very vulnerable. "Are you sure no one will find me in here?"

"In one standard hour, everything is going to begin. I'll try to stop Daith before then. Afterwards, I'll come back to get you and Torrak if I can. If he's still alive."

"Why don't you just stop Commander Xiven? If he's the problem, then once he's stopped, Daith will be fine and my friend won't be dead."

"The problem is Daith because she holds the power. Commander Xiven thinks he can control her, but I don't think he can anymore. Xiven has warped and confused her. Even if I kill him, she will still continue with the plan because she can't see anything except her pain."

Kalil wanted to protest, but to what end? He didn't know Daith. He only knew his friends were in trouble and this man could help them. And stop others from dying.

Except he knew how much Daith meant to Torrak. The way he'd spoken about her...she seemed too important to lose.

"I know it won't make sense, but give Torrak a chance to reach her first. Please. Give him the hour before everything starts. He might be able to change her mind."

Cenjo thought it over. "I'll wait as long as I can, but I'm not holding out much hope. He won't have much time to talk to her before Xiven takes her to the bridge. In one standard hour, no matter what happens, I'm going to do what I must."

Cenjo almost left when Kalil called out one last question.

Cenjo nodded toward the back of the office. "Second door."

After Cenjo ducked out, Kalil hobbled over and entered through the second door. Standing on one leg, he clumsily undid his pants.

He, and his bladder, had never been so relieved in their entire lives.

* * *

Torrak had been sitting on the cold floor of the holding cell for four standard hours. Four hours since Daith and Xiven had left the room.

Four hours since Daith had killed Faan.

Torrak sobbed and yelled until his head hurt and then turned his back, unable to look at Faan's lifeless body any longer. And in that time, several insights of truth hit him.

He knew he couldn't save Daith.

He knew he wouldn't survive.

But he also knew Xiven wasn't prepared for Sintaur to fight back, and Torrak only hoped Nuis, Preeaht, and Opute would be enough opposition.

Torrak felt the ship's engines rumble beneath him.

"Here we go."

* * *

Nuis and Preeaht met early in the morning, both completely exhausted after they spent the entire night arguing with government officials.

"How are plans with the ground troops?" Nuis asked.

"Everyone is in place, at least everyone who believed me," Preeaht answered. "Several of the smaller outlying cities won't give any support. Most of them said they didn't want to leave their industries and businesses to fight in a war we couldn't guarantee would take place." Preeaht sighed and growled. "Not that I blame them. I don't know what I would do if someone raced into my meeting room spouting about an Aleet Army resurrection and attack without any proof. I convinced four of the major cities to prepare, but only two out of the thirty-three military bases will evacuate, even though I insisted they would be targets."

Nuis rubbed his eyes. "Trust me, I understand. I spent six standard hours arguing with Sintaur's main planetary counsel to establish some kind of aerial counter-attack. Except without specific tactical knowledge, I couldn't tell them to do anything more than standard procedures. We don't have any idea what Daith will bring to the table. How can we fight against that?

"Regardless," he continued, "the council finally conceded, but only offered twenty percent of their battle fleet. They claimed most of the military was on leave and didn't want to recall any more soldiers than necessary. Still, they promised those on leave would be on standby, so if fighting did break out, they could be called onto the scene and would arrive no more than four standard hours into the fight. I doubt that will be soon enough, but it's the best we can do."

Nuis and Preeaht talked about a few more details when they heard an alarm go off, followed by an announcement. A large vessel had just entered Sintaur's atmosphere.

Nuis looked at Preeaht.

"Here we go."

* * *

Opute called out orders, rechecked statistics, and fiddled with the controls of his ship, all in an attempt to combat his impatience as he waited. All the ships in his group had been carefully instructed not to fire on the enemy vessel until he gave the order. The Aleet Army needed to believe Opute's fleet was Exarth's group coming to reinforce them.

Opute looked over everything for what seemed like the hundredth time and knew the other crewmembers must be feeling just as restless. Especially since they were a random group of mer- cenaries and smugglers thrown together with one goal—they all had been betrayed by Exarth and wanted to see her dead.

Unlike Torrak and his group who were already in on the action, Opute and his ships had nothing to do but wait the entire evening.

And night.

And most of the day.

And *nothing* felt worse than waiting on the edge of a fight.

He stood to ask for another weapons check, which would be his fifth since the previous night, when he heard one of the bridge members cry out that a ship called the *Horizon* had entered firing range of Sintaur.

"Here we go!"

CHAPTER 40

DAITH STOOD ON the bridge of the *Horizon,* her lips slightly parted, her eyes half closed, her skin tingling.

She was everything.

Channeled fury surged through her, filling her body with fiery warmth. Energy swirled inside her, connecting with everything around her.

She was the energy of the weapons, the rumble of the engines.

She could feel and sense everyone in her vicinity. She could hear every vibration in the bridge.

The ship. The crew.

Everything.

The battle consumed her. Coordinates for military installations on the planet spilled from her lips faster than the tactical team could enter them into the ship's computer and fire. A surge of satisfaction raced through her every time the ship's weapons warmed up and discharged their energy onto the planet below.

She hated everyone for messing with her mind, for invading her dreams, for controlling her life.

And she wanted everyone connected to the Controllers to die for Dru's death.

His image stuck in her mind, like a vidlink display caught in a skipping loop. She could see his face, hear his voice, feel the warmth of his fingers against hers. Even though she could see the bridge of the ship, feel Trey close by her side, and sense the destruction on the surface of Sintaur, Dru's face still hung there, superimposed between two levels of consciousness. A face she could remember with perfect clarity, but would never truly see again.

Torrak had felt her pain. Now everyone below would, too.

Daith, stretched in so many different directions, involved in so many different energies, didn't notice Cenjo until he stood right beside her. Daith turned her focus onto him. The battle held its breath.

"Did you find Torrak's associate?" Trey asked.

Cenjo ignored Trey. His gaze saw nothing but Daith. With a movement quicker than a thought, he pulled a knife from his sleeve.

"NO!" Trey screamed.

But he needn't have screamed. Cenjo's arm stopped centimeters from Daith's chest. The knife trembled with effort, but Cenjo couldn't get any closer. She had stopped him with her mind.

Daith looked at the knife and then at Cenjo. "Why?" she asked. "I thought you wanted this?"

"I *knew* it!" Trey snarled. "I knew you'd become weak. Security! Take the Lieutenant Commander to a holding cell."

The security team on the bridge hesitated.

"That's an order, soldiers. Take him, now!"

The security team pulled Cenjo back, taking the knife from his hand.

"You have to stop," Cenjo told her, struggling against the guards. "You need to know the truth. You need to know—"

Trey hit him sharply across the face. "Get this traitor out of my sight."

The whole bridge watched security drag Cenjo from the room, dazed from the blow. Daith turned to Trey, confused. "What just happened?"

Whatever Trey's answer, he didn't get to say it. An announcement of Exarth's fleet arriving cut him off.

A sinister grin spread across Trey's face. "Open communications to her fleet."

"Open, Commander."

"This is Commander Xiven. Please take care of any menial resistance they might muster up—"

A man's voice, low and rough, interrupted Trey, ringing loudly over the speaker. "Hate to disappoint, but this isn't Exarth."

"Who under the stars is that?" Trey snapped at the communications officer.

The man on the intercom continued. "Even with Jaxx's daughter, you won't win. Give it up, Xiven."

Jaxx's daughter? Daith thought.

"I will give up when every star in this galaxy blinks out of existence," Trey seethed.

"Have it your way."

The Horizon shuddered from a shot.

"Evasive maneuvers!" Trey bellowed at the pilot. He turned back toward Daith. "Can you disable those ships? I want that captain alive."

Daith nodded, but her thoughts felt unfocused.

Part of her searched out the engines of the incoming vessels, using her mental energy to disrupt them and shut them down. But part of her struggled with what had just occurred. Cenjo attacking her...another traitor who seemed loyal...and now this man saying she was Jaxx's daughter....

Time seemed to slow. She watched the pilot's eyelids take a standard minute to open and close. She heard Trey inhale for what seemed like an eternity—a bead of sweat dripped off his eyebrow and fell so leisurely Daith could have walked over and caught it.

And then a wave of displacement hit her. She felt disconnected from reality. Memories of the past few weeks raced through her mind as bits and pieces of information that had made no sense now jumped at her with perfect clarity.

I'm Jaxx's daughter.

Trey had told her he stopped her dreams to break the connection with Torrak. But Dru said her dreams were her memories trying to resurface. And the dreams she had were of being kidnapped and strapped down to a large machine with a huge, white helmet over her head.

What if Trey had really been blocking her dreams to keep her from remembering things? Then Dru's programs were only there to shape and measure her empathic and telepathic abilities. Trey and Dru were training her—seeing how far she could be pushed and what she could do—setting her up for this very day, so she could sense and destroy targets on the planet below.

I'm Jaxx's daughter.

Daith remembered how nervous Dr. Ludd had been at the suggestion her abilities were genetically linked and how both he and Dru only met one other being with the same abilities as she. And the only one both the Aleet Army and the Controllers could find with this leader's powers was her.

Maybe Dru meant to tell her the truth about her relationship to the Aleet Army's leader. Could that have been why he'd been killed? But Torrak killing him made no sense. What would he have to gain? What would anyone have to gain? And then Dru's face popped into her mind.

No. I can't see him right now.

And the image shifted to his death

No. Please. I CAN'T...

—the scorched stomach, the burning pain—

DEAL WITH THIS...

and then the vision continued.

RIGHT NOW!

Dru looked up. He saw who shot him.

It wasn't Torrak. It was Trey.

Trey killed Dru.

Because I'm Jacin Jaxx's daughter.

Trey's mind opened to her. His barriers crumbled like dry sand. She now knew the truth. Jaxx had been the leader of this army and after he died, Trey looked for his daughter to replace him. He needed her to be unstable so he could get as much power out of her as possible in a short period of time. And he did what he had to do to keep her from finding out.

He'd killed his own brother.

Daith stopped.

She stopped blinking. She stopped breathing. Her heart stopped beating.

She was dead.

But somehow she was more alive than ever.

She began to see things—the crew members, mere masses of energy radiating light and heat from their bodies, the panels of the ship were pieces of metal and she knew where they'd been forged, the oxygen in the room shimmered and she could see every atom as tiny pinpoints sparkling amongst the emptiness.

She looked out of the viewscreen. She could feel the energy from Sintaur's sun as it warmed the planet, she could hear the sound of a waterfall in a forest below, each drop of liquid hitting with the forceful sound of a drum, she could see the make-up of every being on the planet—from the hair follicles on their bodies to the crystals of salt in their tears. She felt the entire universe stretch before her, pressing on her with its power. It connected her to everything and everyone, drawing her energy into itself and exhaling its life back into her. The past and the future were at her fingertips.

She thought she could sense everything before, but this moment opened her up to ideas and shapes she had never thought possible. She saw and heard everyone's mind at once. The voices thrust down on her in a garbled accumulation of pain and joy, nonsensical yet linear, with a sound like a static hum in her head. The sound grew. It drowned out her own thoughts, consuming her mind. She melted into a puddle of feelings and emotions.

She heard everyone in her head except herself. One with them, she swayed in a musical swirl of energy beyond anything she could ever dream.

She didn't have to care anymore. She didn't have to think.

Nothing mattered.

Nothing mattered.

Nothing....

Daith...

A voice pierced the blended clutter of energy.

Daith's mind trembled with exhaustion. She was falling, being pulled under. She was....

Let it go...

Daith focused on the voice, familiar. Nearby.

Torrak.

I don't know how...

Let it all go...

A tremor rippled across her skin. She took all the energy that filled her, all the thoughts and emotions that ripped her apart, all the broken dreams, shattered souls, and moments of ecstasy that filled her and...

...she screamed.

The sound welled up inside her and coursed through her, erupting from her body. The noise made everyone on the bridge cover their ears and cower in pain. Panels exploded, doors burst open. She felt everything in her head spew through her mouth as if expelling a poison from her body. She shook, swayed, nearly fell over, but still the sound came, until the last of the universe's energy had been forced from her. The scream died slowly. Her vocal chords were raw and torn.

Daith's mind returned to the present. Only a few moments passed, but it seemed like a lifetime. She wiped her hand across her face and it came away covered with sweat and blood. She looked over at Trey, his eyes wide with concern, his lips pressed together tightly.

"Are you okay?" he asked. He watched her carefully. She knew how terrible she must look. Her hair clung to her face with static electricity, her face red and wet. "Do you want to sit for a moment?"

She trembled with fatigue and her vision blurred, but she knew she couldn't sit. Though Trey had been able to block his mind before, his thoughts were now laid open and free for her to peruse.

She felt his pain when he found Jacin's body, lifeless.

She saw the deal he made with a beautiful and terrifying woman, Exarth, skin pale as snow, eyes black like space.

She watched contempt contort his face when he fired the electro-volt weapon, killing his brother.

Killing Dru.

She knew the truth behind his lies. His illusions.

And she knew she had to get out of there. Now.

"No," she rasped, "I'm all right. Simply trying to do too many things at once."

"You should rest then," he said.

Daith shook her head. "I have to finish what I started." She smiled and opened communications to the attacking fleet. Her voice came out cracked and hoarse. "Enemy vessels. If you surrender now I promise no harm will come to you."

The man who spoke before came back on. "We're ready for whatever you can throw at us."

"Very well." Daith closed her eyes and concentrated. She made the Horizon's sensors believe the ships had been disabled. Less than a standard minute later she turned to Trey. "All their engines have been disabled. They are floating dead in space."

Trey looked at the pilot who nodded in agreement. "Sensors register all other ships have stopped moving."

"Great. Let's target their lead vessel and—"

"Incoming fire!" the pilot called out. "Their weapons are still active!"

"Evasive—" But Trey didn't get to finish his order. The ship rocked underneath him. "Render them weaponless!"

Daith sent a message directly to the mind of the captain of the oncoming fleet. Crude, but she made it clear he needed to stand down, that the Horizon surrendered. "Already done," Daith said in a smooth voice. She found her way out. "The hit we sustained did critical damage, but I can fix it," she reassured him. "I have to go to engineering and look at it. I used too much power against the ships."

"Fine," Trey said, dismissing her. "We'll finish off this broken fleet when you finish the repairs." Trey placed his hand on her shoulder. "You've done well. Dru would be proud."

Rage flared up like flames. How *dare* he say Dru's name! She almost snapped Trey's neck with her mind, but a wave of fear hit her. If she killed Trey, his crew would use their hand-held weapons against her and she didn't think she had enough energy left to stop them all. Her vision blurred even more and she had to press her hands together to keep them from shaking. She couldn't hear anyone's thoughts anymore. All she felt were vague emotions.

No, she had to escape.

Daith left the bridge and instead of heading down toward engineering, she made her way up to the holding cells. She walked through the door and approached the guards on duty.

"I'm sorry," she told them.

Looks of confusion passed over their faces.

She closed her eyes and concentrated. Using her mind, she constricted their windpipes. She heard them both gasp for breath and felt their heartbeats slow. When she sensed they'd lost consciousness, she released their airways and heard the rush of air fill their lungs as their bodies began to work again, unconscious but alive.

Daith opened her eyes and blinked several times, hoping her cloudy vision would clear. When it didn't, she cursed softly, headed for the controls, and turned off the electric energy fields that blocked the cells. She watched Cenjo and Torrak each step out, their faces almost identical in bewilderment.

"We don't have much time." She motioned for them to follow her. "Where is your associate?" she asked Torrak.

"I don't know...what's going on here?"

Daith shook her head. "There is no time to explain. We need to leave."

Cenjo stepped up. "Kalil is in my office."

Daith's forehead wrinkled. "*Your* office?"

He smiled. "Like you said, there's no time to explain. Let's go."

"Wait," Torrak called out. He rushed over to Faan's body and, although everyone knew the result, he checked for a pulse. He looked up at Daith, his eyes ablaze. "We can't leave her here." Torrak lifted her to her knees and with Cenjo's help, draped her between them.

Daith turned to Cenjo, her words slurred. "I'll meet you in the shuttle bay. I'll go and get Kalil and be there soon."

"You can't move him by yourself with his bad knee," Cenjo said, grabbing her by the arm. "You can barely stand on your own."

Daith pushed away his help. "I won't need to carry him. Trust me. You have to start up the shuttle."

The three of them left the holding cells, with Torrak and Cenjo carrying Faan, and Daith headed toward Cenjo's office, her skin clammy, her mouth dry. She entered the room and found a young man with a mop of curly red hair, his leg propped up on Cenjo's desk, the knee swollen and purple.

His body clenched as she approached.

Daith offered him the most reassuring smile she could. "I'm not here to hurt you. I'm here to get you off this ship. But first, let me look at that leg."

Daith concentrated on his knee. Her mind screamed in agony while she forced it to work. She redistributed the blood flow, cooled down the swollen tissue, and popped the kneecap back into place. It wasn't perfect, but good enough for him to walk on. Daith wiped at her bloody nose and told him they had to hurry. Along the way, Kalil asked Daith about everyone else.

"Cenjo and Torrak will meet us in the shuttle bay. They are carrying Faan."

"So it's true. She's dead."

Guilt hit her in a wave. She stumbled, trying to block the anger and confusion that emanated from Kalil. "I'm sorry. You can hate me later."

The two of them found Cenjo and Torrak waiting outside the

shuttle.

"I can cripple the ship," she said, "but if we don't leave soon, I won't have the energy left to do it." Daith's head pulsed in pain and blood dripped from her ears. Nearly blind she stumbled, gripping the edge of the doorway.

Kalil and Torrak made their way onto the shuttle. Cenjo hesitated, right outside the door.

"What about Xiven?" he asked. "Somebody needs to make sure he doesn't continue to fight."

Daith sighed. "We won't have to worry about that."

"Why not?"

"Because he's here."

Cenjo spun around to find Trey, an electric-volt weapon in his hand. A dozen crewmembers stood behind him.

"Going so soon?" he asked.

Daith nearly collapsed. She'd been so close. "Trey, it's over. I know everything."

Trey smirked. "And you played your part perfectly. The citizens below saw a vidlink recording of you on the bridge and know you're behind this attack. My pretty little puppet performed well. And now, you aren't needed anymore."

Daith felt Cenjo tense beside her. She put her hand gently on his arm.

"Ah, yes. I haven't forgotten about you, Lieutenant Commander." Trey's voice dripped with disgust. "Back on her side after trying to kill her? How can she believe you now?"

"You're one to talk. Did you start planning the takeover of the Aleet Army before or after Jaxx's death?" Cenjo snapped.

Trey's face darkened. "Jaxx was brilliant, but a fool. He could've fixed everything. But he couldn't handle it. That's why I had to take over. I knew I could succeed where he failed."

Something clicked inside Daith's head. She took a step forward, her legs unsteady. "Was it hard for you to see Jaxx fail?"

Trey looked at her. "What?"

"He didn't live up to what you wanted him to be. He broke like anyone one else would have. But in your eyes, he wasn't supposed to. He should have fixed everything, like he did on your planet."

Trey scoffed at her. "You don't know what you're talking about. You don't remember any of that."

"No, but I don't need to." Daith kept talking to keep him distracted. She probed ever so gently into his mind. With emotions and adrenaline so high, his thoughts came to her easily. "What did it feel like to have this icon of yours let you down? After all the work you put into this cause, *his* cause, and then to have Jaxx give up, leaving you all as targets, not taking responsibility for his actions?"

Trey's breathing quickened.

"Or maybe it's because you blame yourself for his death?" Daith continued. "That you couldn't do more to help him. That he wouldn't let you help him."

Trey tried to laugh, but it sounded forced. The crewmembers around him shifted uneasily.

"You had nightmares about it. For years."

Trey's smile faded.

Daith pressed on. "You saw him decide to give up on his life, his mission. *Your* mission."

Trey's jaw clenched. "Get out of my head." She felt him try to reestablish his block, but it wouldn't hold.

One of the guards looked at Trey. "Commander?"

Trey threw the guard a look that silenced him instantly. "Shut your mouth," he said to Daith, his weapon shaking. "You don't know anything about what happened to me."

Daith took another step forward. "You keep telling yourself that in war you have to sacrifice the few to save the many. But the few became real faces, those you knew." Daith began to pull the names from his mind. "Your mother—"

Trey fired, but his weapon hissed in a display of blue sparks before powering down. She had shorted it out with her mind.

Beads of sweat popped up all over Trey's face.

"...Jaxx, Riel, Dru," Daith continued. "I'll bet no one knows you sometimes forget whole parts of the day. I bet none of your guards know you can't sleep more than three standard hours a night because of your nightmares. You have no friends. You have no family. You have no one who knows your deepest darkest...

...secret."

Trey's eyes widened in terror. "Don't!"

But Daith found the memory. "No one knows the guards who beat and raped your mother did it to you first. And she had to watch."

No one moved.

Trey began to shake and the crewmembers around him all looked uncomfortable, tightening the grip on their weapons.

"How dare you," he seethed. "How dare you judge me and my actions? I wanted to bring peace. I wanted to do what your pathetic father couldn't do, didn't have the GUTS to do!"

"You don't know what I went through," he continued, spittle forming in the corner of his mouth. "You can't imagine what it's like for a twelve-year-old to go through what I went through. And Jaxx didn't punish those men! He changed their thoughts—like that was good enough? But what about their victims? Didn't they deserve justice? Didn't my mother? Didn't I?

"It would have been for the best!" Trey screamed. "Everyone would have been safer and happier and no one would ever have to go through what I did. EVER!"

Trey lunged toward Daith, startling one of the edgy guards.

The whole room stood, frozen, as Trey looked downward, a large smoldering hole in his chest. The smell of burnt flesh filled the space.

"I didn't mean to!" the guard exclaimed, dropping the weapon. "It just went off!" He bolted from the room.

"What...?" Trey's gaze returned to Daith, his eyes glassy.

He crumbled to his knees. Daith rushed over to him, sliding onto the floor.

"I can save you." The words came from her lips without her knowing why. She hated this man. He'd stolen her past, her life, her soul. He killed Dru. He used her.

But something inside her ached. He'd been through so much pain, so much terror. A desire to help him, fix him, save him blotted out everything else inside her.

Because if he could be saved, after all the horrible things he did, then maybe so could she.

Daith prepared herself to repair his wound, but the power wouldn't come. She could barely see anymore. Her concentration wouldn't hold. She couldn't even feel his fingers on her hands.

Trey shook his head.

"Don't save me," he gasped. *I want the pain to stop.* She heard his words in her head.

Daith wanted to object, but she didn't know what to say.

One of the guards called for Doctor Milastow, but everyone knew she would arrive too late.

Trey turned his head and spat out a glob of blood. *Don't let the men who hurt me get away with it... don't let them hurt me anymore.* He brushed her face with his bloody hand. *Dru loved you, you know.* A spastic cough forced its way through his lips.

Daith swallowed, finding it hard due to the lump in her throat.

His eyes fluttered. *I'm sorry. Tell my mother, I'm sor—*

Trey's hand dropped from her face.

CHAPTER 41

THREE STANDARD HOURS had passed since Cenjo issued an unconditional surrender and the *Horizon* docked on Sintaur.

Three hours since Daith, Torrak, Kalil, and Cenjo had all been rushed to separate hotel rooms under heavy guard to await trial.

Three hours since Trey's death.

Daith had done nothing but lay on the hotel bed and stare at the ceiling. She felt totally alone. Her body began to repair itself as she lay—her sight returned, her head stopped pounding, and her balance came back.

But she didn't care.

Soon she would stand trial for the destruction of hundreds of homes and buildings, irreparable damage to an entire fleet of ships, and the deaths of thousands of innocent civilians. She would see Torrak, the only real connection she had to her past. How could she face him after she'd killed Faan? And she continually battled the urge to tap into the energy connection she felt on the bridge. It pressed on the edges of her mind, tempting her with power and insight, but her fear overpowered the urge.

She would never access her abilities again.

Daith hoped they locked her away for the rest of her life. She didn't deserve to be free after what she'd done. She wanted to curl up in a windowless room and rot for eternity, content only because she knew she would never be able to hurt anyone again.

A hard rap at the door interrupted her thoughts. Daith sat up slowly, stiff from tension, and told whoever to come in. A guard entered, followed by a governmental official.

"My humblest greetings, Miss Tocc," the Sintaurian said with a low bow. "I'm sorry I hadn't come earlier to greet you. I've been a bit busy, as you can imagine." The official walked toward the bed. "My name is Appointed Official Losa, but you may call me Losa. I hope the accommodations suit you?"

"They're fine."

"Good. If there is anything you need, please don't hesitate to ask. You have, I assume, been told you are to stand trial tomorrow morning?"

Daith nodded.

"Very good. I believe Judge Illu is presiding over the case. She has been informed of the situation and instructed to expedite the trial. It will, of course, *not* be vidlinked for the public, so there is no need to worry about that. But it should be over with quite painlessly, I imagine, and you'll be free to be on your way."

Daith's eyebrows furrowed. "I don't understand."

Losa wrung his hands. "I'm sorry. I hope I didn't offend you. Were you not briefed on the trial tomorrow?"

"Not specifically."

"Oh, my," Losa said. He took a seat next to her on the bed and patted her hand. "Well, you see, we understand what happened so you won't be convicted of anything. The trial is a formality," he explained, talking to her as if she were a child. "We know the vidlink broadcasts were fakes. We know you couldn't have done those things and you were framed by this Commander Xither, or Xiven was it? No matter. He is dead and he is the guilty party." Losa frowned at Daith's surprised expression. "I'm terribly sorry. Have I offended you somehow?"

"I don't mean to contradict you, Losa, but you are gravely mistaken. I did do all those things. That image of me on the broadcasts was true."

Losa chuckled and waved away her words. "Please, my dear, there is no possible way you could have done those things."

Daith stared at him in disbelief. Didn't he realize her power? Didn't he know how dangerous she was?

"The guilty party simply made you think you were doing those things," Losa continued. "Xither confused you and manipulated you to think—"

Losa and his guard smashed against the wall, pinned. The bed spun beneath Daith while she hovered half a meter above. The lights flickered and the windows imploded, showering the room with shards of glass. After a few moments, the bed slammed back down and Losa and his guard were released, falling ungracefully onto the carpet.

"Do you still think it wasn't me?" she asked.

Losa and the guard fled the room, locking the door behind them.

Daith pressed her fists into her eyes. Why had she done that? She'd been so angry at them for not making her take responsibility for her own actions, for dismissing her like some sort of naïve child, and she wanted to prove he couldn't trust her and then she...

...lost control. Again.

A string of thoughts floated through her mind.

I told myself I'd never use those abilities again, and look what already happened.

It will never end for me, will it?

I will never be free from these...these curses.

They will always control me.

I'm a danger to everyone around me.

I should just die.

The next morning, Daith's eyes opened to the sound of loud knocking on her door. She sat up slowly, rubbing her head. She didn't remember falling asleep.

"Come in," she said. Four guards entered, heavily armed, their weapons trained on her.

She sighed at how little they knew the uselessness of their weapons.

"We are here to escort you to your trial," one of the guards said.

They left the hotel and transported Daith to the courthouse. When they arrived, they stood outside the doors to the trial room. As they waited, Daith turned her head and followed the tall black and grey marbled pillars on either side of the polished silver doors. The pillars stretched all the way to the ceiling and flared out like crowns of flower petals at the top.

The guard next to her cleared his throat and signaled for Daith to enter. She walked into a huge room with a high, curved ceiling, the same silver as the doors. The tables in the room were all the same black and grey marble as the pillars, with the exception of the crimson judges' table, accompanied by a brilliantly white throne-like chair.

An empty room, except for a young woman who sat at one of the tables toward the front. Her short, spiked, copper hair stood out against her dark skin. She stood and waved Daith over.

"Good morning, Miss Tocc. My name is Ufi Ro. I normally work in the treasury department, but they couldn't locate other counsel on such short notice. I'll be handling your case today."

Ufi's feelings of purity and willingness to help poured from her, grating on the edge of Daith's mind.

The door to the left of the judge's table opened and a large bundle consisting of a coat and several scarves entered the room. The shape shimmied out of the over-garments and a heavy-set woman wrapped in a satiny pink dress plopped down in the white chair.

"Good morning, Miss Ro. Good morning, Miss Tocc. Please, be seated." The woman's words came crisp and businesslike. She leaned her pudgy arms onto the table as Ufi Ro stood.

"Judge Illu," Ufi Ro began, "I would like to begin by—"

"Miss Ro, please sit down," Judge Illu told her, her voice soft. Ufi Ro snapped her mouth shut mid-word and sat down. "Thank you." Judge Illu shifted her gaze to Daith, her eyes narrowing as if taking in every detail. She then looked back at Ufi Ro. "I hope I didn't offend you Miss Ro, but there have been some changes you are not aware of. We held a briefing this morning concerning the...event that took place yesterday in Miss Tocc's hotel room."

Ufi Ro shot up. "I object to this. I wasn't informed—"

"Sit down, Miss Ro," Judge Illu snapped, each word echoing in the large room. The judge immediately softened her voice. "My apologies, of course. Did not mean to offend.

"You were not informed," Judge Illu continued, "because this case is unlike any other that has occurred on Sintaur. Appointed Official Losa and the other city delegates want to dismiss this trial completely and escort Miss Tocc off the planet, permanently."

Ufi Ro started to stand, but the look on Judge Illu's face made her sit back down.

"However," Judge Illu went on, "I told them to stop running from something they fear."

Daith hadn't expected the judge to say this. She wanted to

explain how they *should* fear her, but before she could choose the right words, Judge Illu leaned over the table, her second chin almost touching the crimson stone, and spoke to her directly.

"I am going to ask you a few questions, Miss Tocc. You can lie, cheat, or manipulate me if you wish. If that is what you plan to do, say so right now, leave my courtroom, and get off my planet. I will not waste my time or anyone else's. I am interested in the truth, Miss Tocc, nothing more, nothing less."

Daith wanted to shrink down in her chair away from Judge Illu's piercing gaze. She wanted to run out of the courtroom and take the judge's offer to leave the planet. And yet something stirred in her that made her want to stay.

"I will answer truthfully."

"First question," the judge began, her tone pensive. "Did you cause all the damage and casualties shown on the vidlink broadcast?"

"Yes."

"Second question. Did you do these things knowingly and willingly, regardless of any mental or emotional manipulation that may have occurred?"

Daith swallowed. "Yes."

Judge Illu slid her hands under her chin. "Then answer me one more question, Miss Tocc, because what I have been told does not fit with your previous answers. You were winning the battle. You had the power to stop our ships and destroy our cities. But that isn't what happened. You confused your own ship's sensors to believe the enemy fleet had been disabled. You sent a cease-fire and surrender to that same enemy fleet. These two acts caused the battle to end. And from what I've been told by witnesses, you risked your own life to retrieve three prisoners and a crewmate. You also confronted the man in charge of this entire operation and even after his betrayal, you offered to help save him from dying.

"So my question, Miss Tocc, is this: why?"

Tears rimmed Daith's eyes and her vision of the judge blurred into a mixture of white, pink, and red. "It doesn't matter."

"That doesn't answer my question."

"Don't you see? It doesn't matter what I did afterwards. Look at what happened." Daith angrily pushed the tears from her eyes. "I killed your families. I demolished your homes. I did it all and I enjoyed every moment of it. Fun, even. Definitely easy. And I could do it again at any moment. Whenever I want. Whenever *it* wants." The doors burst open and a blast of wind swept through the courtroom. Ufi Ro's papers blew out from under her hands and Judge Illu's coat and scarves swirled above their heads. The wind raged, moving the chairs around the court—they squealed and scraped against the ground. Ufi Ro ran screaming from the room.

"This right now? This is *nothing*." Daith continued, motioning around her. "I'm not even trying. Do you understand that? Do you?"

Judge Illu gripped the edges of the desk. Her stare remained on Daith, ignoring the mayhem around her. With a huge intake of breath, Judge Illu opened her mouth as wide as she could.

"ANSWER MY QUESTION!" she roared.

"I CAN'T!"

The wind stopped. The papers settled. The scarves floated softly to the floor.

Daith cried into her hands. Tears of shame wetted her face. "What does it matter what I did after? How can I live with what I've done?"

"You have presented me with a difficult case, most likely the hardest one I've ever had to pass judgment on, but I have come to a decision." The judge paused. "I knew your father."

Daith felt like she'd been slapped. She looked up. "You *what?*"

"Oh yes. It's been...well it's been fourteen years already. I met

261

him when he came to Sintaur to help with negotiations to end the civil war plaguing our planet. He only stayed here for about a month, but we spent quite a bit of time together."

"I believe what I learned from him applies to you. He was a fairly quiet man, always in his own mind, trying to piece things together by himself. Incredibly brilliant, driven, and ambitious, but very caring, too.

"Your abilities, they are like the colors of life. Some everyone can see, some only certain individuals can see, and some are hidden among all the other ones. Your father tapped into those hidden ones and saw more than anyone could, but instead of embracing them, he tried to force them into something he could control. He wanted to help everyone. He wanted to fix everything. But it's not possible. There are too many differences. Joy for one brings sorrow to another. And from that sorrow might blossom a passion that creates joy."

"What does this has to do with me?"

"You saw all the colors too, didn't you? That's why you stopped the war. That's why you saved those with you on the ship. That's why you still wanted to save the dying commander. You saw everything."

Daith thought about her experience on the bridge, how she felt so much around her, how she sensed everything and everyone. How all her experiences before paled in comparison to the new connection she achieved.

"But I can't control it," Daith said.

"Of course not," Judge Illu said, matter-of-factly. "Whoever said it could be controlled?"

"It makes me a danger to others."

"As a judge, I've seen the worst of many individuals. Everyone has the potential to harm someone else or help. You face those same decisions only with larger consequences. You chose to harm the citizens of this planet. You chose to burn down our facilities. But unlike many who enter my courtroom, you were able to escape from your own prison. You saw past the anger and despair and opened your mind to every possibility. And once you saw everything, you made the choice to stop."

Judge Illu stood, her hefty bosom swelling. "Here is my ruling. Your punishment is to live with what has happened and what you have done for the rest of your life and to share what you've experienced with others. It will not be easy—it will be painful and unbearable at times, but you will do it. It will remind you of your strengths and weaknesses. It will be a guide to you so you can be a guide for others. You lived through something no one else has. You are forever changed. Share those experiences. Be one with your abilities. Do not control them, do not force them, do not push them. They are a part of you and will always be there. Always."

CHAPTER 42

OPUTE HAD BEEN packed and ready to leave Sintaur for four standard days. Meaning he was wearing his clothes and twirling the password encrypted datachip he took from Lang's killer.

Opute spent the time in his hotel room doing nothing but watching vidlink broadcasts. Hour after hour the media showed shots of Daith's terrifying scene from the bridge on the *Horizon*, pictures of buildings on the planet's surface burned to the ground, and sob stories from one citizen after another about loved ones they lost.

And then in the blink of an eye, the broadcasts changed.

Now the pictures showed rebuilding efforts by the government, clips from Judge Illu who had presided over all the trials and found Daith and her associates free of guilt, and shots of the new "heroes", including Torrak, Kalil, Nuis and Preeaht.

Opute had declined an interview.

Opute wanted to get back to his own life. He might not have

settled things with Exarth, but he helped avert a war, owned six battle cruisers, and received a comfortable sum of money from Sintaur's government.

Not bad for a few weeks work.

He was waiting for Torrak to finish up with some publicity event. Opute offered to take Torrak and everyone else back to their respective homes, since their ship had been wrecked beyond repair.

With that thought, he heard a knock at his door.

"Think and it will happen," Opute mumbled under his breath. "Door's open," he called out.

Opute heard the door creak, but to his surprise, it wasn't Torrak. It was Daith.

She looked into the room, her vibrant green eyes wide with curiosity.

"I bet you're ready to get off this planet," she said.

"You have no idea."

"You'd be surprised." Daith walked into the room, her steps soft on the plush carpet. "Probably weren't expecting me," she said as she sat in a chair next to the bed. Her hands cupped her knees, her feet raised on tiptoe.

Opute arched an eyebrow. "Not really."

"I'll get straight to the point then. I wanted to meet you."

"Me? Why?"

"You probably don't realize this, but you helped tip the scales during the battle. I know you felt very confident about your odds— what with the surprise attack and your assortment of new battle cruisers—but you would not have won."

"You say that now, but who knows how it would've turned out."

Daith smiled softly, her eyes dark. "I do. I would have destroyed your ships without a second thought."

She may be right, but his pride made him think that *maybe* he could've had a chance.

"So what did I do that changed things so much?"

"You told me I was Jacin Jaxx's daughter."

Opute waited a moment. "That's it?" he asked.

"That's it."

"No offense, but so what?"

"While on the *Horizon*, Trey—Commander Xiven—went to great lengths to keep that piece of information from me. Without it, his story of who I was, why I had the abilities I did, and the reasons why I should help him all made sense. However, that phrase revealed so much. It opened my mind, allowed me to see past the lies to the truth, and let me make my own choice, a *different* choice. My mind expanded into the universe in ways I don't understand—pulled into something both beautiful and frightening at the same time."

"You almost didn't come back either," said a voice from the doorway.

Opute turned and saw Torrak looking through the open door.

"I didn't mean to interrupt," Torrak said.

"I was leaving soon anyway," Daith replied, rising from her chair.

"No," Opute chimed in, motioning for Daith to stay seated, "I'm going to leave. I think you two need to talk." Opute grabbed Torrak by the arm and pulled him into the room. "This guy is the one who came for you. I joined up for my own personal reasons and *by mistake* said the thing that kept you from killing everyone."

"You mean you didn't sign on to rescue the damsel in distress?" Daith asked, a sparkle in her eye.

"Me? Not in a million. I only wanted Exarth."

"Exarth?" Daith asked.

"She's responsible for our friend's death," he said, motioning to Torrak. "That's what got me involved in the first place." Opute shook his head. "Not that it matters. I don't think she really exists. I've searched for her a long time."

"From what I've seen, she might be worth the search. She's quite beautiful."

"I wouldn't know," Opute said with a snort. "All I know is—wait—*what*?"

"You've seen Exarth?" Torrak asked.

"I saw a flash of her in Trey's memories. Moon-white skin, long ebony hair—really very lovely."

"She's...she's real?" Opute sank down onto the bed. "I can't believe it. After all these years—and so much effort—I really thought she couldn't be real—and I gave up...."

Daith walked over to the bed and put her hand on his shoulder. A wave of heat spread from her fingertips through his body, calming him.

"You've been hurt by Exarth, more than once."

Opute clenched his teeth. "You don't know the half of it."

"I may know more than you think. But please remember revenge can never bring back the ones you love. Trust me, I know." Daith's gaze flitted for a moment toward Torrak.

"Exarth deserves to die for what she's taken away from me."

"Maybe. But sometimes things aren't always what they seem."

The warmth subsided in his body and Daith sat again.

"I guess I'll see you on the ship," Opute told Torrak, lost in thought.

"Be there soon," Torrak replied.

After Opute left, Torrak turned to Daith. He had no idea where to start. What should he say? I'm glad you're okay? Are you coming with us? I hate you for killing Faan?

Luckily for him, Daith broke the silence.

"I don't really know where to start."

"That's okay. I don't either."

Daith picked at her nails for a moment before taking a long breath. "I'm sorry...I mean, for what I did to Faan."

"No small talk, huh?"

"Guess not."

Torrak paused. His chest ached. "What are you going to do now?"

"I don't know. I thought I'd start by trying to reconcile with who I've heard is my closest friend."

Torrak felt torn. He'd come all this way to find her, to help her, to *save* her, and she destroyed someone in his life that could have meant everything to him. He wanted to tell her they'd still stay friends, that he forgave her and knew it wasn't really her who had done it, but he couldn't. Maybe it still hurt too much. Maybe it would be better with time. But for the moment....

"Look, Daith," he began, "you're welcome to catch a ride with Opute and us back to Fior and see your sister, Valendra—although her memory of you may not be the best..." Torrak rubbed his hand across his forehead. "This is a mess, isn't it?"

"I suppose it is."

The two of them fell quiet.

Daith spoke. "I guess I just wanted to say thank you for helping me when I was on the bridge. The sensations I felt...."

"I saw some of it."

Daith's fingers tightened on her lap. "You did?"

"Yes. In the holding cell I could see the bridge. It was...in my head, but it wasn't. Like my mind opened to yours and you could see everything inside, but it didn't feel like a violation."

"That's when you told me to 'let it go'."

"Yes. I could feel you expanding with energy. It seemed too much for you to handle. But I didn't want to at first. I was so angry at you."

Daith's eyes rimmed with tears. "I'm really sorry."

Torrak shifted uncomfortably on the bed. "I know. But I don't know if that changes anything."

"Yeah. I also think I'm not ready to go back to Fior yet," Daith said abruptly.

Torrak looked at her, surprised. "Don't you want to get back to your life?"

"It doesn't feel like my life anymore. What I've been through— I'm different now. And what I've done.... There are too many lives I destroyed. I don't know how to live with that. I don't know how to fix it."

"I don't think you can." Torrak didn't want to sound so harsh, but he couldn't help it. His whole body hated Daith right now, even though he cared so much about her. She was right. Everything had changed. And she knew that, too.

Kalil's head peeked through the open door. "You ready to...oh."

Daith stood. "Guess this is goodbye."

Torrak swallowed, not wanting things to end sourly. "Look me up when you come back to Fior."

Daith gave a sad smile. "Yeah...sure..."

EPILOGUE

DAITH STARED OUT the window. She looked through the thickened moisture-protected glass and marveled at what she saw. Lush and diverse plant life blanketed the scene, from the completely clear plaga plant, over four meters tall with translucent sacks, which hung off its limbs, to a complete contrast seen in the morta bush, with a black oily coating on its leaves to keep out the excessive rainfall. Scents filled the entire atmosphere, stimulating her nose and causing her skin to tingle.

"What was I thinking?" Daith said. "I can't do this. What am I supposed to say to them? What would *you* say if you were me?" Daith's gaze shifted from the outside view to Cenjo. He sat on the floor, numerous datapads around him.

"How am I supposed to know?" he answered. "I can't keep my own thoughts together, much less pretend I'm you. Counselor Imah doesn't seem to realize that although thought-transference is instantaneous for telepaths, writing takes time." Cenjo stretched out his legs and scratched at the stubble on his face. Two years had passed since that fateful day on Sintaur and although he sometimes said it itched like crazy, he always had some sort of facial hair. Daith thought he did it to separate himself from the clean-shaven man he'd been during his time with the Aleet Army.

"And the types of things he wants?" Cenjo continued. "I mean he expects me to write down feelings and emotions as if I could touch them. It's like explaining colors to someone who's blind!"

Daith smiled. The two of them came to Tela about a year ago and their lives finally felt like they had direction. After Sintaur, Daith felt lost. She stayed for a while on the planet, but eventually she went back to Fior. Torrak and Kalil, with Preeaht moving into his room with him, began their lives again, both reentering the Academy, but Daith felt stuck. Her abilities far surpassed any professor at the Academy, she was too well-known for anyone to hire her, and the media enjoyed broadcasting her life story whenever anyone caught a glimpse of her going to buy food for the week or visiting her sister.

That situation had been the hardest of all for Daith. Valendra couldn't remember anything about having a sister and no amount of memory retrieval or therapeutic work made a difference. Every time Daith visited, she had to start all over again. Valendra's memory cells had been destroyed by the memory erasing serum she'd been given and any new memories were erased right away. And though she and Daith tried to reconnect, a gap remained between them, a space that couldn't be filled. She felt like she'd lost her family all over again.

Daith sunk into a deep depression. Yes, Torrak and Kalil visited her when they could, and her friendship with Torrak grew, but Faan's death always hovered over her, expanding the rift between them. Daith couldn't forgive herself for what she did and the guilt and shame of it intensified every time she saw him. She missed Cenjo and

Dr. Ludd. And of course, she still missed Dru.

Daith came to realize she couldn't return to her old life on Fior. She lived for a year in a shadow of what her life once had been and she didn't know how to get out of it.

The answer came when she received a vidlink call from Cenjo. He remained on Sintaur to help with the rebuilding efforts and had recently been contacted by Counselor Imah from Tela who wanted to reach Daith. Contact from Tela to someone off-planet happened very rarely. They were a secluded race, most of whom didn't know how to use their vocal chords since they communicated telepathically, but Imah told Cenjo he wanted to change that. He'd been inspired by Daith's story and wanted to meet her.

Cenjo told Daith he'd been invited as well. Apparently Imah wanted to document the history of the Aleet Army and wanted an insider's perspective. Although a controversial idea on Tela, Imah knew his fellow citizens could no longer isolate themselves. He believed if they had been more involved with other planets, there would have been a chance they could have sensed Daith and helped her. Imah always regretted not following up on Jacin Jaxx after he received a vidlink call from him years before. He didn't want that to happen again.

Daith agreed to visit Tela and meet Imah. She wasn't really sure why. Maybe curiosity or that she needed someone to tell her what to do next with her life. Either way, she went. Relief flooded her to hear Cenjo would be there as well. Like her, he had no direction, and no family. He'd been a part of the Aleet Army for so long he didn't know what else to do. He truly believed what Jaxx did had been worthwhile, and now to document that history was a chance for him to finally wrestle with and defeat his own darkness.

Once they arrived on Tela, they met with Counselor Imah. Imah worked very hard to communicate vocally, especially for Cenjo's benefit, but every so often an image or feeling would emanate from him only Daith could translate. Daith explained her own situation, her fear of her power, and Imah offered to help work with her and her abilities.

Daith accepted Imah's proposal and the next several months were as intense a training as Dru had put her through. The only difference was, with the support of other telepaths around her, Daith never overexerted herself. They could assess her mental and physical state simply by extending their senses.

Exhausting, exhilarating, terrifying, and encouraging all at the same time, Daith learned how to trust and listen to herself again, letting the energies flow through her instead of treating them like something she had to keep separate from herself.

Even through her training, however, Daith sensed something amiss. She enjoyed exploring her own gifts, but to what purpose? She didn't want to spend the rest of her life seeing how far she could reach with her mind or how long she could levitate an object.

Daith brought these concerns to Counselor Imah and he offered a solution. Since she and Cenjo arrived, others had been more open to contact with outsiders and vocal communication. Imah wondered if Daith would be interested in teaching young students to communicate vocally as well. Many students never even learned to use their vocal chords, or if they did, it usually wasn't until many years later and the sounds were rough and difficult to understand.

Daith accepted the job.

As she now prepared to teach her first class, anxiety hit her full force. But seeing Cenjo there, she remembered she wasn't alone. Even if she made mistakes, she had friends who cared about her and beings like Imah who wanted to invest themselves in her life and well-being.

Daith let out a breath. "I know better than you think what it's like to try to explain colors to those who can't see."

Cenjo looked up and grinned. "And I know what it's like to try to train a bunch of students how to prepare themselves for the real universe," he said. "It isn't about telling them what to do; it's about showing them what else is out there and then letting them find their own path. Trust yourself and you'll be fine. And if they do something like glue you to your chair, you'll have a funny story to tell me later when I'm going crazy trying to organize these datapads."

Daith playfully pushed him with her foot as she left the room, but she felt better. Whatever happened next, she knew who she was and it wasn't someone she hated anymore.

Right before she entered the classroom Daith heard a man's voice, sad but strong, flow through her mind. It wasn't someone's actual thought; more like an echo of a thought.

Daughter, the voice whispered. *Do not fear the colors.*

Daith recognized the voice, remembering it from many years ago.

I won't, Father. Daith didn't know if her own thought could reach across time and space the same way, but part of her believed, on some other plane of existence, her father heard her.

She took a deep breath, opened the door, and entered the room.

"Good morning class. My name is Teacher Daith Jaxx. Are we ready to begin?"

Thank you so much for reading IDENTITY!
Here's a sneak peek into the next Eomix Galaxy novel,

COILED VENGENACE

Available Now!
www.ChristaYelichKoth.com

CHAPTER 1

White.
White everywhere.
Lights, eyes, clothes, skin.
Machines, needles, doors, locks.
Even the toys.
White.
Exarth's eyes snapped open and adjusted to the hotel room's dim

light. They focused on the domed cream-colored ceiling above her and locked onto the empty metallic light socket in the center. Twisted shadows seemed to be caught mid-crawl along the peeling bits of paint.

It was just a dream, she thought, willing her breaths to slow. You aren't in that hospital anymore. Only a dream.

She shifted her view and looked at the individual lying next to her, his blue skin having paled and puckered throughout the night. Red, vacant eyes stared up at nothingness atop his face, which expressed a mixture of pleasure and shock. His uncovered chest and arms were dimpled and scratched—souvenirs from a sexual conquest he would never get the chance to brag about.

"Ughhh...." Revolted, Exarth pushed the corpse away from her. The rigid body slid ungracefully off the bed and landed with a sick thud onto the floor.

Exarth threw off the covers and shuddered when the cool air met her bare skin. She made her way through the bedroom to the washroom, using the inklings of light that seeped around the edges of the opaque curtains to find her way. She didn't know the exact time, but it didn't matter. Her next appointment wasn't scheduled until that evening.

She entered the washroom and stood before the reflector unit, admiring her naked body—small, but by no means frail. Taut muscles rippled when she moved. Any teeth marks and bruises on her skin from her enthusiastic partner had vanished, her body having repaired itself during her brief sleep. Her icy white skin, a stark contrast to her long dark hair, remained smooth and supple as usual.

Exarth slid her delicate fingers over her hair, which hung straight to her waist. Light in the washroom glinted off its surface, revealing subtle multi-colored tones among her dark locks, like an oil spill made of silk. She popped in a pair of black contacts to hide her color-changing eyes, which at the moment swirled between the greens and blues of pleasure.

She dressed quickly, turning her back toward the room with her recent lover's corpse. She hadn't even been that attracted to this one, but her fury at the news she'd received the day before prompted her to vent her frustration, which led to...whatever his name was... instead. The few moments of gratification, however brief, gave her an escape from the rage that swelled inside her. But then he'd looked at her as if she meant something to him—his eyes full of joy and adoration after their pleasurable physical act—and she'd snapped his neck without a second thought.

Not that she would have kept him alive anyway.

Why do they always have to spoil the moment by getting emotional? she thought.

Still, her climactic release and solid few hours of sleep had done wonders for her mood. Though often quick to anger, Exarth now felt focused, ready to deal with the bad news she'd received. One last look around the room confirmed she hadn't left anything behind. She pulled a small circular device from her jacket pocket, set the timer, and lobbed it onto the bed.

As she exited the building, the device detonated, blowing apart half the hotel. Chunks of debris flew around her. Dust spewed through the sun-streaked air as bystanders shrieked in fear, protecting their heads, and running for cover. Pieces of shrapnel hit her body, tearing into her skin. She didn't care. The wounds wouldn't take long to heal.

Exarth smiled.

It was going to be a good day.

About the Author

Christa Yelich-Koth is the award-winning author (2016 Novel of Excellence for Science Fiction for ILLUSION from Author's Circle Awards) of the Amazon Bestselling novels, ILLUSION and IDENTITY from the Eomix Galaxy Novels collection.

Aside from her novels, Christa has also authored a graphic novel, HOLLOW, and 6-issue follow-up comic book series HOLLOW'S PRISM from Green-Eyed Unicorn Comics. (with illustrator Conrad Teves.)

Originally from Milwaukee, WI, Christa was exposed to many different things through her education, including an elementary Spanish immersion program, a vocal/opera program in high school, and her eventual B.S. in Biology. Her love of entomology and marine biology helped while writing her science fiction/ fantasy aliens/creatures.

As for why she writes, Christa had this to say: "I write because I have a story that needs to come out. I write because I can't NOT write. I write because I love creating something that pulls me out of my own world and lets me for a little while get lost inside someone or someplace else. And I write because I HAVE to know how the story ends."

You can find more about Christa and her other books at:
www.ChristaYelichKoth.com